Edgewater Road

ALSO BY
SHELLEY SHEPARD GRAY
AVAILABLE FROM BLACKSTONE PUBLISHING

THE BRIDGEPORT SOCIAL CLUB SERIES
Take a Chance
All In
Hold On Tight

THE DANCE WITH ME SERIES
Shall We Dance?
Take the Lead
Save the Last Dance

THE RUMORS IN ROSS COUNTY SERIES
Edgewater Road

SHELLEY SHEPARD GRAY

THE RUMORS IN ROSS COUNTY SERIES

Edgewater Road

BLACK STONE PUBLISHING

Copyright © 2022 by Shelley Shepard Gray
Published in 2022 by Blackstone Publishing
Cover and book design by Alenka Vdovič Linaschke

The characters and events in this book are fictitious.
Any similarity to real persons, living or dead, is coincidental
and not intended by the author.

Printed in the United States of America

First edition: 2022
ISBN 978-1-7999-2369-5
Fiction / Romance / General

Version 2

CIP data for this book is available
from the Library of Congress

Blackstone Publishing
31 Mistletoe Rd.
Ashland, OR 97520

www.BlackstonePublishing.com

*In loving memory of my first agent, Mary Sue Seymour,
who touched a great many hearts just by being herself.*

"Before the coming of this faith, we were held in custody under the law, locked up until the faith that was to come would be revealed. So the law was our guardian until Christ came that we might be justified by faith."

Galatians 3:23

"I don't know exactly what the future holds, but I'm stepping forward with grit anchored in grace."

Julie Bender

DEAR READER,

Thank you for picking up *Edgewater Road*. I hope you enjoy getting to know Jennifer, Lincoln, and all of the other assorted characters in the novel. I know I certainly enjoyed writing the book.

This book was something of a labor of love for me. I'd been thinking about the first scene in this novel for quite some time, but I wasn't sure what to do with it. No matter how many times I tried to incorporate it into the project I was working on, it didn't seem a good fit, so I put it aside again.

About three years ago, I finally decided that Jennifer and Lincoln needed a book of their own, even if no one ever read their story but me. And then, somehow, that first scene became three chapters, then a hundred pages, and then something that I really cared about.

I was a nervous wreck when I sent the first fifty pages to my agent, asking what she thought. I got even more nervous when we decided to send it out to editors. I had no expectations and couldn't have been more surprised (or delighted!) when the folks at Blackstone asked to publish it.

I received my contract at the beginning of 2020. Just a few weeks later, my husband and I were essentially quarantined in our new home at the base of Cheyenne Mountain. As uncertainty swirled in the outside world, I focused on this book. It became something of a lifesaver for me, and I don't think I'll ever think about Jennifer cleaning out closets without remembering all the cleaning I did as well!

Now, looking back, I wonder if this book's journey—so filled with uncertainty and missteps—was meant to follow Jennifer and Lincoln's storyline. The main characters had to not only take a leap of faith, but to also dig deep into themselves in order to find happiness, freedom, and love. I can't help but think that many of us have done that very same thing a time or two.

I've always considered it a blessing to be viewed as the person one hopes to be . . . Perhaps, though, what is important is that those dreams are given a chance.

Here's to hopes and dreams—and to the Lord and the many people in our lives who help make those dreams a reality.

Best,

Shelley Shepard Gray

PROLOGUE

"That's her, boss," Bo said under the cover of a large black umbrella. "That there is Jennifer Smiley."

If Bo had uttered anything else, Lincoln probably would've asked him to repeat it. It was raining that hard. Storming, more like it. And, since they were currently standing in the middle of a graveyard next to Ginny Smiley's final resting place, Lincoln might have simply shrugged.

But this young woman was his longtime neighbor's grand-daughter—the woman dear to Ginny's heart. Jennifer was the only person the cantankerous old woman had guarded like a Doberman. As close as he'd been to Ginny, she had never gifted him with the honor of meeting her beloved granddaughter and namesake. All his life, whenever Jennifer was in residence in the sprawling white farm-house next door, John Lincoln Bennett was supposed to stay away.

That's just how it was.

"Ah," Lincoln finally said. Bo raised an eyebrow but kept

his silence. Lincoln hardly noticed, though. He was too busy staring at the woman he'd always been curious about.

She was hard not to look at. Jennifer stood among the crowd of fifty or so mourners on the hill. While almost everyone else was wearing jeans and boots—it was pouring, and they were standing on grass and mud—Jennifer Smiley was in a prim black dress, black patent leather heels, and a black raincoat with vivid purple lining. Her umbrella was covered in some kind of abstract swirling black-and-gold design. Underneath that nylon covering, golden hair hung in a cascade of curls down her back. She was a beauty—there was no doubt about that.

And, while most everyone else had also come with at least one other person, Jennifer was completely, utterly on her own.

That's when it hit him. She *was* completely alone in the world. Ginny had been her grandmother. Ginny's son Eric—Jennifer's dad—hadn't been around in years. Maybe a decade. And Jennifer's mother had never really gotten along with Ginny. At least that was what everyone said.

When more than a couple of people began to shift uncomfortably, Pastor Dan cleared his throat. "Everyone, if we could gather a little closer together, it might be easier to hear."

Dutifully, everyone scooted forward, stepping carefully in the sloshy, wet grass. About thirty or so umbrellas clanked together as everyone vied for space in front of a plain cedar coffin, the pile of muddy sod and dirt, and a six-foot-long hole in the ground.

Well, everyone moved closer but Ginny's granddaughter. She seemed frozen in her spot. Twin spots of pink painted her cheeks.

Pastor Dan looked uncertain whether to begin or wait another moment.

"I think she's stuck, Boss," Bo muttered.

Lincoln guessed he might be right. The woman's spiked heels had dug into the ground like drill bits.

"I'll get her, Pastor," Lincoln murmured as he strode to her side. "Hey," he said in a quiet tone. "Let me give you a hand."

Jennifer looked at him in surprise before nodding. "Thank you."

When she held out her hand, he took it, then rested his other hand around her waist and gently pulled. After a second of fighting, the earth finally let go of each of her heels. Though it was tempting to simply pick her up and carry her to Pastor Dan's side, he knew that wouldn't fly. Instead he murmured, "If you keep on the pads of your feet, you might be all right."

"Yes. I've got it." She smiled slightly as she placed one slim hand on his arm. Together, they stepped forward.

The crowd silently watched their approach. Dan looked relieved. Jennifer stopped just on the outside of the group. Then released a ragged breath.

Even though he was only wearing a ball cap instead of carrying an umbrella, Lincoln stayed where he was. Catching the pastor's eye, he nodded.

Pastor Dan opened up his Bible. "Everyone, thank you for coming out today to celebrate Jennifer Ruth Smiley's life. Ginny, as she was known to all of us, asked for a simple graveside service." He cleared his throat. "She insisted on it, actually." He glanced Jennifer's way. "Jennifer wanted to respect her wishes. So, even though the sky is practically falling on our heads, I can't help but think that Ginny would be kind of pleased that we were following her directives to a T."

Beside Lincoln, Jennifer relaxed.

Lincoln was glad about that. Still, he decided to stay where he was. Just in case she needed him.

For most of the next fifteen minutes, Jennifer stayed silent and dry-eyed. She stood stoically while Dan relayed Ginny's charitable work in Ross County. She didn't move a muscle when the pastor told everyone about the old gal's stint as an army nurse during the Korean War. Hardly blinked when Dan said that Ginny always tried to do good for people in need.

But when Pastor Dan led the group in "Amazing Grace," his voice loud and clear and fervent, Jennifer seemed to pale a bit. When Lincoln felt her sway, he reached out and took hold of her hand. She gripped it hard.

Lincoln kept his hand in hers while everyone finished the song, during the last prayer, and while Ginny's coffin was lowered into the ground. Only after the groundskeepers moved away did the first tears fall from her eyes.

"Jennifer, it's time," Dan said quietly.

She looked startled, then seemed to collect herself all over again. "Hmm? Oh. Yes."

After rocking forward to release her heels from the mud, she walked to the big hole in the ground, reached down, grabbed a handful of almost-dry dirt that had been in a covered bucket, and tossed it on top the casket.

Seconds later, Lincoln did the same, and then led her over to the side. Knowing that the other forty-eight people were about to come forward to share their condolences, Lincoln leaned toward her again. "Do you need anything, Jennifer? Everyone's about to come over here to pay their respects."

"Thank you, but I'll be fine." She smiled tightly as she dug in her purse for a tissue. "Thank you for your help, and for helping me get unstuck. I, uh, I guess I wasn't thinking when I put on these heels."

"I think you're doing just fine. Don't worry about it."

A burst of gratitude mixed in with those tears in her eyes.

"You've been very kind." She wrinkled her brow. "I'm sorry. I don't believe we've met before."

"We haven't." He held out his hand again. "I'm Lincoln. John Lincoln Bennett." While she shook it, he waited for some sign of recognition in her pretty, light brown eyes. "I've lived next door to Ginny all my life."

After the space of a heartbeat, her cheeks flushed. "Oh! My grandmother mentioned her neighbor, but she never told me your name. I'm sorry. I should've asked."

"No worries." Ginny Ruth Smiley had been one of the most important people in his life and she'd never even mentioned his name to her precious granddaughter. That stung.

Jennifer was looking up at him like he was the kindest man in the county. "It's nice to meet you, Lincoln," she said. "Thank you for coming."

The words, so polite and proper, grated on him even though he knew better than to blame the girl. She seemed to mean every one of them.

"You take care now," he said, just as Colin Wallace, Ginny's banker, approached.

Jennifer's eyes widened and her lips parted. She looked about to tell him something, but old Mr. Wallace strode forward with his hand outstretched.

Lincoln stepped out of the way but remained nearby as Bo joined the others in line. As the minutes wore on and the crowd began to dissipate, Lincoln continued to watch Jennifer. She stood tall and proud, looked each person in the eye, and let all those strangers take her hand, hug her close, and share their stories and reminiscences. She let them speak and smiled politely, all while that beautiful golden hair resting on the back of her trench coat got soaked and her heels sank farther and farther into the ground.

It was one of the most impressive things he'd ever seen.

Without a doubt, Jennifer Smiley was remarkable. She had a spine of steel and was so very beautiful. And so very alone.

"Think we should stick around and make sure she gets home okay?" Bo asked. "She's gonna be your neighbor now, you know."

For anyone else, Lincoln would've nodded yes. But he got the feeling that Jennifer wasn't that type of woman. She didn't lean on anyone, especially not perfect strangers. No, especially not strangers who were real far from perfect.

"I reckon Pastor Dan will get her home. She'd probably prefer that anyway."

"Whatever you want, Boss."

When there was hardly anyone left, they turned and walked back to his truck. Lincoln got in, took off his hat and realized he was soaked to the skin. Huh. He'd almost forgotten that it was still pouring down rain.

CHAPTER 1

This had been a bad idea. Staring at the five vehicles parked haphazardly in the long driveway leading to her neighbor's farmhouse, Jennifer pressed hard on her Camry's brakes and wondered if she could get away with turning around.

But the two guys drinking beer on the front porch had already seen her. One of them waved.

If she turned around, Jennifer knew that John Bennett would find out. And when he did, he wouldn't let it slide, because that was the way he was. Shoot, he'd probably show up at her front door tomorrow morning and ask her a dozen questions about why she hadn't parked and gone in.

He might even decide to stop by later that night.

Though she'd only spoken to John a couple of times, Jennifer had already gotten the feeling he didn't suffer fools. Or liars, which was what she would be if he asked why she'd decided to show up at his house without calling first. Jennifer wasn't typically a liar, but she knew herself well enough to realize that she'd feel so foolish, she'd start making up all kinds of excuses that were as flimsy as tissue paper.

Since there were no good options, she decided to go inside and do what she came to do.

Feeling a weight on her chest, Jennifer carefully pulled off to the side of the driveway, leaving plenty of room to turn around. That wouldn't be hard to do. Lincoln's house was on a full two acres, just like her own. There was plenty of space for parking.

And, it seemed, parties.

Turning off the ignition, Jennifer came up with a plan. She was going to walk up to John's front door, say hello to his friends, deliver this really bad idea, and then hurry home.

Feeling the men's eyes on her, she walked around to the passenger side, opened the door, and pulled out her reason for being there. One triple-layer chocolate cake with a chocolate mousse filling and a creamy white seven-minute frosting. It was a beautiful dessert, if she did say so herself.

She'd baked it for Lincoln. As a thank you present. She'd thought it was the kind of gift her grandmother, Ginny Smiley, would have delivered back in the day.

But now that Jennifer thought about it? She was starting to get the feeling that MeMe wouldn't have done such a thing after all. Another example of how her grandmother had been filled with a whole lot more gumption than Jennifer ever had. Well, until now.

The longer she lived in MeMe's old Victorian farmhouse, the more aware Jennifer became that she hadn't really known her grandmother.

Then again, there was *a lot* to know about MeMe. She'd had a fascinating life. Even at eighty years old, she'd been far more confident and vivacious than Jennifer.

Yep, Jennifer was plain, store-brand vanilla, while her grandmother had been one of those crazy Ben & Jerry's ice cream flavors that are filled with ten different mix-ins and cost twice as much. Side by side, there was no comparison.

"Hey."

Startled, she turned and found herself face-to-face with one of the men who'd come over to help her unload her U-Haul when she'd moved in next door a week ago. He'd shown up barely ten minutes after Lincoln had stopped by. Lincoln had pulled in her driveway to say hello, practically acting like she wouldn't remember the way he'd helped her get through her grandmother's funeral. After he'd shrugged off her thanks, he'd focused on the fact that she was attempting to move into the house all by herself. That she was completely alone once again.

He had frowned when she'd told him that she was fine and didn't need a single thing. Didn't need help.

But mere seconds after that, Lincoln had sent a text, prompting his friends to arrive—including this fellow.

Now, looking at the man dressed in a long-sleeved T-shirt and worn jeans, Jennifer couldn't remember his name. All she could recall was that he'd been a lot easier to talk to than John Bennett.

"Hi . . . I'm sorry. I know we met at the funeral and again the other day, but I seem to have forgotten your name. Was it . . . Ben?"

He scowled. "Bo."

"Oh. That's right." She smiled weakly. "I won't forget it again." That was, if she had a reason to talk to Bo anytime soon. "My name is Jennifer."

"I didn't forget." She watched him study her face, drift down her torso, then finally come to a stop on the cake server clutched between her hands. "What you got there?"

"This? Oh, it's a cake."

"You brought a cake?"

"It's a thank-you cake. For John."

His brow wrinkled. "Who?"

"Oh! I mean Lincoln." She shook her head. "He introduced himself as John at the funeral. I guess it stuck." When Bo continued to stare at her, she added, "So, like I said, I baked a thank-you cake for Lincoln." Yes, she had now stated that she had a cake in her hands three times.

When Bo tilted his head, like he was trying to comprehend such a thing, she rushed on. "I know. I bet he would rather have a six-pack of beer or something. And I should've called before I drove over. I didn't know he was having a party."

Bo looked over his shoulder like this was news to him too. "Huh. Yeah, I guess you could call this a party."

When he looked back at her, she realized that the short heels of her cute mules were slowly getting covered in mud. When was she ever going to start wearing decent shoes? "Hey, you know what? Maybe I should deliver this later."

"No way. Lincoln's probably wondering what's taking you so long."

So long? "To do what?"

"To come up to the house. Come on." He turned and started walking.

Her heart sinking with every step, Jennifer followed.

The closer she got to the door, the more she lamented her decision, which was saying a lot because she already regretted it an awful lot.

There had to be at least a dozen people standing on the front porch now, and they were all looking at her like she was a strange creature that had just appeared from the woods. Even the other men who'd helped her unload the van looked surprised to see her.

And no wonder. She was wearing a pair of navy wool slacks, an ivory sweater, and beautiful, impractical, turquoise suede mules. In her hands was a plastic cake carrier. She looked like she was going to a church social. Not this . . . this . . . whatever *this* was.

Right as she reached the front steps, one of the men tagged Bo. "What you got there?"

"Jennifer here has a gift for Lincoln." He looked down at her hands. "It's a cake," he added, saying it as if it was a foreign word.

"She going in?"

Bo nodded. "Yeah. Where's he at?"

The guy shrugged as he directed another long glance in her direction. "Ain't no telling . . . but I wouldn't bring her inside."

"Don't see as I've got a choice. I'm not going to just leave her standing out here."

Yep, they were talking about her like she wasn't standing right there in front of them. Jennifer was starting to feel like a stray dog no one wanted around.

It was time to finish this errand and get back home where it was safe and quiet, and where her shoes weren't in danger of being ruined.

Jennifer cleared her throat. "I'm going to head on in. I'm sure my delivery won't take but a minute."

Bo looked appalled. "Hey, now—"

Ignoring him, she walked through the door.

And entered a whole new world.

Though the house wasn't much to speak of on the outside—an old white-washed sprawling farmhouse—inside it was decorated in vintage fraternity row. Mismatched couches, scarred coffee tables, beer cans littering surfaces . . . and she was pretty sure more than one couple was making out in the back corners.

There was also a group of men playing cards at a massive table near the kitchen. Lincoln was one of them.

As she stood there, gaping at everything in wonder, the door opened and shut behind her.

"Come on, then," Bo said, sounding irritated. "He's over there. Let's get this over with."

When he started walking, she kept by his side, though it was a bit of a challenge, given that Bo was a good six inches taller, and she was in mules covered in mud, and holding a three-layer cake.

Her shoes made little clacking noises on the wood floor.

Lincoln looked their way. And then he did a double take.

After saying something under his breath, he threw his hand of cards on the table and stood up.

"Here he comes," Bo said.

"Yes. I noticed."

As he came closer, Lincoln pulled out his cell phone and studied the screen with a frown. Then he shoved it into his jeans pocket.

"Jennifer, what's wrong?" he asked.

Oh, any number of things. Starting with the fact that she was holding a chocolate cake while a couple on a nearby couch next to her seemed to be minutes from pulling off the rest of their clothes. She really hoped they'd wait at least ten more minutes.

"Nothing's wrong," she said in an almost cheerful voice. "I brought you something."

Lincoln glanced at his phone's screen again before he studied her closely. "I'm sorry. Did I miss your call?"

She met his gaze and noticed for about the fifteenth time that his eyes were *really* blue. Dark too. Like lapis.

The woman on the couch giggled.

Oh! Jennifer needed to get out of this room. Clearing her throat again, she attempted to find her voice. "John. I mean, Lincoln, I'm sorry I didn't text or call. I guess I should have. Anyway, here." She thrust her container toward him.

He took it easily enough, but he held the red Rubbermaid cake server like it had a bomb about to go off inside of it. "What is this?"

"It's a cake, Lincoln," Bo announced. "She made you a freaki—" He looked over at her again. "A chocolate cake."

Lincoln was still holding the container gingerly, like it might explode. He frowned. "I don't understand."

"It's a thank-you cake." When he still only stared at her, she added, "You know, as a thank-you for helping me during the funeral and for calling all the guys to help me carry all my boxes and furniture into the house last week. It was really nice of you."

"You don't need to thank me for either of those. Not a big deal."

"Well, it was to me. You and all the guys made my life a lot easier." She smiled at Bo, so he'd see that she hadn't forgotten that he carried her desk inside.

Lincoln ran a hand through his coal-black hair. "No need to thank me for helping you when I can. I promised Ginny we'd look out for you."

Ah. He hadn't gone out of his way for her on his own. It had been because of his friendship with her dead grandmother. And . . . that made the awkwardness of this whole errand complete.

Swallowing the lump of embarrassment, Jennifer nodded. "Well, I think I'll be going now. Have a good night." Turning around, she closed her eyes. *Have a good night?* She wasn't at one of her mother's friends' houses.

Was she ever going to learn to be less self-conscious? A little more easy-going and relaxed? A little more like her grandmother?

She increased her pace. Kept her head down as she walked

by the couple on the couch. Ignored the stares as she strode to the front door, her heels once again clicking against the hardwood, each step echoing in the suddenly quiet room.

"Jennifer."

She paused, mentally debating whether she wanted to turn around and face Lincoln in front of all his friends or keep walking.

She decided to get the heck out of there.

She opened the door. Felt the cool breeze bite her cheeks.

A large hand gripped the edge of the door as it swung open. "Jennifer, wait," Lincoln said. "Please."

She could feel his breath on her neck. Goosebumps rose, not from the cold air but from his proximity.

"Yes?"

"Jennifer, turn around, babe."

Babe? She wasn't a fan of that word, and especially wasn't a fan of being on its receiving end.

So why had a little part of her insides melted when she heard it from his lips? Why did she pivot on her heels to face him again, as if she had no other option?

Now, they were barely standing eight inches apart. Close enough that she had to raise her chin to meet those blue eyes. Close enough to smell the faintest hint of soap on his skin. "Um, yes, Lincoln?"

Humor lit his gaze before he visibly put his game face back on. "I'm gonna walk you out."

It was dark. She might have social issues, but she wasn't a fool. She nodded. "Thank you."

Taking her arm, he guided her out and pulled the door shut behind him. Almost immediately, she could hear the noise level rise inside the house.

The five men on the porch abruptly stopped talking and watched them.

Lincoln acted as if they weren't even there. "Where's your car, honey?" he asked in a soft voice.

She pointed to the driveway, where her reliable gray Camry still sat at the end of a long line of vehicles.

"How come you parked so far away?"

She shrugged, not wanting to admit how close she'd come to turning around.

He sighed and started down the stairs, still holding her arm in his heavy hand, like he was afraid she'd dart off without him.

They stayed silent as they walked. She was doing her best not to thank him a second time for walking her out in the dark. And John? Well, who knew what was on his mind?

When they reached her vehicle, he held out his hand. "Key?"

"Oh, there's no need." She patted her pocket. "It's keyless entry."

"You going to be okay getting home?"

She was a grown woman. It was a three-minute drive back to her grandmother's farm. The farm that was barely a mile away. So, all in all, it seemed like a pretty silly question.

But it still made her feel cared for—mainly because she couldn't remember the last time anyone had cared enough to ask if she was going to be okay doing anything. "I'll be fine." Looking up into his eyes, she smiled softly. "Now, you have a good night, John."

"My name's Lincoln."

"I didn't forget." Unable to stop herself, she chuckled at his irritated expression before opening her door and slipping inside.

Lincoln stepped away, but she knew he was watching as she turned around and slowly drove back onto the main road.

She'd been the one who'd delivered a thank-you cake, but she had the strangest feeling that Lincoln Bennett had given her something too.

She just wasn't sure what it was.

CHAPTER 2

John Lincoln Bennett had a migraine coming on. All the signs were there. A relentless pounding behind his eyes. The shooting pain across his brow. His ears were starting to ring, and his vision was getting blurry.

It was gonna be a bad one.

Having a migraine wasn't exactly an unfamiliar thing—he used to get them all the time back when he was a kid. Though, he didn't remember those headaches bringing him down like he feared this one was about to do.

It was probably because his situation had changed.

When he was a kid, eleven or twelve, the headaches had gone hand in hand with riding the school bus home. Whenever he knew his mother was working late, he'd sit on that vinyl seat, ignoring all the other kids as they talked about their plans for the afternoon, and he'd mentally prepare himself for what was about to come.

If his Pa was home alone, waiting, then it was likely he was going to whip Lincoln's butt for some imagined slight.

Boy, he'd hated those interminable forty-five-minute rides. He'd sit there, staring blankly out the window, knowing there wasn't a thing he could do to stop the inevitable.

Even at a young age, Lincoln had known his father's actions weren't right. But he'd been stuck. Too little to fight back and too young to leave for good. Lucky for him, the headaches had eased right about the time he'd been big enough to hit back. It had only taken one good punch to dissipate his Pa's abuse *and* the pounding behind his eyes. He learned a good lesson that day— that appearing weak never did a man any favors. He had learned the same lesson a time or two back when he was incarcerated too. In prison, any sign of weakness would make you everyone else's target. Real quick, he'd made sure the walls he'd erected around himself were hard enough never to be penetrated . . . until he'd discovered that there was something even stronger and more powerful than tough skin and a good right hook.

And that was why he wasn't pleased about the new, pointed tingling at the back of his neck. On top of the pain, it brought back memories he'd just as soon forget.

Experience told him that he needed to get some Excedrin and a hot shower real soon, or he'd be out of commission for the rest of the day. He didn't have time for that. He had work to do and a mess of men to keep tabs on.

But first, he had a cake holder to return and some awkward feelings to explore with his neighbor.

Doing his best to ignore the sledgehammer against his brain, Lincoln rapped lightly on Jennifer's front door. He'd return the container, chat with her for a few minutes to be polite—for Ginny's sake—and then get on his way.

After a few seconds slid by, he glanced at her Camry to make sure he hadn't dreamed it up, then knocked again a little bit louder. Which, of course, made his head start pounding worse.

"Coming! Hold on!"

Her shout was punctuated by the rushing of footsteps along the wood floor. Boy, she sounded like a teenage girl, so bright and innocent.

It was a mystery how Ginny could have a granddaughter like Jennifer. Ginny had been a lot of things, but innocent had never been one of them. Though the old girl had done him more than a couple of favors, she'd also been loud, tough, and cranky. He'd always described her as the type of woman who could hold her own in a bar fight.

Not for the first time, he wondered what she'd thought of her sweet, pretty, cake-baking granddaughter. He shook his head in wonder, only to be reminded that his head didn't appreciate the motion.

He was frowning at a fresh wave of pain behind his eyes when the door opened, at last, revealing a whole new neighbor.

Of course, that was a bit of an exaggeration, but it sure felt right. The other three times he'd seen her, Jennifer had been all tricked out—wearing tailored clothes that cost good money, her thick blond hair curled and falling about her shoulders in pretty waves, and nothing had prevented him from getting a good, steady look at her light brown eyes and the flecks of gold that decorated her irises.

But now?

This gal had on gray sweats, her hair in a messy knot at the top of her head, and she wore Buddy Holly glasses.

She looked . . . approachable. And sweet. Real sweet.

And, given the way her mouth was set into a small O, she was also surprised. "John! Hi."

"Hey," he replied before he remembered that he was supposed to be annoyed by her calling him John.

When she stood there gaping at him for another second or two, he shifted his stance and held out the container. "I brought this back for you. Here."

"Thanks." After setting it on a step, she turned back to face him. Waiting.

It looked like he was going to have to say something or turn around and leave. He was no good at small talk, but he figured he should at least try a little. "So . . . how are you?"

"Currently? I am beyond embarrassed. I can't believe I answered the door looking like this." Looking down at her gray sweats, she sighed. "Sorry for the scary sight. I've been working all day on my computer. I wasn't planning on having company."

She considered him dropping off her stuff as having company? Though his head was still pounding, and he was feeling awkward as all get out, he tried to set her at ease. "I don't care what you look like." When she pulled back slightly, he realized that he'd sounded like a jerk. "I mean, I like your glasses."

She looked self-conscious as she ran a finger along the rims of her thick black frames. "Thanks. I usually wear contacts, but sometimes it's nice to take a break from them, you know? Plus, like I said, I didn't plan on seeing anyone today."

"Well, now you have."

She smiled at him warmly, like he'd just told her that Christmas was coming early. "Yes. I guess so."

Shoot. There was that pull again. Part of him wanted to stay and chat. Confide that he had a headache and it was gonna be a bad one. Ask if he could avoid his life by staying in her clean, sweet world for a little bit longer. She wouldn't even have to talk to him. He'd be happy just to park himself on her couch and watch her work.

But she was still standing in the doorway looking wary,

like it had finally hit her that he'd entered her world and he didn't belong.

Alrighty. It was time to get this duty over with and get on back to work. Just as he was about to turn, he realized his mother would have reminded him to compliment the cook. "I don't want to keep you or nothing. I just wanted to thank you for the cake. It was real good."

And just like that, everything about her warmed up another notch. "Really? You liked it?"

He grinned. "A homemade chocolate cake? I liked it a lot." He was tempted to tell her that he couldn't remember the last time he'd had anything that someone had gone out of their way to make for him.

But that seemed like too much to share.

When Jennifer smiled back, he felt rather than saw her eyes skim over his body. Maybe she was just as affected as he was by the tension that seemed to buzz between them.

"I'm glad," she murmured. When her eyes met his again, she smiled wider. And, for the very first time, that smile seemed to reach her eyes.

He stilled, almost mesmerized. Remembering the way she'd let so many people touch her and chatter while she'd stood in the rain, Lincoln was reminded again that she was something special. Maybe even something more than he'd originally thought. Maybe even a whole lot more.

Sensing that maybe she needed a break from her life as much as he did, he gently nudged her out of the way, closed the door, and then walked right inside.

Right away he noticed how different the living room looked from the last time he'd been there. Ginny had kept a pair of couches in the room and not much else. Jennifer, on the other hand, was using it as her new home office.

The girl had arranged the fancy-looking office furniture they'd carried inside a week ago into two neat rows. Files and reference books covered the back row while a computer, printer, and a really big monitor stood neatly in the center of the front. He also noticed a headset, cords, and an open file resting on the shiny dark wood.

"What is it that you do again?"

"I'm a medical transcriber."

"What does that mean you do, exactly?"

Her eyes widened, looking almost owl-like behind the lenses before she seemed to come to a decision. "Hey, um Lincoln, would you like a cup of coffee?"

He had a heck of a headache, a thousand things to do, and an unnatural attraction to his next-door neighbor—who reminded him of one of those Disney princesses his mother had been so fond of. He should keep his distance.

But before he knew what he was doing, he nodded. "Yeah."

"Come on back, then." She picked up the cake holder and led the way down the narrow hall to the kitchen where he'd spent many an hour with her grandmother.

He might have taken a better look around if she didn't have the word PINK emblazoned on her butt.

Without asking, he took a seat at the oak table and finally looked around the room. There was a bright white monster mixer on the counter, a plate of cookies, and about ten assorted plates leading a trail to the sink.

A peppermint candle was burning, creating a little glow in a corner. But wafting over everything was the scent of fresh coffee.

"You know, your grandma always had a pot of coffee going. No matter what time of day."

"Did she?" She flashed a smile. "I do the same thing." She pulled out two cups. "So do you take your coffee black?"

"Yep, with one spoon of sugar."

She pulled out a delicate-looking china sugar bowl and carefully measured one spoonful into his mug. "Just a little bit of sweetness needed, hmm?"

"You could say so." Memories haunted him, this one coming from his time spent in the pen in Madison. The prison cooks brewed coffee that tasted like dirty water. The first time he'd taken a sip, he'd almost choked, but eventually he learned to appreciate it. The one thing that abysmal coffee ever had going for it was that it was hot. He never could abide lukewarm coffee. Of course, there was never any question of getting milk or sugar in his brew—he hadn't been living at the Holiday Inn.

He noticed that she drank hers completely black. "No milk or sugar for you?"

"No. My mother always told me adding those two things would make me fat." She kind of smiled, but it didn't reach her eyes. "For whatever reason, I've followed her advice. Of course, maybe she should have warned me that cookies could also do the trick."

The girl was curvy, but those curves only enhanced her looks, as far as he was concerned. Thinking about her being told to stay away from even a spoonful of sugar in her coffee seemed like a crime.

But instead of going there, he focused on Ginny. "Huh. Your grandma would pour so much cream in hers, her coffee would turn white. I used to say she had coffee with her milk."

Jennifer's eyes warmed again. "That was MeMe. She didn't do much by half, did she? She sure enjoyed everything about life."

"That she did." He smiled at her again. "So you're a medical transcriber?"

"Yes." She sat down next to him. "Physicians send me tapes and I type them into the patient portals and transcribe them on electronic charts."

"It sounds tedious."

"Oh, it is. But I like it. I'm good at details, and I'm good at double-checking my work." She paused, then added, "I like to feel like I'm helping people, even though they never probably realize it."

He thought that was kind of a sorry way of going through a job—working day after day on something without a hint of being appreciated. But who was he to judge? "You been doing it long?"

"Three years. At first, I was just going to transcribe records until I found something better. But, then, I thought, what's wrong with the job as it is? It pays well enough, I get to work at home, and I don't worry about any of it on the weekends."

"You might have something there." Realizing that he smelled something floral wafting off her skin, he took a sip of coffee. Then another one. Anything to stop himself wondering if it was her shampoo or lotion or perfume . . .

She noticed the way he was chugging it. "There's plenty more, if you'd like."

"Thanks. This is real good."

"Thank you. I put a little bit of cinnamon and chocolate powder in the grounds. I think it keeps it from being bitter."

No, it kept it from tasting like any other coffee that he'd ever had. "Huh."

"What about you?"

"You mean my job?"

"Well, yes." She pushed her frames back up on the bridge of her nose. "What do you do?"

"The majority of the time I manage a couple of properties around here." When Jennifer leaned forward, like he was saying something of interest, he added, "Two are down by Lake Mary and I rent them out as an Airbnb." Among other things.

A wrinkle formed on her brow. "Oh."

"You seem surprised about that."

"I guess I am." When he kept staring at her, she waved a hand. "I mean, it seems like you have a lot of friends. I thought maybe those guys worked with you in construction or something."

"A couple of them do work for me. I'm usually remodeling one or more of my places at a time." He almost stopped at that, but he wasn't one to sugarcoat reality. Setting his empty cup down, he added, "But most of the guys you saw the other night are on their own. I'm just trying to help them out."

"With what?"

Lincoln couldn't help but gape at her. "You really don't know about my past?"

She shook her head. "MeMe never said much about you. I mean, other than her neighbor was a good friend." She paused. "Oh! She also told me more than once that she trusted you a lot."

He would've been a little hurt that Ginny hadn't said more about him . . . if he wasn't well aware of the type of woman she'd been. In addition to being loud and bossy, Ginny kept more secrets than a sailor on shore leave.

Leaning a little forward, ignoring the pain searing his brow, he decided to lay it all on the line. "Jennifer, I know those guys from the prison up in Madisonville. When they get out, they spend time with me."

"Really?" She looked like she was trying to laugh, like she thought he was joking with her.

"I wouldn't lie about that."

"I'm sorry. I didn't mean to sound rude. I'm just surprised. I mean, how would you know a bunch of prisoners?"

"Because I was a prisoner once, babe. I spent three years inside."

Her cup clunked as she set it down. "You were in prison?"

"Three years," he said. Just like he hadn't said it already.

Right there in front of him, every bit of warmth he'd spied in her eyes vanished like a flame in a thunderstorm. "What did you do?" she asked.

Her voice now sounded thready. Nervous.

He stood up, poured himself another cup, and took another long sip of the delicious coffee to buy himself some time. He'd been sentenced for three to five on a second-degree assault charge. Knowing he'd more or less deserved the punishment for what he'd done, Lincoln had never shied away from it. But now, staring into Jennifer's wide eyes, he decided to gloss over it a bit. A girl like her might get scared off about a word like assault. "I was . . . well, I was an accessory to a crime."

Her brow furrowed. "I'm sorry, but I don't understand what that means."

"It means I was at the wrong place at the wrong time, but I wasn't innocent." That was as much as he was willing to talk about.

"Did my grandmother know about this?"

"Well, yeah." Just how much of a bubble had this girl been living in? "Ginny used to visit me twice a month." Like clockwork.

"MeMe went to the prison?" Her voice rose an octave.

"Wasn't like I could Uber over here every other week, babe."

She ran a hand through her hair, causing the makeshift knot on the top of her head to slip away. Thick golden waves tumbled down around her shoulders. It wasn't curled or fussily styled but it was still gorgeous. Remembering his sister Annie's habit, Lincoln guessed that Jennifer had put it up wet and it had dried on its own.

All that naturalness transformed her. Made her look less stark, younger. Sweeter, maybe.

Well, it would've if she wasn't looking at him like he was a serial killer.

"Why would she visit you there?" she whispered, obviously still trying to come to terms with his news. "Did MeMe volunteer at some church organization or something?"

"I reckon she drove over to the prison because she cared about me, Jennifer."

"You two were close."

"Uh, yeah. Like I've said, we lived next door to each other for most of my life. She was around when I was born." She'd babysat him when he was a little thing. Patched him up when his father had taken all his problems out on him. She'd also lectured him nonstop when he'd started feeling his oats and gotten stupider with each passing year.

"Oh. Of course."

There was a note of emptiness in her voice now. He hated that. Hated feeling like he suddenly wasn't good enough to share her space.

Even though it pained him something awful, he cleared his throat. "Like I said, your grandma was around for me a lot. Just like I was around for her when her loser son took off and left her high and dry."

Jennifer flinched as if he'd struck her. Which, of course, he'd intended. "John, Ginny's *loser son* was my dad."

"I know." Of course he knew that. But he sure wasn't going to take his descriptor back. Eric Smiley had been a worthless waste of space.

Looking troubled, she got to her feet. Picked up her cup. Set it back down. "I'm sorry, but I need to go." She shook her head. "I mean, you need to go. I've got to get back to work." She smiled tightly. "Those records can't transcribe themselves, you know."

26

His mouth went dry as he walked his coffee cup to the sink. "Yeah, sure." His heart felt heavy, and he hated it. Hated that he was thinking about his feelings instead of his pounding head. Hated that he'd come over to return a plastic container and somehow ended up chatting with a woman he barely knew about things he never talked about.

But most of all, he hated that she was condemning him for something that he couldn't change. It didn't matter what he was doing with his life now or what he would ever accomplish in the future. He was an ex-con, and that label was never going to disappear.

Practically marching in those purple socks, she led the way to the front door and held it open. "Thank you for returning my cake holder."

"It was not a problem." Just to needle her, he said, "I mean, I wouldn't want you to think your ex-con neighbor was stealing it or anything."

Her cheeks colored. "I didn't call you a thief. Don't put words in my mouth."

"I won't do it again—if you ever decide to get a more open mind."

"It's open."

"From here it feels closed as tight as a steel trap."

Her lips thinned. "Look, I appreciate you helping me move in here. And all you did for my grandma. But, um, I'm just not sure if we have much else to say to each other."

Each prissy sentence felt like a weak slap in the face. It didn't exactly hurt, but he wasn't real thrilled about it either. "Why don't you just say what you're thinking?" He stepped a little closer, crowding her with his size on purpose. "How about you say what's really on your mind," he half-whispered. Goading her. "Say that you don't want to know me anymore because I served time."

The January air was chilling the room, but her voice was even colder. "It's not just that, John. I mean, you're right, I am kind of taken aback by your news. But that's not the reason."

"What is it?"

A line formed on her brow as she visibly struggled to phrase her response. "It's like this. I . . . I'm not like my grandma."

"And you thought what . . . that I thought you were?"

"No. But what I'm trying to tell you is that I'm . . . well, I'm a quiet sort of person and you . . . well, you're not. I just don't think we have much in common."

He knew she was right, just as he knew he'd already missed the narrow window of opportunity to save himself from twenty-four hours of extreme pain. But because both of those things were chipping away at the small amount of kindness he had left, he blurted out exactly what he was thinking. "Jennifer, you might be quiet, and I might not, but that ain't our real problem with each other."

"What do you think it is? Do you even know?"

"Oh, I know. I think your problem is that you work all day by yourself in your grandma's old living room and don't do much else. Your problem is that I live in the real world, and you don't even want to see it."

A shadow fell over her features. He wasn't sure if it was a trick of the light or if it was something else, like a reaction to the way he was speaking to her. She straightened her shoulders. "If that's the way you want to think about me, John, then so be it. I can't change your opinion."

"Jennifer, no offense, but instead of looking down on me, you might want to think about who your grandma really was, and how you got this house in the first place."

She nudged her glasses up again. "What are you saying?"

"I'm saying that maybe me and the guys at my house aren't

the only people on Edgewater Road who've done things they aren't proud of," he said as he stepped out onto her front porch. "I'm saying that everyone's got something they want to hide from the rest of the world. Everyone has secrets."

"Especially you, it seems."

"Maybe I do. But I don't believe that I'm the only one. I'd bet you've got a slew of your own secrets." He bent down slightly to meet her troubled gaze. "But you know what? Your grandmother did too."

"MeMe?"

"Don't look so shocked. Face the facts, Jennifer. Ginny Smiley was no saint. She wasn't even close." The moment the words had left his mouth, he regretted them. Jennifer had loved the Ginny she'd known. He should've let her have that.

There was no real reason for Jennifer to ever discover that while her grandma had indeed been a nurse, served in Korea, birthed a no-good son, and helped out a slew of people, she had also done some very bad things.

Including being one of the reasons he'd gone to prison in the first place.

CHAPTER 3

It hadn't been an easy decision to call her mother. Though Jennifer got along with her well enough, their best conversations stayed clear of controversial topics. That meant they didn't talk about politics, religion, Jennifer's unfortunate "rebellious stage" (her mother's description) when she was fifteen, her missing father, or Ginny Smiley.

They usually discussed only the weather, *Dancing With the Stars*, and the latest sale at Macy's. Because there was only so much Jennifer could take of those three topics, they didn't talk all that much. Maybe once a month?

But every once in a while, it was necessary to go off their script. It usually felt a lot like free-falling without a parachute, but some things just couldn't be helped.

Like the questions she was about to ask her mother. She needed some answers and she needed them fast. For the last two days, Jennifer hadn't been able to get Lincoln's parting words out of her mind. There'd been something in his tone and words that made her realize that choosing to never push too hard or dig too deep into her family's past hadn't done her any favors.

Instead, she was fairly sure that her decision to live most of her life on the surface had only served to isolate her more than her natural tendencies already did.

That was why, with a firmness of heart accompanied by a healthy sense of dread, Jennifer had picked up the phone and called her mother. And, after discussing the January weather (it was cold) and her mother's new boots bought during the after Christmas sales (they'd been 60 percent off), Jennifer gripped her phone tight against her cheek and dove in.

"Hey, Mom . . . What do you know about MeMe's life?"

Jennifer could practically hear a new tension crackle on the line. "What do I know about Ginny? Well, um, that's a pretty big question, Jennifer."

It sounded more like her mother considered it a *loaded* question. "Mom, I mean specifics. Like, did she have any unusual hobbies or anything?"

Her mother kind of chuckled. "If she did, she sure didn't tell me. She was a pretty secretive person, you know."

Jennifer hadn't known, but she was sure learning that there had been a lot more to her grandmother than she'd realized. Feeling like she was grasping for straws, she pressed. "Anything at all would be helpful."

"Well, all right. I don't know much more than you. Let's see. Ginny was a nurse for thirty years, including two years when she volunteered to help in a MASH unit in Korea. She married, he died right after the war, and they had a son named Eric, who is your father."

"But what was she like? What did she do with her time?"

"I'm not really sure." As if she sensed Jennifer's dismay, her mother spoke again. "We weren't close, Jen. But you know that." An edge had slipped into her tone. It wasn't new or unfamiliar, but it felt just as sharp as it used to when she was criticizing Jennifer for acting too full of herself. "What I don't understand is why you're asking me all about her now."

"Because I feel like she was this person that I should've known . . . but never did justice to. And now I'm living in her house—which she willed to me. I've found myself walking around these empty rooms really feeling her loss." Hating that she sounded so emotional to her mother, she tried to sum things up as neatly as she could. "I feel like I should've known her better, Mom. I feel like I missed out."

"I think you knew her as well as anyone did. Like I said, she was private."

"I should have seen her more. I wish I had."

Sounding even more defensive, her mother sighed. "When you were little, I was a single mother working full time. I didn't have time to drive you three hours north to visit her."

"I know . . ."

Sounding even more defensive, her mother added, "For the record, even though the only two things Eric ever did worthwhile were impregnate me and then leave, I didn't blame Ginny."

"Of course not."

"And I never told your grandmother that she couldn't come visit us. If she had wanted to make the effort to drive south, I would have made sure you were available. I promise you, I would have. But she kept her distance, Jennifer."

The hurt in her mother's voice sounded so fresh, Jennifer felt tears prick her eyes. Even after all this time, Ginny Smiley was a sore subject. And here she'd gone and opened that wound and then poked at it. "Mom, I'm—"

"I never told you this, but Ginny had a lot of excuses too.

There were a couple of summers when you were home and I was so slammed at work, I called and asked if I could drop you off for a couple of weeks. More often than not, she'd say that it wasn't a good time to have a granddaughter underfoot. She was always too busy." The bitterness her mother never tried very hard to hide came back full force. "Doing what, I don't know. I mean, she was retired."

Jennifer guessed that MeMe had been keeping busy with her garden, taking care of this falling-down house, and visiting prisoners at the nearby penitentiary. "I'm starting to think that MeMe actually was busy, Mom. This house is old and needs a lot of work." For a moment she considered mentioning those visits to the prison but decided against it.

If she brought it up, she'd have to talk about Lincoln, and she wasn't ready to talk about him. Thinking of his dark blue eyes and the way he seemed to take in everything around him the way most people took in a good dose of air, Jennifer realized she had no idea about how she would even begin to describe the man.

Her mother sighed. "I know I sound hurt, and I guess I was hurt about her distance for a time. In those early days, I felt so alone, what with your father neither giving me money nor the time of day . . ." She coughed. "That said, even though it hurts to admit it, you're probably right that she wasn't making up excuses. She always did sound regretful. I believe she was. She lived alone in a big house in the country. Even twenty years ago, it needed constant upkeep and was always so stubborn. I remember her refusing to accept a helping hand when the nearby church sent over volunteers to rake all her leaves in the fall. She preferred to spend hours outside raking and bagging leaves instead of accepting the smallest amount of help. It drove me crazy."

"Wow. I didn't know that."

Her mother chuckled, but the sound was more bitter than anything else. "I don't know how you would have. I never told you, and I'm guessing she sure didn't. Ginny wasn't a fan of being seen as weak."

"Hmm."

"Oh, Jen. Look, I'm sorry if I'm bursting your bubble about your grandmother. I promise that Ginny wasn't a bad person—not at all. I think our problem was that she and I just never saw eye to eye."

"Like her keeping this old house."

"Especially that. One time, when she brought you back home after you spent a week with her, you went straight to your room and cried because you didn't want to leave her. I went so far as to suggest that she sell that old place and move in with us."

"You did?"

"I really did, Jennifer. You loved her, and she loved you." She sighed. "It doesn't matter what I offered, though. Ginny always said she couldn't leave Edgewater Road."

"Couldn't."

"I don't know why she never sold it, but I guess she had her reasons."

Her mother stopped abruptly, and Jennifer knew why. They'd very recently had almost that same conversation—except this time she had been the stubborn one who didn't want to sell. "How did she get this farm in the first place? Do you know?"

"I think her first husband and her bought that land in 1948 or so."

Jennifer latched on to that bit of information like a lifeline. "What? MeMe had more than one husband? What happened, Mom? Did they get divorced?"

"Um, I don't believe so." She paused. "I think he died soon after they got married."

"She was a young widow? That's so sad."

"Oh, yes. Young would be the operative word, too. I think she was still in her twenties when he passed."

And MeMe had kept it a secret all this time. Why, though? What had she been afraid of people knowing? Was there more to the story? "I can't imagine that. It's strange that I never knew."

"She was enormously private, Jen. It was a sore point with me, if you want to know the truth. I always felt like I only knew part of what was really going on in her life. Then, when I'd say something about it, she'd act put out, like I was being selfish."

"Wow." Jennifer was collecting tidbits from her grandmother's past like she was on an Easter egg hunt. "All of this is really too bad."

"You're right. It was too bad." Mom paused. "I would've helped if I could, but—" She cut herself off. "Anyway, um . . . back to her being a widow. Her first husband's death. I don't think it was that big of a surprise though. You see, he was older." Her voice lowered, became softer. "I think something happened to him in Japan or something during the Second World War. PTSD, you know."

Jennifer waited for her mother to relay how, exactly, the man had died, but she didn't add another word. To fill in the gap, she murmured. "Well, Ginny's second husband was nice. I remember Grandpa Gil."

"He was. He was a good man. He was formerly Amish, you know."

Jennifer's mouth was practically hanging open. "Ah, no. I didn't know that."

"Gil grew up on one of the big farms nearby. You're knee-deep in Amish country now, dear. In any case, he was good to Ginny. Very kind." She took a deep breath. "Ah, Jennifer, where are you going with all of these questions?"

Her mother's voice was guarded again, which was such a shame. It made talking to her about the house and her situation even harder, because it felt like she was pulling teeth to get the most basic facts.

And that was what Jennifer wanted. She didn't want to hurt her mom, but she wanted to know about her family's history. She wanted to know why her grandmother would leave her a house but keep so many secrets that they were practically strangers.

She also wanted to know how her father could have walked away from her before she was ever born, how he could've gone through his life without ever caring enough to seek her out. And she wanted to know *why* her mother never spoke about her time spent with Eric Smiley.

But most of all, she wanted to know how a man she'd only met a couple of times could trigger such a reaction that she felt wrung out when he left her side—so restless that she was badgering her mother with questions that Jennifer knew she'd never want to answer.

"I don't know," she finally murmured. "I guess there's something about living in MeMe's house, using her stove, storing my clothes in her closet, but not knowing much about her." Even hearing that out loud made Jennifer wonder what kind of person *she* was. Was she trying to form a connection that had never existed when her grandmother was alive?

"Well, like I said, as much as she came across as a simple farm woman, she was anything but. She was a mess of contradictions." After a pause, her mother added, "Sometimes I felt like trying to get to know her was like trying to get through a labyrinth. If I said one wrong thing or pushed too much, she would shut me down, and then I'd have to start all over again."

Hating that her mother felt that way, but also wondering if maybe her mother hadn't been completely mistaken in her assessment, Jennifer said, "Do you think it's wrong that I'm trying to learn more about MeMe?"

"Jennifer, you know I didn't want you living there. You're far away, and I miss you."

Her mother had sidestepped the question. Neatly avoided the topic in the hopes that Jennifer would drop it.

Just like she usually did.

Biting back her frustration, Jennifer said, "I miss you too, Mom. But—"

"I also think you've never been particularly good at being around other people, and now you're putting yourself in a position to be even more isolated. I'm worried that now you're going to spend your life either working on your computer or working on that blasted house. It's not healthy to be alone twenty-four-seven, Jen."

Her mother's comments sounded eerily like Lincoln's split-second assessment of her. But Jennifer thought they were both wrong. Yes, she was quiet by nature, but she wasn't a recluse.

Why, from the time she'd moved in, she'd seen other people a lot. She'd had some former inmates help her move in, she'd delivered cake to a scary party, and she had served coffee to the man who had been responsible for both things. That was a start, right?

Determined to stick up for herself, Jennifer said, "Mom, I know it's not healthy to stay by myself all the time. In fact—"

"No matter how much I might do something differently, I've finally realized that I can't change you. I've decided to try to accept your decision and support you as best I can."

Ouch. "I see. Well, um, thank you."

Mom continued, her voice sharp. "Obviously, this hasn't been a particularly easy pill for me to swallow, but I know you feel strongly about being there. I hope you'll be happy."

She was floored. In mom language, that was almost an apology. Almost.

Floundering for words, she said, "Mom, I'm just trying to find some answers, you know?"

"I know," she replied in a soft voice. "Now, stop worrying, honey. What will happen will happen, right?"

"All right."

"All right?" She chuckled. "That's it?"

"I . . . I guess so. Everything you're saying makes sense. I think I need to stop second-guessing myself and start accepting things." And start accepting the fact that if she wanted to find more answers, she was never going to get that information from her mother.

"Jennifer, hearing you say that . . ." Her voice softened. "Well, it sounds good, you know?"

"Hey, Mom, thanks. I'm glad we talked."

"Me too, honey. I know we seem like two really different women, but don't forget that twenty-some years ago I fell in love with your dad. I spent a lot of time on that farm—at least for a couple of months. I uprooted my life on a dream. I wanted so badly to be happy with Eric. It's not the same thing, of course, but I can't help but reflect that your situation isn't all *that* different."

"I guess it isn't, is it?" She had uprooted her life, all because she was full of hope, wishing for a dream to come true. "I keep forgetting that you moved here without knowing anyone." At one time, her mother had spent quite a bit of time on this farm and quite a bit of time around Ginny. And Ginny had supported her a whole lot more than Grandma Emma when Mom had gotten pregnant.

"All I'm trying to say is that while I didn't want you to move, I can understand your motivation," her mother added quietly.

"That's enough, I think."

She chuckled. "If we can agree on that, then maybe there's hope for us after all, Jen. Just remember that I love you and want you to be happy."

"I love you back, Mom."

After they spoke for a couple more minutes, Jennifer hung up the phone. Unbidden, tears pricked her eyes. Why was it that she could only now—after moving two hundred miles away—finally have an honest conversation with her mother?

She walked back into her office and thought about putting on her headphones and getting back to work, but she couldn't do it. Instead, she wandered into the worn farmhouse kitchen and pulled out some sugar and flour. She'd make some cinnamon rolls and take them to the fire station or nursing home or something—anything to keep busy.

Three hours later, she'd just pulled the tray out of the oven when Bo knocked on the back door. "You decent, girly?"

"Absolutely. Hi, Bo," she said with a smile, just to show that she hadn't forgotten his name yet again.

"Howdy, Miss Jennifer," he said with a nod. He stuffed his hands into the pockets of his jeans as he stared at her.

"Long time, no see," she teased. Bo had on his usual uniform of a white T-shirt, faded jeans, black boots, and a half-zipped black hoodie. And, as usual, his blond hair, dark eyes, and ruddy-tan good looks took her a minute to get used to. He was that handsome.

When he didn't grin at that, she started to worry. "Is everything okay? May I help you with something?"

"Huh? Oh, no. Nothing's wrong."

"Oh."

After a pause, he gestured behind him. "Mason and me were driving by and decided to see if you needed help with the driveway."

She peered beyond him and smiled awkwardly at the younger guy, who looked to be not much older than twenty-two or twenty-three. "Thank you, but, um, what's wrong with it?"

"It's covered with snow," Mason said.

"Really? I saw it had started snowing, but I haven't looked out front for a while. I've been baking." She smiled awkwardly when she realized she was chatting with them like they were inside her kitchen instead of out in the freezing weather. "Thank you for asking, but I can clear my own driveway. I'll get to it."

Bo shook his head. "Where's your shovel?"

"It's out in the barn." She wrinkled her nose. "I mean, I think it is. Why?"

"'Cause we're gonna get that driveway cleared." Just as he turned away, Bo looked around the kitchen. "What's that smell?"

"I made cinnamon rolls." Looking at Bo's and Mason's wistful expressions—she realized that she hadn't talked to another person face-to-face since Lincoln stopped by. With her mother's words still ringing in her ears, she made a sudden decision. "When you two finish clearing the drive, would you like to have some?"

"That ain't necessary," Bo said.

"It isn't necessary for you two to stop by and offer to help me out, either, but you did. Won't you come in and help me eat some? Honestly, it would be my pleasure, and I made plenty."

Mason grinned. "Oh, man. That would be great. Thanks."

Bo nodded. "Thank you, ma'am. We'll be back after the drive is cleared."

They turned and walked back down the path, leaving Jennifer to watch their retreating backs—and to come to terms with the fact that she was now going to be feeding two former inmates from the local penitentiary.

Which meant she wasn't going to be sitting alone in this big house with only work for company.

With some surprise, she realized that she was pleased about this.

Who knows? Maybe MeMe would've even been pleased about that too.

CHAPTER 4

"These rolls are good, Miss Jennifer," Mason said.

"Real fine," Bo agreed. "I ain't never had anything like them before. I mean, beyond the ones you pop out of the can."

Seeing someone enjoy what she'd made from scratch made her happy. She smiled at the men sitting on the other side of her grandmother's worn oak table. "Thanks, but it's nothing. I like to bake, so I bake a lot. You did me a favor by sharing them with me."

After consuming another gooey cinnamon roll, Mason leaned back against his chair with a satisfied sigh. "My grandma used to cook up stuff like this. Every once in a blue moon, she'd give me one. I'd forgotten all about that."

Thinking about how MeMe had probably served these men from this very table, Jennifer felt a real sense of satisfaction. She might not be as outgoing or hip as her grandma, but at least she could carry on this tradition. "I'm glad you guys stopped over.

Like I said, I needed some help eating them. Plus, it's the least I could do for all your help with that driveway."

"It weren't nothing," Mason said.

Bo took the last bite of his roll, looking at his empty plate longingly before pushing it a few inches from him. "Ginny was a real good cook, but you might even be better, girl."

"Thank you." Inside, she beamed . . . and outwardly she felt herself flush with embarrassment. Boy, maybe she really was desperate for validation.

"It's the truth."

"I never met Ginny, but everyone said she was a real nice lady," Mason said.

"She was. The best."

"I got out after she passed," Mason added. "I always thought that was too bad."

Got out. As in "got out of prison." Feeling her way around the conversation, because she'd never had the occasion to share small talk with ex-cons, she said, "Were you up in Madison-ville like Lincoln?"

Mason nodded. "I was locked up for four. Bo here was in for three."

"I see." A new tension rose in the air, lingering against her uncertainty. She could almost feel the men tense, preparing themselves for a look of condemnation. She wasn't going to do anything of the sort . . . but what did one say to that? "I bet you're real glad to be out."

Mason, all two hundred pounds of him, looked her right in the eye. "Uh, yeah," he said without breaking a smile. "I guess you could say that I'm real glad."

Oh, Lord. "I'm sorry. Boy, I really just put my foot in my mouth, didn't I? Please forgive me if I hurt your feelings." Rushing on, she said, "No offense, but could you guys help me out in case I start chatting with some of the other men who might have been there?"

They exchanged a look. "Not sure I'm following you, ma'am," Bo murmured.

This was getting worse and worse. "I meant, should I never mention Madisonville? Am I not supposed to talk about it? The last thing I want to do is offend someone."

Mason blinked. Then grinned at her. "Sugar, all of us have come to terms with the fact that we were in the pen. It's not like we can pretend it didn't happen. You can talk about it whenever you want. I don't care. And, ah, shoot, you can say anything you want, here especially. After all, this here is your house."

"You call her Miss Jennifer or Miss Smiley," Bo uttered in a tone that didn't invite argument.

Mason looked down at his clean plate. "Sorry, Miss Smiley. Meant no disrespect."

"No, I'm the one who owes you an apology. You've been nice enough to come over here and shovel off my whole driveway. I don't want to repay the favor by being rude."

Mason grinned at Bo. "Can't say I've ever had a pretty thing like you say she was worried about hurting my feelings before."

"Shut up. You know Lincoln don't want you saying things like that to her," Bo said. His voice wasn't harsh, but there was something in it that made Jennifer take notice. Well, the tone and the fact that he'd just said Lincoln didn't want any of his friends calling her a pretty thing.

Turning back to her, he said, "Like Mason said, I don't reckon there's a thing you could say that's going to cause a bunch of hard feelings. Especially not about Madisonville, anyway. We were there, so it's a part of us now. Pretending we weren't isn't going to change a thing."

It's a part of us now. Something about that phrase resonated deeply, like he was speaking of so much more than just his years spent in a correctional institution. Had that been what *she'd* been doing? Pretending parts of her past didn't exist?

Feeling a little shaken by the direction of her thoughts, and even more awkward, she stood up. "Hey, would you two like any more rolls for the road?"

A half smile played on Mason's lips. "For the road, ma'am?"

She almost frowned but quickly realized that he was messing with her. Chuckling softly, she replied. "Oh, you know what I mean. You could take a couple back home with you. You could heat them up in the morning for breakfast."

Bo answered immediately. "I think cleaning you out of five was enough. Obliged, though." He got to his feet. "We'd better get going."

"I understand. Well, um, thank you both for shoveling the drive. It would've taken me all afternoon to do it myself."

Bo shook his head. "Girl like you shouldn't be out shoveling. I'll pass the word around that someone needs to come over and see to your driveway when it snows."

"That's not necessary."

"It ain't no big thing," Mason replied. "Especially since we got to eat after."

Slipping back on his coat, Bo nodded. "Lincoln will be pleased that we took care of the drive. Don't worry none."

She walked them to the front door. "Well, thanks again."

Mason gave her a kind of salute before walking out, Bo right on his heels.

When she was alone again, Jennifer picked up the plates and thought about the guys—and how strangely nice it had been to sit with them in the middle of the day. And she couldn't help but think about Bo's comment, the one about how Lincoln was going to be pleased with them. And the way he'd reprimanded Mason when he called her sugar, saying how Lincoln wouldn't be happy about that.

Both of the comments had taken her by surprise. Given the way Lincoln had left the day before, she'd been sure Lincoln was ready to wash his hands of her. Maybe he was, but was all this a part of his mission to honor her grandmother?

If that was the case, did it even matter? She wasn't sure.

Picking up the coffee cups, she wished that weren't the case. Bo and Mason had been friendly. But no matter how she spun it, she knew they hadn't come over because of *her*. No, they'd come out of obligation. Or because Lincoln had ordered them to.

Right. She wasn't suddenly making lots of friends for the first time in years. She needed to remember that.

Stewing on that thought, Jennifer rinsed the dishes, placed them in the dishrack, and then glanced at her computer.

The monitor was lit, practically calling out to her to get back to work. But for the life of her, she couldn't seem to care. For the longest time, work had served as her companion. And because she worked from home, it was close to being her roommate too.

Which, she now realized, was a pretty sad thing.

Walking away from her desk, she glanced out the front door. It was still snowing outside, the scent of cinnamon and sugar filled the room, and she had nothing pressing on her agenda.

What to do?

Maybe go for a walk in the snow? Just as she reached in the hall closet to grab a coat, an old box that had been stashed on the top shelf toppled to the ground with a *thunk*. As it landed, the lid popped off and a pile of papers slid onto the ground.

Well, there was her answer. Just like her memories and Bo and Mason's history, there were some things that just couldn't be ignored and forgotten.

Such as Ginny Smiley's packrat tendencies.

Her grandmother had been a great woman—undoubtedly brave and with more than a little gumption and grit—but a good housekeeper she was not. Not only had she left her belongings unsorted for what looked like years, it also didn't seem to have occurred to her to vacuum the carpet or sweep away the dust bunnies on the closet floors or back corners either.

Mentally preparing herself for confronting a packed closet full of bittersweet memories, *and* a mess of spider webs, grunge, and other mysterious flotsam, she decided to tackle the large hall closet first. At least here she would still be out in the open and not in a tucked-away bedroom.

After grabbing both a cardboard box and a large garbage bag, she waded in. She was now ready—mentally and otherwise—for whatever she might see.

CHAPTER 5

"You two have been gone for hours," Lincoln said as he watched Bo stride through the front door, Mason trailing behind Bo like a lost puppy. "Where were you? I thought you were going out for firewood."

"We did. But then we got sidetracked," Bo replied.

"Is that right? What sidetracked you?" Lincoln didn't want to jump to conclusions, but he'd had his fair share of men who spent their first couple weeks out of the pen on the straight and narrow, but all too soon old habits, temptations, and boredom gripped them. He wasn't worried about Bo, but this Mason kid was another story.

From the moment Lincoln had met Mason in Madison-ville's parking lot, he hadn't known what to do with the guy. He seemed lost and aimless. Every couple of days, the kid jumped from one idea to the next, ricocheting like a pinball before crashing and burning. Lincoln had seen his kind before. There were more than a few men who simply didn't want to change. They took advantage of Lincoln's help and connections, said all the right things, and then took off once they found easy money or easier acceptance.

He wasn't positive that was Mason's story . . . but both of these guys should've known that they were going to be questioned if they couldn't account for large chunks of time.

Bo stopped in his tracks but didn't look offended. "Nothing to worry about, boss."

"That's right." Mason nodded. "Miss Jennifer's driveway needed shoveling."

"You went over to Jennifer's?"

Humor lit up Bo's eyes, but his voice was as quiet as ever. "Yep."

For some reason, her having the guys over without notifying him didn't sit right. "Why were you over there in the first place? Or, did she call you?" Yes, he sounded like he was accusing them of something, but there was a part of him that didn't want any of his men to go over there without his knowing. He and Jennifer might not get along, but that didn't mean he didn't feel protective of her.

"We haven't exchanged phone numbers, boss," Bo said. "At least not yet."

Lincoln knew Bo had added that little jibe just to mess with him. It was probably nothing less than he deserved. His questions had been out of line.

Now he just felt like a jealous fool. But instead of admitting that, he folded his arms over his chest. "Anytime you're ready to give me some answers, I'm ready to listen."

"Bo and me were driving back when we noticed that there was a good five inches of snow coating her driveway," Mason explained. Puffing up a bit, he continued. "When me and Bo knocked on her door to see if we could help her out, Jennifer hadn't even noticed it was snowing." He grinned. "She practically trotted over to the window just to make sure we weren't lying. It was funny as all get-out."

"She'd been busy baking," Bo supplied.

"Anyway, the girl needed help," Mason added. "Even after Bo got out of her that there were snow shovels in the barn and it was no trouble, she still hemmed and hawed like she was putting us out. Eventually, though, she gave in and seemed real grateful."

Even though Jennifer Smiley's driveway was not his problem, Lincoln bit back a rush of guilt for not thinking about clearing it on his own. "I guess she needed a hand. That's good you stopped by."

Mason nodded. "It sure was. It didn't take Bo and me no time to clear it off. Plus, Miss Jennifer made it worth our while."

Hating that his mind was already heading toward a mess of inappropriateness, he bit out, "In what way did she do that?"

"Weren't nothing bad, boss," Bo said, his tone laced with warning.

Seemingly oblivious to the tension brewing around him, Mason said, "Miss Jennifer invited us in for cinnamon rolls."

"You ate cinnamon rolls with her?"

Mason nodded. "Yes, sir. She'd just baked them. And man, oh man, were they good. She must have used real butter."

"Huh," he said, fighting back yet another sting of jealousy. It wasn't like he needed to be sitting around eating baked goods. But that didn't mean any of his guys needed to be doing that either.

"Just to let you know, we didn't linger. Just long enough to be neighborly," Bo added as he finally hung his hoodie on one of the hooks by the door. "You know, I was thinking . . . Next snow, we ought to have some kind of rotation in place to help her out. Girl like her, on her own, shouldn't be out shoveling. That driveway is a good half mile long."

"Yeah, we could do that, I guess," Lincoln agreed.

"Don't know why we wouldn't," Bo continued. "All of us took turns helping Ginny out when we could."

There was a difference, though. Ginny had never been all shiny, innocent, and new. Ginny Smiley had been around the block and knew how to take care of herself. She was tough as nails and twice as sneaky.

Jennifer, on the other hand . . . well, he didn't know much about her. Other than that, she kept to herself and wasn't exactly a fan of ex-cons.

Even though he would never admit it to anyone, there actually were a couple of men in his employ who did *not* need to go visiting Jennifer without supervision. Some temptations were too hard to resist, and if she got hurt by one of the guys, he'd never forgive himself. "Don't you go sending men over without letting me know, Bo," he warned.

Bo raised his eyebrows but only nodded again. "Gotcha. Everything that has to do with Jennifer will go through you first."

When Lincoln noticed a couple of the other guys who were in the vicinity step closer and exchange looks, he knew he needed to take it down a notch.

Here he was, standing in the front hall interrogating two of the men because they'd had the nerve to go shovel a woman's driveway. He didn't understand it, but he was feeling protective of that girl—and he needed to get a handle on it.

"Miss Jennifer even offered to send some cinnamon buns home with us so we could heat them up for breakfast," Mason said, as if Lincoln hadn't already heard enough about their field trip. "Bo said no, though. Said something like we couldn't be taking advantage of her good nature."

Lincoln took a deep breath and changed the subject, hoping that would calm his nerves. "I sent y'all out for firewood. Where is it?"

"Couple of the guys were standing around when we parked, so I asked them to take care of it. They're adding it to the wood-pile now."

"Good." He rolled his neck a bit before turning away and walking into his office.

When he was alone and sitting behind his desk, he wondered what he was going to do about his new neighbor. There was a part of him that was drawn to her like a prisoner to a decent meal. Kind women like her didn't cross his path very often, and her sweet disposition was so welcome, he wasn't exactly anxious to push her away.

On the flip side, he knew Jennifer was dangerous to know. He and Ginny Smiley had had a convoluted relationship on the best of days. On the worst, he was both resentful and disappointed in her public persona. She'd come across to most people as a do-gooder—a woman intent on helping some of the less fortunate men in the county.

But he had known that it wasn't just her aptitude for good works that motivated her. It was also a good deal of old-fashioned guilt. The woman had been involved in things no one had any inkling about, and she'd been so foolish half the time . . . And when he'd stuck out his neck to help her, she'd backed off so quickly, like she hadn't wanted to get the blood from *his* deeds staining her pretty clothes.

That was his quandary.

Though he couldn't deny that he'd deserved to serve time, there was a lot more to the story of how he'd ended up behind bars than Jennifer knew. But . . . did she really need to know the whole story? He wasn't sure.

"Lincoln?" Two raps on his door interrupted his little journey into the past.

"Yeah?"

Easton, his foreman on most of the remodeling he did, stuck his head in. "That Amish boy is back to see you. What do you want to do?"

"Wayne's here?"

"Wayne Miller. None other."

"What does he want?"

Easton rolled his eyes. "What do you think he wants, boss? He wants to talk to you."

Lincoln lumbered to his feet. At least twelve-year-old Wayne was smart enough to know that he needed to stay on the outside of the building, where he wouldn't be subjected to the sights and sounds of men who had forgotten how to behave around decent folk.

Unlike Jennifer and her useless, fancy turquoise shoes.

"Where's he at?"

"He's standing near the porch, talking to Seth."

Seth was former Amish. "He's only talking to Seth?"

"Well, yeah," Easton threw over his shoulder as he started through the door. "As of three minutes ago."

No telling who else could have shown up and decided to corrupt the kid in that time. Mumbling to himself, Lincoln followed Easton out of his office, glared at Bo talking to three new guys about work details, walked past two men sitting on the couch eating chips, then strode out the door.

As he feared, Wayne was sitting on the floorboards of the covered porch chatting with not only Seth but two other guys like they were long-lost friends. About a year or two ago, Lincoln had put some fancy restaurant-grade heaters out there. One of them was on, so between the contraption and the porch being covered, it was almost pleasant.

The kid looked up at him with a grin. "Hiya, Lincoln."

"Hey there, Wayne. What brings you by?"

He jumped to his feet. "I came over to see if you had any work for me."

After gesturing to Seth to stay but the other men to leave, Lincoln said, "I appreciate the offer, but don't you have enough to do with school and your chores?"

"*Jah.*" Looking down at his feet, Wayne scratched an ankle. "But I need some extra cash."

"How come?" He hated putting a twelve-year-old on the spot, but Lincoln had learned that no good ever came of letting the guys keep secrets from him.

For a moment, Wayne didn't look like he was going to answer, but then he mumbled. "*Mei daedd* lost one of our horses two nights ago."

"What happened?" Seth asked quietly.

"We had that ice storm, and they were out in it. Annabelle slid on a patch of black ice and broke her leg." His bottom lip quivered for a second before he shook it off. "*Daedd* had to put her down."

Seth murmured something to the boy in Pennsylvania Dutch.

"I'm real sorry about that, Wayne," Lincoln said.

"Me too, even though I ain't never really liked Annabelle. She was as stubborn as all get-out, but she was a real fine horse."

"The stubborn mares are the smartest," Seth said. "I had a mare once who I could tell was smarter than my brother."

Lincoln felt his lips twitch as Wayne grinned. "Half the time Annabelle knew where we were supposed to be going before we did."

"I'm glad you told me about your mare," Lincoln said.

Wayne shrugged. "Anyway, we're out a horse. *Daedd*'s gonna go to the auction next month, but he wants a good'un. So I told him I'd help make some money to pay for it." After hardly waiting to take a breath, Wayne continued. "So that's why I'm asking. Do you have any work for me?"

Lincoln didn't want him working around his house. The boy was impressionable and the men he was mentoring weren't fit company for sheltered Amish boys. "I don't know if I do, Wayne."

"Oh."

"Look, I could lend you some money." Knowing he had a couple of hundreds tucked in his wallet, he reached inside his back pocket.

"*Nee,* that's not what my father asked me to do." He slowly got to his feet. "He won't hold with me accepting money I didn't earn."

"Even if it's just a loan?"

"*Daedd* says a loan is just charity in disguise."

Lincoln didn't necessarily agree but he wasn't going to press the point. "Thanks for stopping by. You want a cup of coffee? It's cold out." He'd learned a couple of weeks ago that Wayne enjoyed a good cup of strong coffee as much as any of them.

"*Nee. Danki.* I better go."

"He should go to Miss Jennifer's," Seth said. "That woman's got more work that needs to be done than an old lady at the plastic surgeon."

Lincoln fought back a smile. Seth's sayings were as random as they were true. "You know what? You got a good point, Seth. I'll talk to her."

"Who's Miss Jennifer?" Wayne asked.

"She's a woman who moved into Ginny Smiley's place," Seth replied. "Ginny was her grandmother, her *Groossmammi.*"

Obviously appreciating the Pennsylvania Dutch help, Wayne tilted his head. "Is she young?"

"Not that young. But she works on a computer all day,"

Seth said. "She could probably use your help outside." Grinning, he added, "I don't think she knows the difference between a rake and a hoe."

Wayne brightened right up. "I do. I'll go ask her right now if I can do something for her."

"I'll ask her, Wayne," Lincoln said.

"When? 'Cause I need the money now."

"How about tomorrow? I'll take you over there in the morning."

Impatience flared in Wayne's eyes, but he tamped it down fast, proving to Lincoln that the boy was more mature than the majority of the men who were working for him. "What time?"

"Nine."

Seth coughed. "Kind of early to go calling, ain't it?"

"Watch it, Seth." .

Wayne's eyes widened at the exchange, but he nodded. "I'll be back at nine tomorrow. *Danke.*"

"You're welcome. Don't forget that we're friends, 'kay?" After Wayne nodded again, he added, "You want a ride, son? It's cold out there and the snow's blowing. Seth here could give you a lift."

Wayne met Seth's gaze, paused for a few seconds, then shook his head. "I think it might be best if I went home on my own. Seth showing up might bring up a lot of questions."

"See you tomorrow then."

Watching the boy ignore the two men smoking nearby, Lincoln said, "How come he said that? Do you know Wayne's family or something?"

"Or something. Wayne's mother is my aunt."

Lincoln blinked. Fought back the slew of questions that were surfacing, mainly how did an Amish boy turn into an *Englischer* who'd spent time behind bars?

"I see," he finally said before walking back inside.

It was a lame response, and one that didn't give him much satisfaction either. Lincoln didn't like secrets like Seth's. It opened him up to being surprised, and he didn't much care for that.

However, Lincoln was learning that they all had secrets—some of them more than others. He'd also learned that the Lord didn't give a man more burdens than he could bear.

It was time he remembered that.

CHAPTER 6

The doorbell chimed at nine fifteen on the dot. When Lincoln had texted her the previous evening, asking if there was any way he could stop by in the morning and bring someone to meet her, Jennifer couldn't refuse. Not that she would've anyway, but there was something in the way Lincoln had phrased the request that had gotten her attention.

It had been . . . sweet. And confusing. After all, the last time they'd talked he had acted mad that she'd been shocked about him being in prison and housing a lot of other ex-cons. She'd felt bad about her reaction afterward, especially after sitting down with Bo and Mason. She wished she would have listened more and controlled her expression *a lot* more. However, she'd also been a little dismayed that he'd gotten so mad about her reaction. She couldn't have been the first person he ever met who didn't know any ex-cons.

Now, as she ushered Lincoln and the Amish boy inside, she was curious. Both about why he was hanging out with an

Amish youth and why they'd decided to come over to visit her at nine in the morning.

The boy was holding his black felt hat in his hands. Lincoln looked ill at ease. And the boy? Well, he looked more than a little anxious. And cold.

Ignoring Lincoln, she tried to put the boy at ease. Smiling softly, she said, "I'm so glad to see you both. I was just thinking about how much I needed a break from my computer."

"Jennifer, this here is my friend Wayne."

She smiled at Lincoln before focusing back on the child. "It's nice to meet you, Wayne. Like Lincoln said, I'm Jennifer."

Wayne nodded his head. "Hi."

After looking down at Wayne, Lincoln announced, "We've got a business proposition to talk to you about."

"I'm anxious to hear about it. You know what? I don't get a lot of company, so I went ahead and made a coffee cake. And Wayne, I make really good hot chocolate too. Would you two like some cake and coffee or hot chocolate?" When the boy gaped at her, she felt her smile falter. "It's still warm."

Lincoln placed a hand on the boy's shoulder. "I can't say that I'd ever turn down coffee cake. Let's take off our boots, boy, and sit a spell."

As Jennifer watched them pull off their boots and coats, she was even more aware of how she was dressed. It had snowed during the night, so she had on a long bulky fisherman's sweater, leggings that looked like they were suede but weren't, and heavy socks. She'd arranged her hair into two long braids. And she'd impulsively decided to wear her glasses today as well. There had been a part of her that had known she'd done it for Lincoln— because he'd mentioned that he liked them on her.

Wayne kept staring like he was trying to figure her out. No doubt she looked a little silly.

"I'll meet you boys in the kitchen," she called out as she decided to busy herself with the cake. "Wayne, would you like hot chocolate, or maybe a glass of milk? Lincoln, I made a pot of coffee. What would you boys like?"

"Coffee's good, Jen," Lincoln said. "Wayne?"

"I'll take a coffee too. Please."

"Oh! Well, okay, then." She put three mugs on the table as the men sat down.

Wayne went directly to the coffee and took a fortifying sip. "It's *gut. Danki.*"

"You're welcome," she said as she placed three plates and forks on the table. "I'm surprised you drink coffee. I always thought of it as a grown-up drink." And now she sounded both condescending and old-fashioned. She paused for a moment when she realized Wayne was quietly saying a prayer—and that Lincoln looked to be praying as well. "I hope you enjoy the cake too," she added when their eyes opened again.

"You made a real good point about the coffee," Lincoln said. "See, the thing is, Wayne here is kind of a grown-up twelve-year-old."

"Oh?"

Wayne didn't reply, whether it was because his mouth was full of coffee cake or because he didn't know how to answer, she didn't know.

Moving his plate to the side, Lincoln folded his hands on the table. "We're over here because he needs a part-time job, and I thought the two of you might be a good fit."

"Oh. Well, I'm not sure . . ."

After swallowing his monster bite, Wayne spoke up. "My *daedd's* horse got killed. He needs a new one."

"Goodness. I'm very sorry to hear that."

"I'm real good at yard work," Wayne continued. "Paying me wouldn't be charity."

"I see." Jennifer was at a loss for how to respond. Wayne might be mature for his age, but he was still just a young boy. She wasn't comfortable being responsible for his welfare. Then, of course, there was the yard work he was anxious to do. She glanced out the window but decided not to state the obvious, which was that everything outside was covered in a good four inches of snow.

While Wayne continued to wait patiently for her to say something more worthwhile, Lincoln folded his hands around his mug. "You mentioned the other day that you were clearing out Ginny's attic and cellar. Wayne could help you carry that stuff out."

"I'm strong and I wouldn't ask for anything either," the boy blurted. "I mean, nothing except for the money you would owe me."

Everything inside of her turned to mush. What was it about this boy that just grabbed her by the heart and didn't let go? Glancing up at Lincoln, she noticed that his expression had softened. He was fond of the boy.

"You know what? That is true. I guess it would be good if I got busy and worked on making the house mine. Then, when the snow clears, maybe you could help me get the yard in good shape."

Wayne's chin lifted. "I can do that."

"Should I speak to your parents first? I'd hate for them to worry about you being at a stranger's house."

Wayne turned to Lincoln.

"That won't be necessary, Jen," he said.

"Are you sure?" She'd never heard of a mother who didn't want to know where her kids were at all times.

"*Mei Mamm* has her hands full with my younger brothers

and sisters," Wayne said. "Plus, she knows I need to help pay for the horse. They cost a lot, you know."

Feeling a bit lost in the conversation, Jennifer said, "I suppose horses are expensive."

"It's real good of you to want to chat with Wayne's parents, but they know I'll look after him," Lincoln said.

"Oh. Well, then . . . yes, of course, Wayne. I'd be happy to hire you on."

The boy's whole posture changed. He leaned back against the back of his chair and almost smiled. "Thank you," he said after Lincoln gave him a small nudge.

"You're very welcome." Noticing his empty plate, Jennifer brought over the rest of the cake and sliced him another piece. "I hope you'll eat a little more, Wayne?"

He looked toward Lincoln.

"No need to ask me. If you'd like some more, just let Jennifer know."

"Jah. *Danke,*" Wayne mumbled.

She didn't know a word of Pennsylvania Dutch, but she could certainly ascertain that he'd just said "yes" and "thank you." Feeling pleased, she smiled at him. "I was hoping you'd take some more. Here you go."

Noticing that Lincoln was eating his now as well, she finally ate a bite of her own cake and felt a sense of accomplishment. It was moist, and it held the faint tang of sour cream and buttermilk and the added sweetness of Mexican vanilla.

"I've never had a cake like this," Lincoln said. "It's good."

"Thank you. It's a new recipe."

Lincoln turned to Wayne, who was looking antsy now, having already polished off his second slice of cake. "Boy, I need to talk to Jennifer for a minute or two. Want to go take a peek in her barn? Last I remember, it was filled to the rafters."

"It still is," Jennifer said. "You're welcome to go out there and look around if you'd like."

"Okay." He picked up his hat, which he'd set on the floor next to his feet, and headed to the front door, where they'd left their coats and boots.

"Not so fast," Lincoln called out. "You need to thank Miss Jennifer here for the food and the coffee."

"*Danki* for the *Kucha* and *Kaffi*."

Lincoln nodded. "And now in English?" he said quietly. "Your words don't mean much if she can't understand them." He winked.

"Thank you for the cake and coffee."

"You're welcome."

As Wayne started heading toward the door again, Lincoln turned toward him. "I'll come get you in ten. Stay in the barn. Hear me?"

"*Jah*." He looked at Jennifer, blushed, then pulled on his coat and boots. About two minutes after, he was out the front door.

After she heard it close, she raised her eyebrows. "You continually surprise me, Lincoln. How did you come to befriend an Amish boy?"

"It's a long story, but basically, the kid knows one of my hires named Seth. Seth is former Amish, and Wayne likes him a lot."

"I noticed that you do too."

He looked uncomfortable. "He's a good kid and his parents have their hands full with his siblings. I'm happy to help when I can. Wayne doesn't seem to care that I'm a little rough around the edges."

Jennifer was starting to realize that his gruff ways didn't bother her either. "To be honest, I never thought about hiring someone to help me clean, but now I'm excited about it. He's going to be a lot of help."

"I know he will. Wayne is a real hard worker."

"Ah, how much were you thinking I should pay him an hour?"

"I thought ten or so."

"Ten dollars an hour? Okay."

"I can pay half . . . or all of it, if you'd rather."

"I can't let you do that, Lincoln. I can pay him. I'm happy to."

"He wasn't making up the story about helping his pa buy a horse. They need the money."

"Of course. Horses aren't cheap."

For the first time since they'd met, amusement shone in his eyes. "You're familiar with the going rate of horses?"

"No, but I can take a guess."

He smiled. "When can he start?"

She couldn't think of a reason to wait. "Tomorrow?"

"That's real good. Thanks, Jennifer. I'll let him know," he added as he turned to leave.

Surprisingly, she hated that he called her by her name instead of his usual *babe*. Boy, she'd messed things up with him. She strode to his side. "Hey, John, wait a minute." She rested a hand on his arm, stilling him.

When he looked back at her, his expression seemed carefully blank. "Yeah?"

"I . . . well, I wanted to apologize to you for the other day. I sounded judgmental and rude. I'm sorry about that."

"I wasn't any better. I knew you didn't know I'd been in Madisonville, but I acted like you shouldn't have thought it was a big deal. Worse, I know better than to walk around with such a big chip on my shoulder."

"I shouldn't have acted so shocked."

"No, here I was, looking down on you because your sweet world didn't include a healthy dose of ex-cons. Well, not until you met me."

Now she felt even worse. "John—"

He reached out and gently squeezed her shoulder. "Really, don't worry about it. Most folks are taken aback at the idea of spending time with people who've served time. I knew that. Shoot, I don't know how many times I've reminded my guys that they are going to need to work harder, act better, and try harder than everyone else if they want to get a second chance." Just as she was starting to realize how warm and almost comforting his touch was, Lincoln dropped his hand. "Lord knows that's been my experience."

"I really am sorry. As soon as you left, I felt terrible. I promise, I acted better with Bo and Mason."

Amusement lit his eyes. "I heard. They thought your cinnamon rolls were something pretty special."

She laughed. "They were easy to please. But seriously, John. I mean, Lincoln. Can we . . . Can we try to start over again?"

"There's no reason for that, babe. We're good." His voice gentled. "Now I'd better go check on Wayne. He's probably wondering how long he's gonna have to hang out in your barn."

She smiled at him. And it felt so good to do that. "Tell Wayne I'll look for him around eight tomorrow morning."

"Will do." He paused, then pulled out his cell phone. "I'm going to give you Bo and Seth's phone numbers. Add them to your contacts."

"Why? I mean I already have yours."

"You're all alone here. Something could happen and you might not be able to get me right away. But chances are good that one of us will be available and able to get here in a few."

"That's not necessary. I mean, we're out here in the middle of Ross County. Not the city."

"That's exactly the point, Jennifer. In the city, at least there are other people around to hear you call out. Here? Nobody will hear if you're in trouble." He paused before looking at her intently. "Keep your doors locked. That's important, understand?"

Even though he was being awfully bossy, she couldn't deny that he had a point. "I understand."

Heading for the door, he got back on his coat and boots in a matter of seconds. Then he called back, "Thanks for helping Wayne out."

"Anytime!" Unable to help herself, Jennifer stood in the doorway while Lincoln collected Wayne, then waved at them both as he turned his truck around in her driveway.

Something about their relationship had changed again today. She'd stopped thinking about him in terms of his history and it looked like he'd stopped thinking of her as just Ginny's granddaughter.

She had no idea what this shift meant, but she had a feeling that she was about to find out.

CHAPTER 7

Lincoln felt relieved when Jennifer finally closed her door and clicked the deadbolt into position. She was safe now. As safe as a woman like Jennifer could be living alone on two acres in an old, too-big, creaky farmhouse.

To his consternation, he found that he no longer thought about her living in Ginny's space. Whether it was because her office was in the front room, or there was always a hint of vanilla and spice lingering in the air, he'd already put Ginny into the past and Jennifer in his present.

Or . . . maybe it wasn't all that surprising, since he had started thinking about Jennifer all the time.

Noticing Wayne looking back behind them too, Lincoln said, "What did you think? Is working for Miss Jennifer going to be okay?"

"*Jah.*" In that careful way of his, Wayne took another moment to collect his thoughts. "At first, I was sure you were just making up something for me to do. But when I walked in the barn, I realized that she needs a lot of help."

"Yeah? It was that bad in there?"

He nodded. "There were bridles and bits and harnesses and all kinds of equipment for horses."

"Huh. I can't remember when Ginny kept horses. It might have been before my time."

"I reckon so. They're old." Wayne waved a hand to illustrate his point. "They're in poor shape but could still be used if they were cleaned up. Right now, they're just taking up space."

"You'll have to ask your pa if he knows of a use for 'em."

"You don't think Miss Jennifer would mind?"

"I can't imagine why she would. Like you said, all that stuff is doing is taking up space and collecting dust. She'd probably love the extra room."

Wayne nodded. "She's got a lot of stuff."

Lincoln chuckled. "I've thought the same thing." Pretending to give it some thought, Lincoln said, "You know, it sure would be good if someone got some use out of that stuff—even if it's selling the items to make a little extra money."

Wayne nodded but kept silent.

Making a decision at the stop sign, he turned right. The boy was probably hungry. Boys his age always were.

"Lincoln, my *haus* is the other way."

"I know, but I got hungry. McDonald's is just a couple miles down the road. Want some lunch?"

Wayne frowned. "I don't have any money on me."

"My treat. We'll eat, then I'll drive you home." When Wayne still hesitated, Lincoln murmured, "You might as well agree, buddy."

"All right."

Lincoln almost smiled. Once again, Wayne kept his emotions

in check. He often wondered where the boy had gotten so much control over his emotions. He knew enough Amish folks to realize that not every Amish teenager was as careful with his words. There had been many instances when he wished some of the grown men in his care had even a quarter of the restraint Wayne had.

"So what else was in that barn besides old livery?"

"Dirt and dust. And a lot of boxes and crates." He looked Lincoln's way. "What do you think could be in them?"

"No idea. I guess you'll find out."

Wayne nodded. Then, as Lincoln pulled into the restaurant's parking lot, he blurted, "I did look in one of the cardboard boxes. Just to see if there was more stuff for horses inside."

The boy's voice was tentative now. "What did you find?" Lincoln asked curiously.

"Some bullets."

Lincoln was glad the truck was parked. "Say again?"

"Bullets and gun shells."

"Are you sure about that?"

"Oh, *jah*. There were boxes and boxes of them."

Realizing that Wayne wasn't going to volunteer any more information, Lincoln asked, "Were there any weapons to go with those bullets and shells?"

"*Nee*. But like I said, I didn't open the crates." The kid's throat worked. "Lincoln, what do you think they were for?"

"I couldn't tell you. I don't think they're Miss Jennifer's though. Do you?"

"*Nee*. The box was covered in a bunch of dust. No one's touched them for years, I bet." Wayne pulled in his lip before speaking again. "And well, Miss Jennifer don't really seem like the type to have lots of guns and ammunition, does she?"

"No, she don't." Shoot, he could hardly get the woman to lock her front door.

He might be putting her on a pedestal that she didn't belong on, but he was of the mind that Jennifer Smiley was about the sweetest thing that had appeared in Ross County in ages.

Definitely the sweetest thing that had ever set foot on Ginny Smiley's property.

"Jennifer wants you to start tomorrow. I think I'll send Seth or Bo with you for a couple of days, Wayne. Just to be on the safe side."

He looked affronted. "No need for that. I'm strong. I can handle the barn."

"I know you are, but getting those crates open is going to be easier with two people." Plus, he didn't want that boy anywhere near weapons.

"What are you going to tell Miss Jennifer?"

"The truth. There's some old bridles and such that need to be cleared out and some ammunition that needs to be removed."

The boy's brow wrinkled. "Reckon she's going to be mad?"

"No. My guess is that she's going to be real appreciative of your help, boy." When Wayne sat up a little straighter, Lincoln said, "Now, you ready to get a Big Mac?"

Wayne grinned. "*Jah*. I'm starving."

"Me too. Come on. Let's eat."

● ● ●

Two hours later, he was back in his house and looking at pictures of one of his rental properties out at Lake Mary. Seth had been waiting for him with the photos in his hand and had asked for a private word as soon as Lincoln had walked in the door.

Now they were standing next to Lincoln's desk and studying the pictures that Seth had taken of the rental property. The place was trashed. If Lincoln hadn't had so much on his mind, he would've been furious. Now, it just felt like one more thing happening in his life that he hadn't expected.

"I thought we knew who'd been living here, Seth."

"We did. Well, Mason did. He vouched for the guys."

"How did he know them? Were they in Madisonville?"

"Nope. Mason said he grew up with them." Seth reached for his phone. "I've got even more pics on my phone if you want to see 'em."

"This is enough." He trusted Seth as much as he trusted Bo. He didn't need proof to believe him.

Looking more frustrated, Seth said, "I couldn't believe what I saw when I went out there this morning. Two months ago, the tenants were paying on time, and no one seemed to have any problems with them. Then, yesterday morning I got a call from a patrolling deputy saying that the place looked abandoned."

That wasn't good. Mason knew that if he vouched for the renters then they were his responsibility. "Where's Mason?"

"He's sitting outside. I texted him when you got back since I figured you'd want to talk to him."

"I do." Lincoln stood up and walked around his desk. "Have you already brought this up with him?"

"Not this," he said, pointing a finger at the first picture. "I did talk to him a while back about the late payments. Two days later, I had the money."

That was enough to send warning bells right there. "I wish you would've told me."

"You count on me to manage the properties, boss. I don't like to get you involved."

"I appreciate that, but I don't like being caught by surprise."

"Me neither." Looking pensive, Seth said, "I didn't give Mason a specific reason for this meeting. I just told him that you were calling in a lot of people this afternoon."

"Good. I'm looking forward to hearing how he's going to explain himself."

"I'm looking forward to that too."

Watching Seth get even more upset, Lincoln attempted to control his own temper . . . though it was likely a losing battle. He was pissed about the damage, pissed about Seth getting called because the place looked abandoned, pissed that he was now going to have to spend the next couple of days getting answers and then spend the next few weeks repairing the damage that had been done. "Go get him, but you come back in here too, Seth. I want you to tell Mason exactly what you saw. And, I want him to have to face you and me both when he sees these photos."

"Sure, boss."

Minutes later, following behind Seth, Mason made the mistake of entering the office with a smug smile on his face. "Heard you needed something?"

Lincoln was glad he was seated behind his desk again because he was tempted to shake him hard. "Yeah, I was wondering how you could have made so many bad decisions regarding the Fourth Street property."

Everything in his stance changed. He'd gone from complacent to agitated in thirty seconds.

Unfortunately, though, it didn't look as if Mason had gotten any wiser. He turned to Seth, who was standing against the closed door. "Hey. Did you know what this meeting was about?"

Seth's pale blue eyes were chilling. "I called it."

"I don't understand why you kept me in the dark. I thought we were friends."

"Looks like we're both disappointed, because I thought I could trust you," Seth said in a no-nonsense tone.

"You can."

Lincoln tapped a finger on one of the photos. "You better start talking. Seth got a call from a sheriff's deputy this morning about the house looking abandoned."

Seth folded his arms over his chest and nodded at the photos. "This was the condition it was in." He reached into his pocket and held up his phone. "I've got another twenty in here if you want to see more. As far as I'm concerned, you've been keeping a lot of secrets of your own."

Looking at the photos on the desk, Mason paled slightly but didn't say a word.

The guy's response wasn't what Lincoln had expected to hear. Lincoln leaned back in his chair and waited for a string of excuses and apologies. When Mason stayed silent, only stuffing his hands in his pockets, Lincoln became even more irritated. What was going on with this guy? "Mason, you need to start talking. Seth told me that you found the renters. Is that the truth?"

"Yeah." Mason looked wary. "I went to school with the guys. We've been friends from way back."

Though Seth didn't say anything, Lincoln could practically feel the waves of animosity floating off of him. Seth had every right to be angry too. From the start, Lincoln met with each parolee and told them to leave their pasts in the past. No good would come from reconnecting with old habits . . . unless they intended to get locked up again.

"If you vouched for these friends of yours . . . if you've known them for years, you should have known that their actions reflect on you," Seth said.

Mason looked incredulous. "Look, all I did was find you a renter. Whatever they did ain't my responsibility. I never even hung out with them over there."

"That's where you're wrong," Lincoln said, barely holding

his temper in check. "First, those men occupied the house based on your word. That makes them your responsibility. Second, you're living on my dime, which means everything that affects this group is your business." His voice lowered. "Third, you're sadly mistaken if you think that you're going to speak to Seth or me in that tone."

Seth stuffed his hands in his pockets. "Do you understand all that, or do you need me to repeat it?"

Mason glared as he stood up straighter. "I get it, but I don't understand why you're talking to me like this."

"Sit down," Lincoln said. "It's beginning to become clear that we've got a lot to discuss."

"I'll sit, but I still don't get what you want me to say."

Seth pushed away from the door and took the chair next to Mason. "An apology would be a good start."

"Apology for what? I didn't *do* anything."

It was time to shut this conversation down before Lincoln gave in to his impulses and kicked the guy out of his life. "This is what you're going to do. You're going to go over to that house and clean it. You're going to track down these friends of yours and convince them to pay what they owe me. When you're not doing either one of those things, you're going to be here, helping out in the kitchen."

"And if I don't?"

"If you don't, I'll make sure to call your parole officer and get you moved, since you're my responsibility." He lowered his voice. "But I can promise you this. If you don't elect to get that money, and if you force someone else to clean that house—even after you move out of here, I'll be contacting you."

"This isn't fair."

"Any one of the other men who are working for me would tell you that life isn't fair. But in this case, it absolutely is. You're going to need to earn your way back into my good graces. One payment at a time."

Mason's jaw worked. "You know, I never would've spent an hour the other day shoveling Jennifer's driveway if I would've known you didn't trust me."

Lincoln was coming to realize that if there was a surefire way to set him off, it was hearing any of his men talking about Jennifer. "Don't worry. You won't have to worry about doing that again. Now, are you ready to listen or are you gonna leave? It don't matter to me."

It was obvious that Mason was debating his choices and wondering if Lincoln was threatening him or just giving him a bunch of empty promises. Beside him, Seth was everything Lincoln had ever hoped one of his lieutenants would be: quiet, contained, and absolutely on the same page.

"Fine."

"You sure about that?"

"I'm sure I don't have much choice." Mason moved to stand up.

Seth grabbed his shoulder. "Hold on. We're not done yet."

"What else do you want?"

"To make sure you realize that this is your only warning. We're not going to have a little get together like this again."

"I get it."

After Lincoln nodded, Seth led Mason out of the room.

Only then did Lincoln release the breath of air he'd been holding.

Back when he'd started this, his goals had been almost noble. He'd wanted to give men like him, men who'd made mistakes but were still decent, a second chance. He'd wanted to help them. Share what he'd learned about faith and hope. Educate them about better ways to solve problems instead of just using force. Give them a sense of worth, give them a decent wage.

He'd ached to give the guys some stability, which was something a lot of them had been without most of their lives.

Now, nearly eight years later, his aspirations weren't quite so lofty. Oh, his heart still searched for the good in people, and he often shared some of the teachings he'd learned from the Bible. However, he'd also learned that not everyone could be rehabilitated. Some people didn't want to change. Shoot, some of the men he'd tried to help over the years were just plain dangerous.

But never before had he been worried about one of them hurting someone he cared about.

It might not be true; he might be just imagining things . . . but right at this moment, he was fairly sure that he'd somehow pasted a target on Jennifer's back.

And now she was his responsibility.

CHAPTER 8

Soon after Lincoln and Wayne left, Jennifer logged out of her computer and forced herself to dive into one of her grandmother's closets. She couldn't very well ask Wayne for help cleaning out the house without taking a good look at what they were going to be dealing with. She'd started on an upstairs linen closet last night. After realizing that the majority of the sheets, blankets, and towels were in too bad of shape to even give away, she'd loaded them into a pair of trash bags and carted them downstairs.

Empowered by her success, she'd gotten up early that morning to tackle the hall closet before Wayne and Lincoln arrived. Unfortunately, none of the items inside were as easy to sort and some were just plain confusing.

Sitting on the floor, surrounded by stacks of jackets, old dresses, a nurse's uniform, and a hodgepodge of gloves, hats, and scarves, Jennifer gazed at the two items nestled in her lap.

She'd been prepared to see a lot of things in MeMe's closet. Not these.

One was a letter. The other was a padded envelope filled with thirty or forty receipts and photocopies of checks.

None of which had been from her grandmother's bank account.

No, for some reason, a whole lot of people had been paying her grandmother money. A lot of money. Sometimes a couple of hundred dollars. At other times, the people had paid her amounts in the thousands.

From what Jennifer could discern, MeMe had accepted not only checks but cash too. And, to make matters even more confusing, her grandmother had obviously accepted the money, squirreled it away somewhere, and kept a neat record of it. Recently too. All in the last six years. Why had she done such a thing? And where had all this money gone?

Just as much a mystery was why Ginny had saved all the receipts for Jennifer to find.

It couldn't have been an accident, could it? Her grandmother had been sick for over a year but had always been very lucid. The nurses Jennifer had talked to always mentioned how Ginny was still as sharp as a tack.

Until just weeks before she died, by all accounts, she'd been fairly self-sufficient too. She'd also intentionally left Jennifer the house and all her belongings. That had to mean that Ginny had intended for Jennifer to find these receipts after she'd passed.

At least, it sure seemed that way.

If that was the truth, then it brought forward even more questions. Like, if Ginny had wanted those receipts discovered, why hadn't she brought them up on one of the many occasions Jennifer had visited? And, what was Jennifer supposed to do with them now that they were in her hands?

Even the thought of handling it all made Jennifer feel sick to her stomach.

Staring at the list again, she continued to ask questions. Who could all these people have been? Did they live in the area? And, for that matter, how had they come into contact with her sweet grandmother in the first place? Jennifer wasn't sure if she wanted to know.

But even more disturbing was the letter from Ginny's son, Eric—otherwise known as Jennifer's dear old dad. Even touching the handwritten note had made her feel uneasy.

However, the things he'd written to his mother made Jennifer feel even worse. With a combined sense of curiosity and doom, she'd read his lengthy note. It was long and rambling—four pages of notebook paper filled with surprisingly legible cursive. Sentence after sentence of graphic details about his exploits, all of which sounded like pure fiction to Jennifer. After all, who went mountain climbing in South America or fishing in Alaska unless they were rich?

Eric was most definitely not.

Actually, it was obvious that he wasn't rich at all. Just a man who took from whomever he could and concentrated only on himself. It certainly seemed as if he'd had no problem asking his mother for money to finance his adventures.

It was also glaringly obvious that Eric hadn't been happy about his mother's refusal to give him a cent. At least not lately.

After Jennifer read the note a second time, she understood the awful truth. Ginny might not have given her son much money recently, but she'd given him lots and lots of money, many times before.

That was crushing. Ginny had knowingly given Eric money, even though she knew that he never gave any of it to Jennifer's mother. Or Jennifer herself. Eric Smiley had never paid child support. Nor had he ever taken the time to call her. It was as if he'd forgotten all about her. She slumped. Or, maybe he'd forgotten about her existence.

It was also starting to feel obvious that Ginny had never spoken to her son about his ex or his daughter either. That was a difficult realization.

Jennifer had felt creepy reading the correspondence and, at the same time, empty inside. Not only had she felt like she was invading both her father's and grandmother's privacy—this insight hadn't done anything to make her feel closer to either of them. Which wasn't really a surprise, but it wasn't good either.

If anything, she felt more out of place than she usually did. Even more alone.

Now, as she stared at the two items in her lap, Jennifer wondered what else she was going to discover—and if there was a way she could remain detached from the information she was discovering.

Yep, that was the crux of it. She had been so thankful when she'd realized Ginny had left her this old house. She treasured the gift. But she was slowly beginning to understand that living with guards up wasn't helping her. She needed to push herself a bit. Get out from under her shell. She wanted to stop being so safe and live a little bit more. She wanted to make more girlfriends, push herself a bit . . . maybe even finally sign up on one of those dating apps she'd been exploring but had never gotten the nerve to try.

And, yes, she also wanted to form more of a connection with her namesake.

Which would be wonderful, except for the fact that Ginny was gone, and it was becoming apparent that she hadn't ever really known the woman, even when she'd been alive. Maybe she'd been going about this all wrong. She had been focusing on the fact that she and Ginny both loved this house and that they both enjoyed baking. Perhaps she should be concentrating on the woman herself—the *real* woman, the one who'd never come to see her.

Who'd had an estranged, strained relationship with her own son.

Who had never gotten along with Jennifer's mother either.

Who seemed to have more in common with the man next door than her own namesake.

The realization made Jennifer feel terrible. Why did she feel the need to dig out a relationship with a dead woman who hadn't done all that much with her when she'd been living?

How was she going to be able to accept Ginny's secrets when it was becoming obvious that each piece of information burned like acid in her make-believe hopes for her future.

Furthermore, why had she been so eager to not only accept a house from a woman that she really hadn't known that well, but also to upend her whole life and move here too?

What did that say about her? Well, besides that she was desperate and insecure and hadn't had much to leave behind.

Recriminations filled her mind and dripped down her throat, making it hard to talk and grasp for clarity.

"Hey, Jennifer? You in?" Lincoln's voice, along with his heavy knock, jarred her to her senses.

"Yes!" she called out. "I'll be right there."

"This door better be locked, girl."

From anyone else, she'd be offended. But for some reason, his gruff threat only made her smile. He cared about her safety.

Walking to the door, she snapped the deadbolt back with a satisfying *click*. "Do you hear that?" she said through the thick wood. "Maybe you'll believe me now when I tell you I've been keeping it locked."

"It's appreciated. But right now, I'm telling you that it's real cold. Want to let us in?"

Turning the handle, she looked directly at Wayne and smiled sweetly. "I'm so glad you're here, Wayne. Come on in and get warm."

"Yes'm," the boy murmured as he hurried through the doorway.

Only then did Jennifer let her gaze drift over to Lincoln. When she caught sight of him scanning the area, as if he was hoping to make sure everything was safe and sound, a little bit more of her unease around him melted away. He was rough around the edges but also caring.

"Jennifer, you good?" he murmured.

She realized that she'd been staring. "Yes. I . . . I was just noticing your sweatshirt. I guess you like to fish?" Lincoln was wearing his usual jeans and boots, and the black jacket that he never seemed to fasten, with a worn gray sweatshirt advertising a fishing tournament underneath. It looked incongruous on him, but perfect too.

"Hmm?"

"Your sweatshirt." She pointed to the shirt as he walked indoors at last.

Lincoln looked down at his sweatshirt and kind of chuckled. "Yeah. I guess today I do."

She closed the door behind him, trying to ignore the way she was constantly being drawn to the confusing man—even when he did something as simple as removing a black leather jacket.

Determined to get herself back to rights, she focused on the boy, who had also taken off his coat and was now staring at her in an expectant way. Realizing she should have said something earlier, she smiled at him. "So, Wayne, are you ready to work?"

He blushed as he nodded.

Only then did she notice that she was wearing pajama bottoms sporting penguins and hearts, an old college T-shirt, and thick socks. Her hair was a mess and she didn't have on a lick of makeup. The only saving grace was that she'd remembered to brush her teeth and put on a bra. "Oh, boy. Guys, I'm sorry I look so goofy. I've been cleaning out this hall closet all morning. I guess I lost track of time."

Lincoln's expression warmed. "It's your house. You should wear whatever you want." Resting a hand on the boy's shoulder, he added, "Wayne was going to work in the barn with one of my guys, but I thought it might be better if he worked inside today. Will that be okay with you? The wind is real bad out there."

She smiled at Wayne again. "I think that's a good idea."

"So do you want us to finish up with the closet while you go put on something warmer?" Lincoln asked.

"No," she blurted a little too quickly and an octave higher than she meant to. There was no way she was going to risk anyone else seeing either that packet of receipts or her father's note. When both of the guys stared back at her in alarm, Jennifer realized that she had to get a grip on herself, and quickly, too.

She sure hoped it was possible.

CHAPTER 9

Lincoln had intended to drop the boy off and get on his way. But, after seeing how nervous Wayne was, both about working for a woman he didn't know and being in an unfamiliar place, he decided to stay. He texted Seth and told him that he didn't need to come to the barn. He would start going through those crates in the barn himself.

But then, when the three of them had been standing in Jennifer's entryway, Lincoln had gone and changed his mind again.

There was something about Jennifer that drew him to her like he was a lonely kid in need of a few smiles. This woman, with her gorgeous blond hair, soft brown eyes, and goofy ways did something to him. From the way Wayne was still sneaking glances at her, Lincoln knew he wasn't alone.

After a couple of seconds passed and Jennifer still looked a bit rattled, he cleared his throat. "Jennifer, where do you want Wayne to work if not in the barn or in this mess of a closet?"

"I've been thinking about that, and I think I'd like you to help me over here by the fireplace, Wayne. Is that okay?"

His eyebrows rose but he nodded. "What do you want me to do?"

She pointed to two cardboard boxes, a large black garbage bag, and a big paper sack, the kind a person might put leaves in. "I made you a little station over here. See that long row of cabinets? They're all filled with old paperbacks and magazines." She frowned. "And some other stuff that just looks gross."

"Gross," Wayne repeated, like he was trying on the word for size.

She walked over and then—much to Lincoln's amusement—started demonstrating what she wanted the boy to do. "Wayne, I want you to sort everything you pull out. The books that look usable, I want in the boxes so we can donate them. The magazines can go in recycle bag here. And then the gross stuff?" She picked up an old zip lock bag with safety pins and paperclips. "You can throw it away in the black trash bag."

"You don't want to see any of the stuff I throw out?"

"No . . . well, I don't think so." Practically on the heels of that statement, she said, "No, wait. If, um, something looks important or that I need it, you can put it on a stack on the card table. But there shouldn't be too much of that." She closed her eyes briefly. "I really hope there isn't."

"All right." Wayne was still holding his coat. "Where should I put this?" he asked Lincoln.

"Okay if he sets his coat on your couch here, Jennifer?"

"Of course. Wayne, I want you to make yourself at home." Completely missing Wayne's raised eyebrows, Jennifer turned back to him. "Thank you for bringing Wayne over, John. I'll drop him home when he's done."

She was giving him an out. Wayne was going to be taken

care of. No doubt Jennifer was planning to feed the boy too. Lincoln was coming to learn she fed everyone in her circle.

But he wasn't ready to go.

"Actually, I was thinking I'd stick around for a while." He stuffed his hands in his back pockets. "You know, maybe help you out."

Wayne, who'd already started examining books, glanced over at him but didn't say anything.

Jennifer looked mildly affronted. "John, that isn't necessary."

"I'm happy to help—unless you want me to go?"

"Of course not. You're always welcome here. I mean, would you like to help me with the basement? Ginny left a bunch of stuff in the back, and I've been kind of afraid to go see what, exactly, it all was."

The way she phrased that caught his attention. "What are you afraid about?"

"Oh, you know . . ."

"No, I don't. What is it?" He hoped there wasn't more ammunition hidden down there.

"Mice. I'm afraid of mice."

Wayne chuckled before pulling himself together.

Lincoln smiled at the boy, but he wasn't fooled by Jennifer's excuse for a second. There was something that she was worried about in this house and it wasn't a rodent. Of that, he was sure.

But partly for her and partly for Wayne, he played along. "Lucky for you, I'm real good at taking care of mice."

"You are?"

"Of course." He gave her a look that seemed to say mice were no match for "real" men.

"I'm warning you, there might be a lot of them." She grimaced. "Maybe even a rat."

"If there's a lot of vermin, I'll just send Wayne down there first."

"What?" Wayne called out.

Jennifer grinned at him, making Lincoln feel like he'd just accomplished something pretty good. Whatever worry had been clouding her eyes had vanished. "All right, gentlemen. Let's all go tackle the basement together. But give me a minute to put on some warmer clothes."

"Take your time." When she was out of sight, Lincoln walked over to Wayne and picked up one of the books he was sorting. It was some romance novel from the 1980s, complete with a half-naked couple on the front. Honestly, it looked like the viking was about to tear off the girl's clothes. "Whoa," he muttered. Who would have guessed that tough-as-nails Ginny had a secret affection for romance books?

Wayne glanced at the book and blushed furiously. "I don't know what to do with them, Lincoln."

"If they're in good condition, you'd best put them in the donation box. I've learned that you can't go about guessing what people want and don't want."

Wayne set the novel in the box. "Did you mean that about sending me down with the rats?"

"Nah, I'll deal with them." He winked, just to show the boy that he was teasing. "Unless they seem real vicious."

"Sounds good," he said. Looking earnest, he added, "If there's a mess of mice, you're gonna need a shovel to kill 'em, Lincoln. That's what I use in my barn."

Just imagining Jennifer's reaction to him killing mice with farm implements made him wince. "Good idea. If it comes to that, I'll go hunt one down."

"Hunt one?" Jennifer asked, now wearing some rubber-and-leather lace-up boots, jeans, and a thin ivory sweater. She'd let her hair down and put on contacts too. She looked pretty and ready for company now . . . though he was kind of missing the other, just-got-out-of-bed look.

"Hunt down a shovel in case we'll need to kill one of those rats."

"If you do it right, you can chop off their heads, Miss Jennifer," Wayne said.

She paled slightly. "Now I'm starting to get even more worried."

"Let's get down there. Wayne, you know where to find us if you need something," he called out.

Waving a hand toward the stairs, he glanced her way. "I'll head on down . . . unless you'd like to go first?"

Looking like they were about to head into battle, Jennifer shook her head. "No, that's all right. You can lead. I'll follow."

"All right then," Lincoln said as he started the descent. After a slight pause, he heard Jennifer follow. With each step, it felt like something more was happening than just a simple cleaning expedition.

He wasn't sure what it was, but it felt important. Almost life changing.

CHAPTER 10

How had this happened? One minute, Jennifer was surrounded by her father's letter, her grandmother's receipts, and far too many doubts and memories. The next? She was going down into the unfinished basement with her sort-of-scary neighbor while an Amish boy was sorting through her grandmother's hidden stash of romance novels.

All of it was under the heading of "Things She'd Never Envisioned Happening," and yet another example of how different life in Ross County was from her rather staid, organized life back in Cincinnati. She was slowly realizing that her life back there, while fine, hadn't been *good*. It was no wonder she'd felt so compelled to get out of her comfort zone and move into MeMe's old house instead of selling it and pocketing the money.

When she thought of the men who were now on the perimeters of her life, she kind of thought things here were better. Well, except that she sort of had a rodent infestation.

"Do you come down here very often?" Lincoln asked. He led the way downstairs, his heavy boots clunking down each step. The noise had to have propelled any bugs or rodents to run for cover. But then, just as the basement came into view, he drew to an abrupt halt.

Since he was so big, she couldn't move around him. "What are you doing?" she asked.

"Taking all this in." She caught enough of his profile to see he was glaring at the entire room as if it had personally offended him.

"I know. It's bad down here."

When Lincoln finally stepped forward, he sighed. "Jen."

Looking around the small portion of the basement that was finished, she shivered. The carpet was an unfortunate shade of baby blue. She was sure that the last time anyone had cleaned it had been in the previous millennium. The sorry-looking futon in the corner didn't look like it had been treated any better. Okay, it looked even worse—the thought of sitting on the thing made her skin crawl.

Littering the floor were about twenty run-down plastic crates. Each was filled to the brim with more books, an assortment of papers, and what looked like a lifetime of *Women's Day* and *Family Circle* magazines. Even the thought of her militant, bossy, stubborn grandma reading articles on child-rearing, diets, or cheap decorating made her smile.

What was sad was that this was the "good" section of the basement. The other two-thirds of the basement was unfinished. It was dark, filled with spider webs, smelled like mildew, and was stacked with seventy years' worth of discarded junk and memories.

Jennifer refused to be embarrassed about the mess. She hadn't made it and it was going to take a lot of time sorting and cleaning the whole thing out. "I came down here with Bo when I moved in but haven't been back since."

"Bo didn't tell me y'all came down here. Or that it looked like this."

"I don't know why he would have. It's just your neighbor's basement, right?"

A shadow appeared in his eyes, but he didn't say anything. "Come on then. Let's go see the rest of it."

She heard a rustle among the boxes the moment she opened the door to the unfinished section. Instinctively, she stepped back—right onto Lincoln's foot. "Sorry," she blurted.

One arm closed around her, fastening to her waist. The rest of his body was surrounding her, making her feel almost protected. "Hush for a sec. Did you hear something?"

She shook her head. When one of the boxes near the back shifted, she jumped. Behind her, Lincoln's already very solid body tensed.

"Where's the light switch?"

She pointed to a string hanging from the ceiling about three feet away. "It's, um, there."

"You stay here." Muttering something under his breath about safety and Ginny, he strode forward and pulled on the string. The bare light bulb flickered before casting a faded glow over the room.

When a box clattered to the floor, Jennifer squealed. "Sorry," she said, covering her mouth with a hand.

But instead of looking irritated with her girlish theatrics, his gaze was filled with patience. "Go get Wayne, babe."

"Do you think something's there? I mean something bad?" Suddenly she was imagining some creepy man lurking in the back.

He turned to her. His blue eyes looked cool, but his voice remained smooth and quiet. "Something's here. Not sure what, though. Go get Wayne now. Please."

She trotted up the stairs.

Wayne was sitting on the floor, looking like a strange meme

that attested to the power of romances because he had about a dozen of the books surrounding him. He was also reading the back of one of the books.

"Ah, Wayne?"

He dropped the paperback like lightning. "*Jah?* I mean, yes, Miss Jennifer?"

"Lincoln asked if you would come help him down in the basement."

"Oh. Sure." He got to his feet, then paused at the mess. "I—"

"I'll help you sort the books later. Don't worry."

Looking relieved, the boy trotted right down the stairs without another word. Jennifer followed a few steps behind.

"Lincoln?" Wayne called out.

"I'm back here. Come on in, but stay by the door."

Jennifer followed. "Do you want me to help too, John?"

"Nope. I want you to stay over there."

His tone was harsh, almost like he was in danger, which she thought was a bit over the top since they were fighting mice, not some street gang or something. "Um, why?"

"Because—" His reply was interrupted by a string of curse words and a . . . *meow?*

She froze, her mind not computing the noise with what she expected to hear. After a grunt, followed on its heels by a clattering of boxes, she peeked inside.

"Jennifer—"

"This is my basement. I think I have a right to know what is going on." And yes, she sounded a whole lot tougher than she was feeling at the moment.

She wasn't sure what she was looking at. On one side of the space, Wayne was holding out his hands like he was ready to catch a ball, and Lincoln was crouched near a window on the other side. Between them was a mess of boxes and trash.

Then, just as she was about to ask if they were going to try to catch those mice with their bare hands, a streak of gray tore out of a corner and ran her way.

She shrieked and jumped about a foot in the air.

"You aren't helping, Jennifer," Lincoln groused.

"I know. Sorry but . . ." At last her brain computed what was happening. It wasn't a giant mouse or rat running through the room. It was a cat.

"What's a cat doing in here?"

"Jennifer! Block the door!"

She reached to close the door, but the cat jumped to the side. Deciding it was foolhardy to turn her back on it, she said, "Here, kitty, kitty."

It froze at the sound of her voice, seemed to decide she wasn't a threat, and hissed.

Well, it was scared and unhappy . . . but it didn't exactly look like skin and bones. "Hey," she said gently. "What are you doing in my basement, little kitty?"

"Little kitty?" Wayne repeated.

Ignoring the men, Jennifer took a step forward.

The cat arched its back and hissed again, but amazingly didn't run off. Instead, it blinked at her with lovely dark eyes, like it could hardly believe what was going on.

Well, that made two of them. She figured there were two ways this could go—she could either attempt to grab it, which would undoubtedly make it run off again, or she could coax it to trust her. She went with the latter. She'd never had a cat, but she had always been good with animals.

"Aren't you pretty?" she said. It tilted its head. And then, to her delight, it meowed.

"Jennifer, you need to be careful," Lincoln warned. "It could bite you."

"I know. I am. But we're getting to know each other right now," she said in a baby-soft voice. "Which means you two men need to stay away and give me a minute."

"Lincoln, what should we do?" Wayne whispered.

"She's doing better than we were. I guess we'd best sit tight a minute or two."

The cat was still staring at her, letting her get a long look at it. It didn't have a collar, but it also didn't look like a stray. Every stray cat she'd ever seen was feral and wild-looking. This one?

Well, this one simply looked like it had trust issues. Figuring that an offer of food couldn't hurt, she asked. "Would you like some milk? Are you hungry?"

It meowed again. She took that as another sign that maybe they could be friends. Slowly she reached out a hand. It hissed and backed up a step but didn't leap.

"That's right. I'm the best chance you have of getting out of this awful room. I won't hurt you."

When it tilted its head, she smiled and carefully opened the door behind her.

"Jennifer," Lincoln growled from the back of the room.

She ignored him. "Come on, kitty. Let's get you fixed up. We'll get you some milk and maybe tuna." She was pretty sure she had a can of tuna around somewhere.

When it sat down on its haunches, she decided it was time to make her move. Intending to give it a gentle pet, she reached out her hand.

And in the space of two seconds, it leaped, hissed, clawed at her forearm, and then ran out of the room through the open door.

"Oh!" she cried out, turning to follow it. She was fast enough to see that it had run upstairs.

"Jennifer, I told you to keep that door shut."

"Well, I didn't listen."

He climbed over boxes, pushed others to one side and at last made it to her side. "Look at you. You're bleeding."

Yes, she sure was. The cat had gotten her good. It had scratched her bad enough that a line of blood was now running down her arm.

Wayne approached, looked at her arm, and frowned. "Are you hurting?"

"Not too bad."

"We need to rinse that off," Lincoln said. "And then we need to find that . . . that feline and make sure it doesn't have rabies."

She hadn't thought about that. "I bet it might come out of hiding if we give it a can of tuna."

"You don't want to feed it, babe."

"Why not?"

"If you feed it, it's going to stay."

"If it does, I might have a new cat, huh?" she asked as she led the way out of the basement.

"Are you sure you want it? It's a mean one," Wayne said.

"She'll warm up to me." Yes, here she went again, sounding full of herself even though she didn't feel at all confident about cats.

When they got to the kitchen, Lincoln shook his head as he guided her to the sink. While one hand was on her back, he turned on the faucet with the other, obviously intent on getting it warm. "Jennifer, I know you've got a good heart, but I don't think you realize what you're saying."

She was pretty sure she did. Sticking her arm under the hot water, she winced but kept it in place. "Everything needs a home, Lincoln. Even stray cats."

"I'll remember that," Lincoln murmured as he squirted some kitchen soap on his hands, got a good lather, then began washing her arm.

Her arm didn't really sting anymore. Or maybe it did, and

she was just distracted by Lincoln's ministrations. "By the way, did you ever see any mice?"

"I found one in the corner with its head off," Wayne said. He sounded hopeful.

She felt sick. "Wait, the mouse was decapitated?"

"I didn't see any blood," Wayne said, as if that would have made a difference. "I think it's been dead for a while."

There were decapitated mouse bodies all over her basement. "I feel like I've been living above a morgue," she moaned as she rinsed her arm and turned off the faucet.

"That's stating things a bit much, yeah?" Lincoln murmured. "Besides, you should be real thankful for those mice. They kept your new cat from starving."

"I can't believe that poor cat has been down in my basement this whole time."

"I don't think it has," Wayne said. "I saw a cracked window in the corner."

"So it's been coming and going as it pleases."

"I reckon so," Wayne said.

"Well, now we've got to find it." After sticking a piece of paper towel on her arm to catch the rest of the bleeding, Jennifer said, "I better go get that can of tuna open."

"You do that, but then stay out of the way," Lincoln said. "Last thing you need is to get hurt worse."

"If the cat scratches you, you could get rabies too," she pointed out.

"Then I guess we'll be getting shots together, Jen."

He sounded so put-upon, Jennifer almost laughed. Until she realized that he wasn't joking. Not at all.

One day soon, she was going to have to decide what she thought about that . . . because at the moment, she wasn't sure. Not too sure at all.

CHAPTER 11

She didn't have rabies, so that was a plus. The scratch on her arm was healing, her basement had a fewer dead mice in it, and the stack of paperbacks was now boxed and ready to be donated. On the other hand, the act of capturing the cat, stuffing it into a pillowcase, and getting it tested for rabies at the vet would go down in history as one of the worst experiences of her life.

Okay, that might be exaggerating things a bit, but it had been *horrible*. The poor cat was hissing and crying the whole time while it was contained in a cardboard box. Lincoln said he didn't want to take any more chances with the animal until its tests came back.

The vet had agreed to keep Clyde—which she'd named the cat—while they were awaiting the results. Then, yesterday morning, the receptionist had called with the happy news. Clyde was rabies-free, was relatively healthy, and had been neutered sometime in his short life. They'd also given him a bath and a whole dose of shots. He was ready to go home. All she had to do to claim him was pay his fee of $700.

Jennifer had almost told the receptionist to take Clyde directly to the shelter. Almost.

She hadn't been able to do it. For some reason, Clyde was a survivor, and she liked that. Plus, if the dead mice were any indication, he might be handy to have around. That meant a trip to the pet store and spending another three hundred on food, litter boxes, a collar, a crate to transport Clyde in, assorted balls, bells, and cat toys. And . . . the Cadillac of cat playgrounds, something called the Cat Condo.

After Clyde was stuffed into his traveling crate—which he wasn't any more fond of than the blue pillowcase or the cardboard box—Jennifer had unloaded all the loot. She'd decided to put the cat condo in her office so Clyde would no longer have to live alone.

That was a mistake.

"Tell me again why you decided to keep it?" Bo asked when he'd stopped by that afternoon to see if she had any more trash to haul away.

"*His* name is Clyde, Bo," she said as she walked him into the kitchen. "Would you like a cup of coffee or something? The coffee's fairly fresh."

"Thanks, but no." He stuffed his hands in his pockets. "I've got a ton of paperwork to get through, so I can't stay long."

She smiled at him. "I hate paperwork."

"Me too, but that wasn't what we were talking about." He leaned forward slightly. "Why you keeping Clyde, girly?"

"I don't know. No, that's a lie. I actually do know." She sighed. "I decided to keep him because someone had to want him."

Something wistful flashed in the man's eyes before he pushed it back, making Jennifer wonder yet again about

Bo's past. How could a man who was so handsome and so mild-mannered end up in prison? And why was she starting to get the idea that maybe he hadn't had much of an easy time before prison either?

"Have you told Lincoln that the cat is a permanent resident yet?"

"No."

He tilted his head to one side. "Any reason why not?"

"I figured he probably wants a break from me. I sometimes get the feeling that Lincoln regards me as nothing but trouble."

"Come now. You know that isn't the case."

"It just might be." Remembering the cat round-up, she shuddered. "I don't know if I can fully describe how traumatic catching Clyde and stuffing him into that pillowcase was. Poor Wayne. I bet he's had nightmares ever since."

"I don't think so." Bo grinned, flashing a set of perfectly white teeth. "Seth told me last night that Wayne stopped by to tell him all about it. From what Seth said, Wayne acted like your place was a combination of Disneyland and a haunted house."

She chuckled. "While it might be true, I don't think he meant it as a compliment."

"Trust me, for a twelve-year-old boy, it was high praise." He looked around. "So where is it now?"

"*His name is Clyde,* Bo. And I don't know. As soon as I let him out of his crate, he ran and hid. He won't even come out for his food, and it's in a cute dish and everything."

He sighed. "You want me to go look for him, or help you take more stuff to the dump?"

"No, it's fine." She patted his arm. "Thanks for the offer, but I don't have anything to haul away."

"You sure about that?"

"Positive. Between this cat and my job, I haven't had much

time to do any more cleaning. And, before you ask, no, I haven't started gathering the, uh, bodies in the basement."

He grinned. "Wayne told me all about the dead mice. That was classic."

"It was gross." She held up a hand. "And thank you, but no, I don't want you to go down there and start disposing of them. That's for another day."

"Don't worry. I wasn't going to volunteer for that job." He turned, then stopped. "So . . . you haven't been out to the barn over the last couple of days?"

Jennifer was beginning to get curious about his line of questioning. "Nope. And, yes, I know that makes me sound like a slacker, but I haven't done much around here besides shower, work, and try to make friends with Clyde."

His jaw worked. "Gotcha. Well, I'm going to get on my way, but would you mind if I peeked in your barn for a minute before I go?"

"What's going on?"

Bo suddenly became interested in a loose thread on his shirt. "Oh, nothing much."

"Bo, what?" Finally connecting the dots, she said, "Did Wayne find something out there besides bridles?"

He pursed his lips. "I'm afraid so."

"What did he find?"

"Ammunition."

"Like a couple of shotgun shells?" She hadn't seen a rifle anywhere, but that didn't mean much, given the amount of stuff her grandmother had stored all over the house. Realizing that Bo looked worried, she shrugged. "Oh, don't worry. My grandmother was pretty self-sufficient, Bo. I'm sure she had a rifle for hunting."

"That ain't what Wayne was talking about. He said there

was a lot of ammunition in some crates. I want to see what he was talking about."

"I do too." She grabbed her coat and boots from the hall closet and walked to the door. "I'll go out with you."

"I was afraid you were going to say that. Come on then," he said as he opened the front door.

She followed him out, blinking her eyes when they started to water from the cold wind. Luckily, the walk to the barn was short and the door wasn't locked.

Bo gave her a long look about that but yanked the barn door to the side and gestured her to walk through ahead of him.

Immediately, the scents of dust, old hay, and horse filled the air. She sneezed, then sneezed again.

"God bless you," he said as he walked toward a set of crates that had been pulled out. "Do you want to go back and wait for me in the house?"

"No. I want to see what you're talking about." As he grumbled, she took another look around the large space. Small windows, each about one foot by three feet, lined both sides of the barn near the ceiling. Rays of light shone down toward the floor, making the ground almost look like a checkerboard of light and dark spaces.

Other than the collection of saddles and other livery, the majority of the barn was empty—except for the line of over-stuffed shelves near the back wall.

Walking over to Bo's side at last, she saw him holding a cardboard box. "Is that them?"

"Well, it's one of them, Jennifer," he said.

When Bo lifted the lid, she could see that Wayne hadn't lied. The crate was filled with boxes of ammunition. "There must be a couple of dozen boxes in there, Bo."

"I was thinking the same thing."

Still trying to grasp what she was seeing, Jennifer lowered her voice. "Why didn't Wayne tell me about them?"

He put the box back in the crate. "I reckon because he didn't know what to say. I think it took him off guard."

"So Wayne told Lincoln because he knows Lincoln."

"Uh-huh."

Of course, the question now was why didn't Lincoln say anything to her about the find? Was it because he already knew about them but didn't want her to discover them? "Did you come over here to get these crates, Bo?"

Bo turned to her. "No, I did not. I came over here to see what Wayne had found, but this isn't any of my business."

Bo sounded certain. So certain that she wanted to believe him. As they walked back to the barn door, he said, "Where's the lock for it?"

"I don't have one. I cut off the deadbolt that was on there when I moved in and never replaced it."

"You'd best replace it, girly. It ain't safe to have all that ammo laying out, just for anyone to come on in and take."

"I'll get a lock real soon," she murmured after debating whether to point out that so far, the only people who had messed with the ammo had been him, Lincoln, and Wayne.

At the moment, it felt like it might be best just to keep that to herself.

CHAPTER 12

Mason was having a hard time. Looking sideways at the guy, Lincoln wrestled with the different avenues he could take to help the man.

Over the last five years, he'd learned a thing or two about guiding new parolees. Some left the prison like babes in the woods, just as confused about what to do with their lives as they had been when they'd committed their crimes. Other men had become hardened and had chips on their shoulders the size of a boulder. They didn't want help of any kind—not until they were in trouble again.

Still others were looking for someone to care. They needed a coach and appreciated a guiding hand. Some even enjoyed discussing their choices.

Others? Well, some almost needed a good dose of ordering about—something that they'd become reluctantly used to. At first, Lincoln had tried to not do the ordering . . . until he'd realized that giving some of the men fewer choices had been as much of a gift to them as offering them a safe place to adjust to life out from behind bars.

Helping ex-cons was Lincoln's reluctant ministry. He didn't feel qualified, but he also vividly remembered how confused he'd felt the first time he'd gone to the grocery store.

He'd been standing in the middle of the soup aisle, looking at all the choices when a woman with two toddlers in tow had accidentally knocked into him. He'd reacted instinctively, ready to defend himself, until he realized what had happened. Madisonville tended to fill a man with fear, and often the only way men were able to deal with all that fear was with anger. For a spell, Lincoln had embraced all that anger and violence too. But then a couple of do-gooders from the outside had offered a Bible study class. He'd started going as a way to escape his boredom, but those hour-long sessions had soon turned into his saving grace. He still had a lot to learn—there were times when anger still got the best of him—but he'd come a long way.

Years ago, after that woman had bumped him, instead of moving on, he'd stood frozen, his mind warring with common sense, struggling to determine whether the woman had run into him on purpose or not.

Only Ginny's reassuring hand on his shoulder had pulled him out of the tailspin. She'd calmly and patiently shaken her head at his clenched fist, rubbed his back, and whispered something that the minister in prison had said all the time: that it was time to *move on*.

He'd realized that he'd needed someone to believe in him as much as he needed air to breathe. And those two words, *move on?* Well, they'd meant everything.

So he knew a whole lot about how Mason was feeling. But

unlike the two dozen or so other men he'd helped assimilate to life on the other side, this guy was proving a hard nut to crack. Mason was acting like a cross between a lost puppy and a Rottweiler. Clueless, full of fun, but quick to anger.

Bo had walked into his office early that morning to share that the kid had almost gotten kicked out of his apartment the night before because he'd forgotten to pay his power bill and his electricity had been disconnected.

He ended up falling back on his crutch of choice. "Let's go for a walk, yeah?"

Mason, who'd shaved off all his hair in prison and was currently wearing a navy beanie in the frigid temperatures, looked at him like he had a screw loose. "What?"

"You heard me. Come on. We're going for a walk."

For a few seconds, Lincoln was sure the guy was going to dig in his heels and refuse.

And if he did, Lincoln was going to have to give him that. The guy didn't owe him a thing—he could damn well do whatever he wanted. But then with a grumble, Mason pulled on a coat and followed Lincoln to the door.

Lincoln grabbed his coat, too, and led the way to the driveway. "You ever been on this path here?" he asked, pointing to a gravel path that in the summer was half-hidden by weeds and hollyhock bushes.

"Nope."

"Come on, then." He took a deep breath of the cold, fierce air, and let it sit in his lungs before exhaling. Something about that burst of coldness never failed to revitalize him.

He started walking.

After a couple of minutes, Mason cursed under his breath. "What's your hurry, anyway?"

"No hurry. Just like to keep the blood flowing. What's

wrong? You can't keep up?" he teased, hoping to get a bit of a rise out of the guy.

"I can keep up. Just not sure if I want to."

Lincoln slowed down slightly. "Sorry. I start walking and forget that everyone else doesn't care for this as much as I do."

"Yeah. Like me."

"Fair enough." He slowed his pace a little more and decided to dive in. "Guess you can figure that I asked you out here for a reason."

"Yep. I guess you decided to go ahead and send me on my way." He cast Lincoln a sideways look. "Have you already called my parole officer?"

"I haven't called anybody."

"How come? I know you and Seth were real mad about the house at Lake Mary."

"I was mad, and you're right. Seth was madder. But you've been working hard on the place."

"I haven't gotten you all the money back yet."

"You've collected two-thirds of it." Lincoln studied him. "Did you get that from them? Truth, now."

"Some. Not all."

"How'd you come up with the rest?"

"I had it saved."

"Ah."

"If you ain't going to send me away, what did you want to talk to me about?"

"Nothing in particular. I just noticed that you've looked like you've been having a time of it lately. What's been bothering you? As much as the house situation was bad, I got the sense that's not the only thing bugging you."

"It's nothing."

"I'm not judging you. I'm here to help, remember? The day

I picked you up and took you to Denny's, I told you that I'd help you figure out how to live free."

"And that's what this walk is?"

"Maybe. How about you start talking, though?"

"All right." Mason pursed his lips, almost like he was attempting to force his body to comply with Lincoln's invitation to share a weakness. "I've been thinking about Jennifer."

"Jennifer, my neighbor?" And yes, he put the *my* in there on purpose. It didn't matter to him whether or not she was *actually* his or not. What mattered was that he felt protective over her. She needed someone to look out for her, and he figured that someone might as well be him.

"Yeah." Mason looked at him strangely. "What other Jennifers do you think I know?"

"Uh, none, I guess." He inwardly rolled his eyes. Lord, but he sounded like an idiot. "What about her?"

"Well, you know how we shoveled her driveway and then sat down with her in the kitchen."

"I remember. She gave you coffee." There was a faint trail through some prairie grass that led to a dried-up creek bed. Come spring, the creek would be running. But in January? It was just some leftover frost. It was pretty, though. He led the way up the rolling hill, his legs reminding him that he hadn't been climbing lately.

"She did. Coffee and cinnamon rolls."

Lincoln fought back the surge of jealousy that came calling once again. "Don't understand why you're still thinking about that." Suddenly, a thought occurred to him. "Or did something happen over there you and Bo didn't tell me about?"

"No. I mean, not really." He shrugged. "It's just that she opened the door, was all surprised that we were going to help her out, and then invited us in for cinnamon rolls. She had been baking and had a whole tray of them." He paused to take a breath, shoving his hands in his pockets. "We sat at her kitchen table, man."

There was a part of him that was jealous. Jealous about the way he had trouble saying much of anything to her. Jealous about how Jennifer had been practically standing guard when he'd knocked on her door but had invited these guys in like they were old friends.

"This story's real nice and all, but I'm not following you. Why are you telling me about it?"

"Oh. She's been on my mind. This girl, so buttoned-up and all, was serving a bunch of ex-cons like she was having a tea party or something. I couldn't believe it." He looked at Lincoln. "She was treating us like we were normal." Lowering his voice, he added, "She was treating us like she wasn't scared that we'd hurt her or steal anything. Like we mattered, still."

"She should." They were on the edge of the creek. He looked down, noticed some deer tracks along the ground. "You do still matter. Even when you were in prison you mattered." Of course, back in Madisonville, that had been difficult to believe. Most of the guards—and even a lot of their own families—had made it their goal in life to convince inmates that they were forgotten and worthless.

"But, don't you see? That ain't never happened to me before." Mason blinked. "It gave me hope, you know?"

So that was what it had all come down to. Hope. Hope for a different life. Hope that things would one day be different.

"I get it." He was about to try to come up with something to tell him. Something worthwhile, when, all of a sudden, there was Jennifer. She was hiking through the woods, dressed in jeans, boots, a puffy white coat, and a baby-blue knit hat and mittens.

She looked as startled to see them as they were to see her.

"Hi, guys." She looked flustered for a moment, then seemed to collect herself. "I mean, hi there, Mason and Lincoln." She smiled shyly. "It's kind of a surprise to see you here. Do you go walking in these woods a lot?"

Mason just stared at her.

"Not really," Lincoln replied, deciding not to point out that they were technically on his land, not hers. "What about you?"

"I do. I mean, I like to walk when I can. When you have a job like mine, it's good to get out of the house from time to time, you know?"

Though he'd never been one for small talk, Lincoln nodded. "I never thought about that. I guess working from home can get old, huh? I'd have a tough time only having myself for company."

"Sometimes it does. But that's the nature of the job. Transcribing medical records is a solitary occupation." Before he could comment on that—though what he'd say about it, he didn't know—she said, "I guess you guys have the opposite type of lifestyle, don't you? Surrounded by other people all the time."

"You get used to it, though," Mason said, finding his voice at last. "I mean, after being in Madisonville, a guy gets twitchy being alone too long." He winked. "Reminds me too much of solitary."

Her eyes widened. "Oh. Yes. I guess so."

As the tension between them drifted tight, Lincoln felt like rolling his eyes. Mason had gone and given her a bold, stark reminder that she wasn't just standing around, shooting the breeze with two neighbors.

No, she was standing in the middle of the woods in between her house and his with two ex-cons.

That reminder was undoubtedly going to transport her back to being scared of him. And it was going to undo everything he just talked to Mason about.

Jennifer looked his way, seemed to notice that he was

studying her intently, and smiled awkwardly. "Well, I hope you guys enjoy your walk. I should probably get on back home myself."

"Yeah. We've got stuff to do too," Lincoln said.

She smiled tightly. Took two steps, then turned back around. "Hey, ah, Lincoln?" Her voice had turned squeaky.

"Yeah?"

She looked down at her feet before visibly gathering her courage. "I just lied. I wasn't just out for a walk. I was walking over to see you. Or to try to find out when you were going to be home."

"Why? Is something wrong?"

"No . . . though, maybe. You see, it's just that I was doing some cleaning and I discovered something in my grandmother's things that's kind of strange. Since you knew her so well, I was hoping you could take a look. Maybe let me know what it's all about."

"Do you want me to come over now?"

"Do you have time?"

He wasn't sure if he did or not. But Lincoln did know that if he didn't deal with whatever she found and was on her mind right now, it would eat at him until they did connect. "Of course, sweetheart," he said instead. "I've got all the time in the world for you. All you have to do is ask."

He turned to Mason, who was staring at him like he'd just turned into one of the Madisonville guards. "Go on back to the house. And if you see Bo, tell him where I'm at."

"Yeah, boss. I'll, um, I'll go do that."

Looking ill at ease but resolute, Jennifer smiled at Mason again. "I'll see you later, Mason."

Mason flushed. "Yes, ma'am." Then he turned and started back down the path.

Leaving Lincoln alone with Jennifer, who was now walking back to her place—to Ginny Smiley's old house—like she was half afraid to go back.

Or, maybe she was afraid to be alone with him again.

If she was, it wouldn't be the first time a woman worried about such a thing. He knew more than most that sometimes words and promises didn't mean a thing.

All that really mattered was what a person did. Of course, he'd also found out that what someone did could be real bad too.

CHAPTER 13

At six feet, four inches and two hundred forty pounds, Lincoln Bennett was so much bigger than she was, Jennifer sometimes felt like even his shadow dwarfed her. Whenever they walked somewhere together, she couldn't help but notice the way their shadows flitted side by side and meshed together.

And how, sometimes, his shadow completely covered up her own. Of course, most people wouldn't notice such a thing. Or, if they did, they'd simply think about it as a trick of light.

But she couldn't help but dwell on it. Was that the sun's doing, the way they were standing together . . . or was it something else? Maybe a flaw in her own personality? Even after all this time, she struggled to be seen and heard.

"What are you looking at?"

"Hmm?" she asked.

Lincoln motioned to their shadows off to the right. "You

keep looking over at the ground like you see something bad. What is it?"

"Nothing." Looking up at him, she shook her head. "My mind wandered. It's another by-product of working at home by myself, I guess. I don't have someone nearby to make sure I stay on track."

"What's that like?"

"My job? I'm a medical transcriber."

"No, I know that. I mean . . . What is it like for you to be by yourself all day?"

Long. Sometimes lonely. "I don't know. It's what I'm used to. I guess I don't know any different."

"Do you ever wish it was different?"

"Sometimes," she said honestly. "But I don't know. I listen to other people's voices all day long. And, as a transcriber, I keep track of all sorts of mental and physical ailments." She shrugged. "Usually I find silence comforting."

John considered it for a moment, then replied. "It kind of seems like you're getting all the work of an office job but none of the benefits."

"Are there a lot of benefits? I mean I have friends who work in offices, and it's not like they get a lot of positive interaction from their coworkers."

"I reckon you've got a point."

"Besides, I get to work from home in my pajamas if I want to. That's a plus."

She could practically feel his gaze searing through her outer layer of skin. "Is that what you do?" he asked. "You usually work in your pajamas?"

"No."

He tilted his head. "I thought you just said you liked working in pajamas."

It was true. She had *just* said as much. Turning from his gaze, she shrugged. "I do . . . but I don't work in pajamas all that often. I mean, I don't know what I'm trying to say." Frustrated with both herself and the conversation, she looked up at him again. "What about you? Do you like working surrounded by people all the time?"

"I used to hate it. When I was younger, I liked being by myself a lot. But after prison, where there was next to no privacy, ever? I guess I got used to it." His eyes lit up. "These guys? They're needy, you know? After being in the pen for a while, they get itchy if they're alone too much. It's like they expect the silence to bring on something bad."

"Has that been your experience?"

"What do you mean? Because I was there too?"

Boy, she was regretting this conversation more and more. How did her fixation on their shadows turn into *this?* "Never mind."

"No, I don't mind talking about Madisonville. If you want me to?"

"I want to hear about whatever you want to tell me. If you don't want to talk about your past, that's fair. I won't push."

He couldn't help but grin. "That's appreciated, but spending three years in prison ain't the worst part of my past."

Now she felt even worse. "Sorry. Forget I said anything."

"What, you don't want to ask me more about my past? I thought you had more gumption than that."

They had almost reached MeMe's farmhouse, and that was a good thing. She needed to focus back on the papers she found, not on shadows on the ground or the new shadows that had appeared in his eyes.

"My, uh, gumption is just fine, but I don't want to pry." Feeling frustrated, Jennifer added, "Lincoln, I feel like we're talking in circles, and I don't know how that happened. I never intended to upset you."

"Yeah. I think you're right." Some of the gravelly cadence in his voice smoothed a bit. "I'd probably tell anyone and everyone that I am real well adjusted after my time in lockup. Maybe even tell people that it was the best thing that ever happened to me, because I found my faith in there." He paused. "But while there's some truth there, it's not the whole story."

She was impressed by his ability to share his feelings in such an open and honest way. She'd didn't know if she would ever be able to do that. She wasn't sure if she ever *had* been able to do that.

Seeking to lighten things up, she said, "What *is* the best thing that ever happened to you?"

"So far? It was when I met your grandmother."

She didn't know why that disappointed her. Maybe it was simply a symbol of just how screwed up her own life had become—she realized that she'd been secretly hoping for Lincoln to name her, even though all she'd really done in his life was interfere and almost give him rabies.

"My grandmother was pretty special," she said as she led the way back inside the house. When she saw the box she'd set on the kitchen counter early that morning, sitting tall and proud like a talisman, she hesitated.

Did she really want to share her grandmother's dirty secrets with someone who looked up to Ginny like he did? That seemed kind of awful—maybe even cruel.

But what was she going to do otherwise? Tuck the secrets away like she did everything else in her life she didn't want to deal with? So far, she hadn't had a whole lot of luck pretending things didn't exist.

Experience told her that wasn't the way to go, anyhow.

Secrets had a way of being revealed and hidden actions had a way of going public during the worst possible moments.

No, for once she was going to do something proactive, even if it hurt both herself and the person she was telling the news to. She might still have a ton of hang-ups, but she had learned a few things lately. At least, she hoped she had.

"The other day, before you and Wayne came over, I was looking through a hall closet and found this," she said slowly.

Lincoln took the box from her but there wasn't anything in his expression other than a vague interest. "What is it?"

She blew a sigh of relief. It didn't look familiar to him. That had to mean something, she supposed. "My grandmother kept some records in it. And a letter." And yes, she knew she was basically asking him for help while giving him no information.

Immediately, Lincoln's expression turned guarded. "What kind of records?"

"Um, I'm not sure. So I guess this means you didn't know about them?"

"No, I did not." Still holding it in between both his hands, he studied her intently. "Jennifer, stop beating around the bush and talk to me. What did you find?"

"It's an envelope filled with receipts. There's a record book of some kind too, but I haven't had much luck figuring out what it was used for."

He opened the lid and pulled out both. Her father's letter was tucked in the middle of the journal. "What were the receipts used for? Any idea?"

"Money." She swallowed, then at last blurted what needed to be said: "John, for some reason, my grandmother was collecting a lot of money from people and keeping the receipts. This wasn't years ago either. This was recent. She wrote dates on everything."

Lincoln lifted the flap of the envelope and pulled out one

of the receipts. Read the notation, then slipped it back inside. He didn't say a word, hardly showed a reaction.

A full minute passed, though it might as well have been an hour. "Here's the thing, Jennifer," he said at last. "Your grandmother . . . well, she was kind of a conundrum."

"A conundrum?" Jennifer wasn't sure whether she was more surprised by the description or his use of the word. "In what way?"

"She had a lot of layers. There was more to her than met the eye."

"Everyone is like that, John."

"I agree, but she had more layers than most. Plus, they were so well hidden, uncovering them is going to be painful." When she just kept looking at him like he wasn't making a lick of sense—because he wasn't—he kept going. "She was kind of like an onion."

"When people describe other people as onions, they mean they have no good core to find. My grandmother did have goodness in her

"She did. But she also had a lot of questionable layers covering up that goodness." He looked at her intently. "I know that's hard to hear, but it's the truth. And, since I'm sharing so much, I need to warn you about something."

"Which is?"

"That if you are determined to find out who Ginny Smiley truly was, if you intend to dig real deep into her past, it's not going to be pleasant."

Loyalty made Jennifer want to defend her grandmother's honor. But in her heart, she knew Lincoln was right. Her grandmother had never been sweet and biddable, and she'd never gone out of her way to do something if she didn't want to. Knowing that truth wasn't putting Ginny's memory down. It was stating a fact.

If Jennifer wanted to go down this path, it was going to mess up all the carefully erected walls she'd put up around herself.

But Jennifer was starting to realize that the consequences of staying in the dark would be even worse. Living her life safe and secure and contained might make a person's calendar look good, but it did nothing when it came to growth.

And she needed to grow. She needed to start letting her guard down, and allow other people in. Continuing to live her life the way she had been was going to get her nothing but pain and confusion.

"I understand," she said at last.

Surprise, and maybe something like disappointment, flared in his eyes. Then he nodded. "Okay," he replied.

She supposed that said it all.

CHAPTER 14

"Lincoln, just tell me what you know about the receipts," Jennifer said.

Her voice was impatient. He guessed he didn't blame her. If she knew something about one of his relatives and was holding back, he'd be irritated and that was a fact. He sighed before sitting down at the table. "First thing you should know is that Ginny knew practically everyone around here, and she not only knew them, she knew their secrets too."

"Okay . . ." Instead of sitting, she perched against the edge of the counter.

"She also had a lot of money. A lot of money. So if someone needed a loan but didn't have good credit. Or, say, this person needed money quickly, for something in a hurry, but didn't want to answer questions about why . . . they might go to Ginny to borrow some cash."

"And she'd lend it."

"She would, but it came with a price, Jennifer. She wanted the money back with interest, and in a timely manner." Hating the look of dismay that was rapidly filling her expression, he averted his eyes. "But, as you might imagine, not everyone who needed money was able to or all that anxious to pay her back."

"What would happen then?"

"She might pay that person a visit and explain that the money wasn't a gift, and she wasn't going to forget about it either."

Jennifer got to her feet and backed up a step. "What would happen if someone still didn't pay?"

Boy, he hated what was happening. He hated divulging Ginny's secrets, hated watching some of the innocence in Jennifer's eyes vanish, and really hated that he was about to make some of the trust she had for him fade into nothing.

But there was nothing he could do besides finish the story and give her the truth she needed. "If a length of time went by and the person still never paid the money back, she would either threaten to divulge their secrets or send somebody over."

"So my grandmother was a loan shark . . . and she dabbled in blackmail on the side. And if blackmail didn't work, she wasn't opposed to beating someone up to ensure she got paid."

"It wasn't quite that seedy, but I reckon that sums it up."

"I can't believe it. I can't believe she was so shady!" Jennifer started pacing. "I feel kind of sick right now."

"I reckon this is a bit of a shock."

She rolled her eyes. "John, a shock is seeing a cat jump out of my basement. This is plain disappointing." She shook her hands. "I feel tainted. I can't believe I'm living here."

"This isn't going to make what she did better, but I feel like I should point out that she wasn't in the lending business. She might lend money to three or four people a year."

"That's still a lot."

"I know it seems that way to you, but it really wasn't. Especially since most of those people who borrowed paid her back."

She blinked. "So you're saying she might have only blackmailed or beat up one person a year."

"I'm not saying that." But it was kind of true.

After giving him another long look, Jennifer turned to face the window. She seemed to pull herself together. But then she suddenly turned on her heel to face him.

"How do you know so much about all this? Did you borrow money from her?"

"No, I did not. But I owed her. She helped me through a bad childhood and a lot of bad decisions, Jen. If she hadn't been there for me, I don't know what I would've done."

"What are you trying to tell me?"

"That when she needed someone to pay an unwilling debtor a visit, well, she used to ask me to help her out."

Her eyes widened. "I can't believe this."

"It's not like I'm proud of what I did, but I owed her." His heart was beating fast and his palms were sweating. His whole body was preparing for Jennifer to connect the dots and remember that he'd been in prison.

And then, just as if he'd conjured the reaction, her whole being stiffened. "Why did you go to prison, Lincoln?"

"I went to prison because one of the men she asked me to beat up ended up in the hospital, Jennifer." Looking at her directly, he added, "And because I owed Ginny so much, I led them to believe that I was simply a thug who enjoyed beating people up from time to time."

"The police believed that?"

"I doubt it. But the whys of it didn't really matter. What did matter was that I had hurt a guy real bad, and I had to pay the price for my actions."

"What did my grandmother do?"

Lincoln knew what she was asking, but he deliberately pretended to misunderstand. "She visited me once or twice a month until I got out."

"John, don't prevaricate."

"I'm not doing anything but telling you the truth." He sighed, more than ready to finish the story. "In the end, I guess getting sent there changed both our lives for the better. I learned to be a leader and Ginny eventually stopped the foolish money lender business and started helping me plan what I do now, which is give a bunch of ex-cons a support system and jobs remodeling houses and buildings."

She sat back down on the couch. "When you got out, she invested in your business, didn't she?"

He nodded. "Ginny did. If not for her, I wouldn't have been able to start it." That was the truth too. He wasn't proud of the things he'd done. He'd never agreed with what Ginny had done either. But now, looking back, he supposed it did no good to judge. The woman was dead, all the money-lending nonsense was long gone, and he'd paid for his sins too.

Jennifer swallowed. "In that box was a letter from my father to her. I didn't understand it, because he was describing things he'd done that I knew cost a lot of money. I didn't understand how he had so much. But now I know for sure. MeMe gave my dad money. A lot of it."

"She never told me, but I wouldn't be surprised," he said. "Eric was always lazy."

"Lincoln, why didn't you tell me any of this earlier?"

"Why do you think? She was your grandmother. You loved her."

"But still. Telling me would've been the right thing to do."

He shook his head. "No, it wasn't. My past is my business,

and Ginny's past was hers. No way was I going to expose all her bad for no reason."

Her voice rose. "For no reason? Lincoln, I'm living in her house! Plus, you and I are friends, right?"

"You're right, Jen. You and I are friends. But everybody's got things in their past they aren't too proud about. I don't know how it's been in your world, but in mine, no one goes around telling people their dirt if they don't have to."

"I still feel like you should've told me about all this instead of waiting until I discovered it on my own."

Her accusation stung, especially since he could see her point of view . . . to an extent. Standing up, he grabbed his coat. "I know you're feeling confused and hurt, but I also think you're blaming the messenger." Waving a hand at the notebook, he added, "I had no idea Ginny kept all that stuff. I don't know why she did, either. I do, however, know that I was not her keeper and I sure as heck ain't yours." When she still stared at him with a stunned expression, he pulled on his coat and headed to the door. "Before I go, I'll leave you with one last thought."

"Which is?"

"You asked me for the truth, and I gave it to you, even though I knew it would taint the memory of your grandma and make your impression of me even worse. But I still did it, Jennifer. When you decide to stop blaming me for things I couldn't control, I hope you ask yourself what you would've done differently."

Because he couldn't bear to see the pain in her eyes any longer, he flicked the deadbolt and strode out into the cold.

But for once, the air didn't feel any different than it had inside that house . . . or how chilled he was feeling in his heart.

CHAPTER 15

Over a week had passed since she'd asked Lincoln to tell her the truth about her grandmother's life. During that week, Jennifer felt like she'd gone through all the stages of grief and done more soul-searching than she'd done in a while—maybe ever.

She'd also taken a lot of walks, worked a bunch, read two books, and baked several loaves of cranberry-orange bread. She'd ended up taking the bread to the senior citizen center when neither Lincoln nor any of the guys stopped by to say hello. She'd even finished her profile on Match Link, and it looked and sounded pretty good—well, as good as she thought she was going to be able to do. It was time to step out of her secure little world a little bit more. One thing was certain, she wasn't going to ever meet the right guy if she didn't put herself out there at least a little bit. It was just too bad she wasn't quite ready to start dating. Not quite yet.

The only company she'd had beyond Clyde the cat was Wayne, and he was too shy to say much beyond who had picked him up and letting her know what time she should drop him off. He'd worked in the basement the five hours he'd been there, cleaning out more boxes and clearing out the dead vermin. But for some reason, he hadn't even cracked a smile when she'd asked if he'd found any more pieces of dead mice.

So she'd kept pretty busy and had been productive too. But what she'd really been was lonely.

She missed the guys showing up unannounced, missed their jokes and laughter and their appreciation for her baked goods. But what she missed most was Lincoln.

Though the right thing might have been to go to his house and speak to him in person, Jennifer wasn't brave enough to do that. Instead, two days ago, she'd pulled out her phone and texted him.

> Lincoln, I should have thanked you for telling me the truth about Ginny. So, thank you.

Satisfied with the note, she'd pressed Send and stared at the screen for ten minutes, anxious for a reply. None came.

The next day, she texted him again.

> I'm sorry if I acted like I blamed you for her problems or my hurt. I feel better now. Oh, Wayne came over a couple of days ago and Clyde came out of hiding to say hello to him.

After another day passed with no response, Jennifer gave it one last try.

> I kind of miss seeing you around. Would you like to come over tomorrow and see Clyde and Wayne? I was thinking about making some blueberry muffins too.

Lincoln replied about ten that night.

> You need to stop worrying so much. You and me are fine. I'll stop by sometime tomorrow to see you, the boy, and that cat. Save one of those muffins for me. Later.

Few things had ever made her so happy as seeing that text. She was so pleased about it, she refused to wonder why he'd begun to occupy her thoughts so much.

• • •

Even though he had a ton of stuff to do, Lincoln couldn't deny he was eager to see Jennifer again. He hadn't exactly been avoiding her, but he figured they both needed some space after all his revelations. The talk had dredged up a lot of things he'd tried to forget. He also felt terrible about spoiling her sweet idea of who her grandmother was.

He hadn't just been sitting around thinking about Jennifer, though. He'd spent two full days out at the house Mason's buddies had trashed. He, Mason, and another guy named Charlie had repaired walls, painted, replaced broken cabinets, and scrubbed six months' worth of grime from the floors and shower. The hard labor had been good for his body, and it had cleared his mind.

He'd also had some meetings with Bo about a few of the guys and met with a realtor about a prospective house to buy and remodel. It had been a busy couple of days.

And that was why he was almost eager when he decided to walk to Jennifer's instead of driving. He needed some time to himself and some time to think about Jennifer and the way she'd gotten under his skin.

Walking across the snow-covered fields in between his house and Jennifer's, he found himself thinking about how different she was from any other woman he'd ever met.

He wasn't sure what it was about her that he found so darn enchanting. Heck, half the time, he was sure he'd never known a goofier woman. But he was drawn to her goofiness.

The girl wore thick Buddy Holly glasses for the computer, but he was convinced that she couldn't see anything else without them either. She had a fondness for sweats and baggy T-shirts and mugs and artwork showing distant places that she was a fan of but had never seen.

And the things she said! He always found himself either anticipating the next silly, naive bit she would utter or biting his lip so he didn't try to educate her in the ways of the world. The fact was, Jennifer Smiley had reached something inside of him that he'd thought was long gone. Something that had to do with vulnerability and tenderness. By the time he reached her property, the slushy snow had soaked his boots and his cheeks were half-numb from the cold. Out of habit, he glanced over to the barn and saw the door was open.

Relieved to have something to do besides make up excuses about why he was over there in the first place, Lincoln wandered in. The first thing he noticed was the neatly swept floor and the absence of a good amount of crap from the bank of shelves on the sidewall.

"Wayne? You in here?"

When he didn't hear a reply, he walked farther inside, scanning the area to make sure that nothing looked disturbed. "Wayne? Where you at?"

Nothing.

He turned on his heel and strode out, scanning the area. Maybe the kid was out raking or shoveling something. But of course, he wasn't. There was a good inch of wet sludge on the ground.

Growing concerned, he walked to Jennifer's back door. It led to the kitchen and it was the entrance he'd often used to catch Ginny whenever they had business to discuss. Two knocks later, he heard some movement and the faint sound of laughter.

But still no one opened the door.

More perturbed now than anything, he turned the handle and scowled when he realized that it was unlocked. When was she going to take his warning about being safe seriously? Anyone off the street could wander in. "Jennifer? Wayne?" he called out. "It's Lincoln. Where are you?"

His call summoned a rush of silence. Straightaway, every worst-case scenario possible flooded his head. On its heels was a rush of guilt—what if his goal of providing a safe, positive place for former inmates had brought about his worst nightmare? Had somebody gotten to her?

"Jennifer!"

"What?"

He turned to the sound and closed his eyes as he heard the scamper of footsteps. "Jennifer, is that you?"

"Of course it's me. John, what's going on? Are you all right?"

There she was. No makeup on, her hair in a messy topknot she was so fond of. She was clad in tight black leggings, a teal tank top, and the straps of some kind of work-out bra were peeking out. Her feet were bare, and her toenails were painted blue. She looked beautiful and, even better, safe and whole.

He didn't even try to hide the relief he was suddenly feeling. "Yeah, I'm fine."

She was still gazing at him in worry. "Are you sure? Because you seem upset." She stepped closer. Half held out a hand. "Did something happen at the house? Are the men okay?"

Before he could stop himself, he clasped her hand and threaded his fingers in hers. Her hand was soft and slim, just like he'd imagined . . . right before he reeled himself in. Was he really getting all poetic about holding a woman's hand, of all things?

Releasing her fingers, he finally spoke. "Yeah. Everybody's fine. Where's Wayne?"

"He's down in the basement. We were going through another old storage area that my grandmother left full. Luckily, we haven't found any more mice though."

She rolled her eyes and kept talking before he could even summon a smile. "I tell you what, John. When I get to Heaven, I've half a mind to tell my grandmother *exactly* what I think about all her rules and tips for living that she constantly bestowed on me when I was little. MeMe should've taken some of her own advice and bought herself a broom."

"I'll go down and see if I can lend a hand after I talk to Wayne for a second."

"What about?"

"About some of his responsibilities," he replied before taking a deep breath and calling out for the boy again. "Wayne, get up here!"

She frowned at him. "Hey, don't sound like that."

Happy to hear the boy's feet moving down below, he said, "Like what?"

"You know. Mean." Lowering her voice, she sent him a chiding look. "You sound mean and bossy, John."

Luckily, he didn't have to respond to that because Wayne appeared, looking worried. "Yes?"

Satisfied that the boy was taking him seriously, he said, "Were you in the barn earlier?"

"*Jah.* I had to get some gloves and a broom."

"When I got here, I found the barn door wide open."

"I was gonna lock it back up when I put the broom away," Wayne said. "Why? Is that not okay?"

"It's just fine," Jennifer answered quickly. "Don't worry, Wayne, you didn't do a thing wrong."

As much as he hated to contradict Jennifer, he knew that a lesson needed to be learned. "Wayne, you leave the barn wide open like you did, then anyone can go on in. That isn't safe for Jennifer, is it?"

Wayne blinked. "I don't know."

"It isn't. Anyone could come on this property and hide in there. Maybe find a way to hurt Jennifer when no one else is around. From now on, if you open the barn and then do work inside the house, you close that barn door."

"I will."

"Good. Now, go close it."

Turning to Jennifer, Wayne said, "I'm sorry."

"There's nothing to be sorry about. I'm sure everything is okay."

Lincoln couldn't fault Jennifer's kind heart, but he knew he was doing the right thing by making the boy more aware of his responsibilities. He was pleased when Wayne ignored her protests and walked right out. When the door closed after him, Lincoln stepped closer to her. "I know you think I'm being ridiculous, but him leaving it wide open ain't good."

"Oh, stop. This is the country, Lincoln. We're safe here."

"You live next to a slew of ex-cons, babe." Lincoln's worst nightmare was that he was going to take a new parolee on, believe he was trustworthy, and have that guy decide to take advantage of the single woman living next door.

"John, we've already had our discussion about all that, and I'm not going there again today." When he still stared hard at her, she threw him some attitude. "What are you trying to say? That you don't think the men you volunteered to look after are safe?"

"I think that the majority of the men would do whatever they had to do to protect you, but there's always going to be one or two of them that aren't going to make the best decisions all the time."

"So you really think they'd come over here to rob me?"

He stepped closer, close enough to smell the faint scent of vanilla and oranges and something else on her skin. Maybe it was her hair, or maybe it was lotion or some kind of ritzy perfume. But it smelled delicious. Hating that he couldn't seem to stop noticing such things, he bit out, "Jennifer, you aren't a child. You know exactly what could happen to a woman alone when a man bent on trouble wanders over."

Something flickered in her eyes. "I do know. But I can't help but wonder what my life would be like if you hadn't come over that very first day."

He knew. He would've been spending a lot less time thinking about her. "I guess we'll never know."

"I'm glad."

Before he even knew he was going to do it, Lincoln bent down and kissed her. When she gasped, he could hear surprise and pleasure in her voice, and he deepened the kiss—tasting her. Feeling her lips that were as soft as her hands. Hating that he noticed. Loving that the reality was just as good as his daydreams.

He would've stepped away if she'd given any sort of signal in that direction. But when she reached up her hands, grabbed his T-shirt in a death grip, and raised up on her tiptoes, he pulled her closer. Ran a hand down the smooth column of her back. He realized that kissing her felt like coming home.

And even though that thought embarrassed him—especially since he didn't even really know what a genuine home was, he was at peace with it.

Until the back door opened with a creak.

As if he'd been tased, he dropped his hands and stepped back.

Jennifer stepped away from him as well, though she looked a little dazed and was breathing hard. Breathing like she'd just run a marathon, hard.

"It's closed now," Wayne said in a happy tone. "I won't forget again."

"I know you won't." Lincoln motioned with his hand. "Now, come on and show me what you've been doing downstairs."

"Sure thing. You wouldn't believe how much was crammed in one place. Miss Jennifer looked real surprised; I'll tell you that. Ain't it so?" he asked with a look in her direction.

"Oh, yes. I was shocked," she replied with a smile in her voice.

Just as they were about to be out of sight, Lincoln looked in her direction.

She was standing at the top of the stairs, staring at him.

When their eyes met, hers softened for an instant before getting their gumption back. And in that instant, he breathed easier. She didn't regret that kiss. She didn't hate him all over again.

Unable to help himself, he grinned at her before turning away. As much as he knew he shouldn't have gone there, as much as he knew he would probably regret it later, Lincoln couldn't deny that at that very moment, all he felt was satisfaction.

The kind that came from knowing that something he'd imagined had surpassed his expectations. By a mile.

CHAPTER 16

Standing in the hallway, trying to get a handle on her breathing, Jennifer attempted to reclaim her old self. But the buttoned-up, orderly woman she used to be seemed as far gone as the grandmother she thought she'd known. Now, instead of wanting to retreat to the safety of her solitary life with multiple boundaries firmly set in place, Jennifer found herself thinking about everything in a whole new way.

She wasn't sure what that meant. Was she finally getting to know her true self? Or, was it something far different? Maybe her new home and life had spurred the change in her.

Maybe all this deep thinking was a waste of time. After all, there was only one thing she seemed to want to think about—and that was John Lincoln Bennett. Lincoln to everyone else. John to her.

The man who was larger than life. Or at least larger than the way her narrow life used to be.

In a lot of ways, John was too gruff. Too bossy. Too masculine. Too presumptive, too much for her to ignore. He was also absolutely not the type of man she should be attracted to, let alone be interested in. But it was impossible to stop thinking about him.

Let alone kissing him.

But, what a kiss. A curl-her-toes, hot-flash, let-her-mind-go-completely-blank type of kiss.

She stood at the top of the stairs, debating about whether to go downstairs and join them. But then, as she heard faint snippets of their conversation floating upward, Jennifer knew she needed to give them some space. Wayne was practically talking like a magpie to Lincoln. Considering that the boy barely said more to her than *Jah* or *Nee,* it was a bit startling to see that he was so comfortable around Lincoln.

But maybe it wasn't that much of a surprise at all? Lincoln had certainly drawn her to him in a way that she'd never imagined.

Instead of intruding, she went into the kitchen and did what she did best. She started slicing apples and making a pie crust. All so she could find some way to show how much she cared for these two guys she'd never expected to know.

When they came up two hours later, Lincoln smiled when she'd admitted that she'd made them a pie.

"Hate to miss it but I've got to take Wayne home."

"Oh. Okay. Of course. So maybe later. Would you like to come over for a slice tonight?" And yes, she was feeling like a fool, asking him over for pie like she was eighty years old.

For a moment, she thought he was going to take her up on her offer, but then his expression shuttered. "Sorry, babe, but I can't. I've got a meeting."

"Oh. Of course." She smiled tightly, though she felt like maybe she'd just made the fatal flaw in the relationship chess game. "No worries."

"I'll see you later."

"Yes, see you." Handing Wayne his payment, she smiled more genuinely at him. "I'll see you next week, Wayne. Thank you for all of your help."

"You're welcome. Bye, Miss Jennifer."

After she stood at the door and waved them off, she went back inside and dutifully turned the deadbolt. And then she realized that the silence she used to be so excited about now only sounded ominous and like something she didn't want at all.

• • •

After another week passed, Jennifer's optimistic mood had plummeted. Lincoln hadn't stopped by or texted her—not even when she'd gotten up her nerve yesterday to ask how the rest of his week had been. Yes, she'd known that was a silly thing to ask him—he'd never seemed like the type of person who enjoyed small talk—but she had expected some type of response.

The other guys hadn't dropped by either. The only time she'd heard from any of them was when Seth had called to let her know that Wayne wasn't going to be able to help her clean that week.

The lack of communication was even more unusual than Lincoln's absence. She'd gotten very used to one of them knocking on her door on their way to Lincoln's house just to say hello or see if she needed anything.

All that—together with processing the revelations about MeMe—made her start to doubt just about everything she was doing. Except work.

So that was what she'd found comfort in. So much so, Jennifer hadn't even minded the monthly call with Angie, her supervisor, and the five other medical transcribers for central and southern Ohio. All the other women were nice, but they liked to talk and the meetings always ran long. Today, however, she was looking forward to conversing with everyone.

When she hopped on the Zoom call, Jennifer did her best to join in the conversation, but when the topic switched from work to personal matters, she once again felt like she was standing on the outside and looking in. Angie and two other gals chatted about their children, another gal was pregnant, and two others shared funny stories about some recent dates they'd gone on.

"What about you, Jen?" Angie said. "You've been kind of quiet. What's new with you?"

"Not much. I'm still trying to get settled in my grandmother's house."

"It's an old house, right?"

"Yes, but it's nice." Doing her best to summon a cheerier disposition, she said, "The house is on two acres, so I get to enjoy the peace and quiet." When nobody said anything, she added weakly. "It's really pretty out here in the country."

"How are you meeting people?" Angie asked.

"Hmm? Well, I have met some of the people who live next door."

"Anyone else?" Bree, another transcriber, asked.

"Not so much. I've actually been studying those dating apps," she said. "I know a lot of you have had good luck with them."

"That's a great idea," Bree said. "I met my guy on Match Link. Have you tried that one yet?"

"Kind of," she admitted. "I've filled out my profile and uploaded a couple of pictures."

"And?" Bree prodded.

"And . . . that's it."

"I think you made a great decision. Match Link is great

because you get to discover a lot of information about the other person you want to connect with. All you need to do now is pay your fee and get started."

"I will one day soon."

"I met my husband on eHarmony," another transcriber said. "He and I always say that getting on that app was the best decision we ever made. I mean, you have to take a chance if you want to be happy, right?"

"I suppose."

"Jennifer, I hate to sound pushy, but I think you need to stop worrying so much." Angie said. "If you're living out in the middle of two acres and working from home, your choices are pretty limited. You might be missing out on someone really special."

Bree chuckled. "Angie has a good point. I mean, it's not like random men are going to show up at your doorstep, right?"

"Right." She knew she was blushing, since she'd been pretty much counting on that to happen since she'd moved in.

Ten minutes later, after they'd all hung up, Jennifer stood at her living room window and looked at the empty driveway. It was time to face facts. Lincoln might have kissed her, but he didn't want to date her. None of the other guys did either.

And, even if she was interested in going out with an ex-con, it wasn't like they were even flirting with her. And that, she realized was a humbling thought. Even men who had been in prison for years weren't flirting with her. If she wanted to stop spending the majority of her life alone, she was going to have to do something about it.

Sooner rather than later.

CHAPTER 17

Very quickly, Jennifer learned that online dating was an exercise in frustration. She had a lot to learn. She thought it was going to be hard enough to post pictures of herself and write her own profile. But she soon realized that even reading all the men's profiles could be a challenge. In addition, there were all the likes and swipes and scanning.

And then there was the stress of figuring out how to respond and wondering how long she should wait to type her replies. It took Jennifer an amazing amount of time to decide whether or not she even *wanted* to respond to any of the men who had messaged her. So far, she hadn't had the nerve to pursue any of them. It felt like crossing a line that she wasn't sure she wanted to step over.

But after another week of hardly hearing from any of the guys and only seeing Lincoln for five minutes when he dropped off Wayne, Angie's words started to ring in her ears. She couldn't keep sitting around and waiting for someone to knock on her door and ask her out.

Even if she thought that someone could be Lincoln.

Therefore, after two weeks of hedging and fretting, she'd finally started corresponding with Phillip. He was a manager at a local pharmacy chain. She didn't know which one because it seemed listing the chain was a breach of privacy. She supposed it didn't matter where he worked anyway.

What did matter was that Phillip seemed happy about his life and he also had a pretty good job. As they corresponded more, Jennifer learned that he enjoyed hiking, fishing, and going to country music concerts.

She wasn't really into any of that, but Jennifer figured she could learn. After all, all she did at the moment was clean out her grandmother's house and hang out with an Amish teenager once a week . . . and hope that a very handsome man with piercing blue eyes would kiss her again.

Last night had been her first phone call with Phillip and it seemed to go all right. She'd read online that they should keep the phone call to under fifteen minutes. He must have read the same thing, because their conversation ended after thirteen. She wasn't sure if that had been a good thing or not.

She was still staring at Phillip's profile and contemplating how she felt about Phillip's sort of high-pitched laugh when Bo and Seth appeared at her back door.

She was so glad that they'd finally stopped by. She couldn't deny that it was a relief to chat with "real" people who had no interest in dating her. Feeling herself relax for the first time in days, she waved them in with a happy smile. "Hi, guys. What's going on?"

"It's been a minute since we stopped by the house," Bo said. "I'm sorry about that. Lincoln's had some trouble with one of the houses about an hour away, so a lot of us have been living up there for the last couple of weeks."

"I'm sorry about the trouble. Is everything okay now?"

"Good enough that most of us are back home for a while," Seth answered. "How are you? Everything good?"

"It's good enough." Walking to the refrigerator, she said, "I made a chocolate pecan pie yesterday. Would either of you like a slice?"

"You know you don't even have to ask," Seth said.

So happy not to be eating another slice alone, she beamed at them. "Great. Y'all have a seat, and I'll fix you some plates. Either of you want coffee?" she asked as she pulled out two plates. "I made a fresh pot."

"No coffee for me, girl. Thanks, though," Bo said. "Hey, what's this?"

Distracted, she looked over her shoulder. "That? Oh. You can close my laptop if you want. I guess it is taking up half the table."

"It ain't bothering me none." Bo paused. "Jennifer, is that Match Link?"

"It is." She sliced the second piece. "Are you on it?"

Bo looked offended. "I am not."

Seth smiled slightly. "What are you doing on Match Link, anyway?"

She kind of felt like they were making fun of her. "I'm doing what it looks like," she said as she brought over their plates and forks. "I'm trying to find someone to go out with."

"You?" Seth asked.

"Yes, me." She was glad her back was turned to pour her coffee. "And what's that 'you' supposed to mean?" she asked when she joined them at the table.

Bo's cheeks turned a little red. "Sorry, but you're a pretty little thing. Didn't think you'd have a need for such gadgets."

"Dating apps are for everyone, Bo."

"Not me."

Bo looked a lot like Brad Pitt in 1992. Of course he didn't need an app to find a date. Jennifer was just about to point out his good looks when she realized he was serious. "Why not you?"

"They don't allow felons to participate, Jen," Seth answered. He winked. "Go figure, but I guess there aren't a lot of women on the hunt for ex-cons."

She would've giggled if she wasn't positive Seth would be a near-perfect boyfriend for some woman. He was kind, polite, and had a good heart. "I'm sorry about that."

After taking another bite of pie, he shrugged. "No worries. I don't trust those apps anyway. People lie on them."

At least she had a good response to that comment. "Actually, they don't lie. You have to promise to be truthful when you sign up."

Bo scowled. "Girl, everyone lies all the time. It's a fact."

"I suppose."

While the two men munched on the pie, she gazed at Phillip's profile picture again. What if he wasn't as easy-going and normal as he'd seemed? What if he was a big, fat liar? She bit her bottom lip.

"When I talked to Phillip last night, he seemed nice. I hope he wasn't lying through his teeth."

Both men stared at her like she'd lost her mind.

"Oh, for heaven's sakes. Now what's wrong?"

"Are you saying that you talked to some clown from Match Link last night?" Seth asked. "On your home phone?"

"That's what you do, Seth. After you exchange notes and such for a while, you talk on the phone."

"He has your phone number now," Bo stated.

"Well, yes." When Bo continued to stare at her, she tried

to explain the whole online dating thing a little better. "Come on, guys. You two need to stop looking like I did something wrong. It was just an innocent phone conversation. We only talked for thirteen minutes."

After carrying his empty plate to the sink, Bo helped himself to a cup of coffee and sat back down. "Does Lincoln know about you being on Match Link?"

"Of course not. This isn't any of his business."

"It might be," Bo muttered.

Feeling even more embarrassed about their attitudes, she added, "Guys, no offense, but I didn't ask you to get involved with my love life." When Seth's eyebrows rose, she verbally stumbled some more. "I mean, with my dating life. You're the ones who started looking at my laptop's screen uninvited."

"It's a good thing we did, girl," Bo grumbled. "Otherwise, who knows what you'd be doing?"

"Meeting strangers in dark corners or something," Seth muttered as he walked to the sink and rinsed off his plate as well.

"It was a phone call. I know what I'm doing. And, I'd like to point out that you two are being pretty condescending. I don't appreciate it."

"Sorry, Jennifer," Seth said.

Deciding against pressing Bo for an apology, she cleared her throat. "Now, can we please talk about something else? How was the pie? Did you like it?"

"Loved it," Bo said. Gazing back at Phillip's picture, he said, "Why are you online dating anyway? I would've thought you'd have your pick of guys."

"We all know I'm pretty average. And, no, I'm not saying that to get compliments. Besides, it's hard to meet guys when you work from home."

Bo waved a hand. "So get out more."

Jennifer was getting fed up with their unsolicited advice. So fed up, she blurted another hard truth. "I'm sure it's obvious to you two that I need to do something."

A line formed between Bo's eyebrows. "Because?"

"Come on. There's obviously something wrong with me."

Seth studied her curiously. "I don't follow."

"Fine. I'm just going to say it. I currently live next door to a whole bunch of men who are recently out of prison but not a one of the guys I've met has asked me out or even flirted. And no, I'm not asking for any kind of pity flirting either."

"I've never heard of pity flirting," Seth murmured, though his eyes had lit with amusement. "Is that a thing?"

"Shut up," she said with a smile. "I know I'm making a fool of myself. I was just trying to make a point."

Bo and Seth exchanged looks, then Bo cleared his throat. "Girl, I thought you knew what was going on."

"I'm sorry?"

Bo sighed. "First of all, you're pretty as all get-out. Sweet too. Any man in the world would be lucky if you gave him the time of day."

"That's sweet of you to say, Bo. Thank you."

"You're welcome, but listen up, okay? Lincoln is protective of you. He knows not every ex-con is going to stay on the straight and narrow."

"We all know plenty of guys who went right back in," Seth said.

Bo continued. "That's why there's only about four of us who ever stop by."

Jennifer was getting tired of admitting to things they thought she should already know. "Could one of you just *talk to me* instead of these little hints and phrases?"

Bo leaned back in his chair and folded his arms across his

chest. "All right. Here it is, plain as day. Lincoln cares about you. A lot."

"I care about him, too, but we're not dating, Bo. We're just friends." Friends who'd shared one perfect kiss.

"What I'm trying to say is that he worries that one of the guys in his program will decide to come over here uninvited. He's not going to like that you're meeting guys on your own that you know next to nothing about."

"Who I date isn't his problem."

"He might think otherwise." Seth looked at her in an almost grandfatherly way. "No matter what, I promise, you're plenty good-looking enough for a bunch of ex-cons."

"Thanks, Seth." She tried not to roll her eyes and forced a smile.

While Seth smiled back at her, Bo glowered. "All this info-dump means you should probably tell us why you're talking to Phil here if you're Lincoln's girl."

"It's Phillip—and I'm not Lincoln's girl! And all Phillip and I did was talk, and I don't know if we're very compatible. He really likes hunting, fishing, and country concerts."

Seth smirked. "That's what he put on his profile in order to catch a girl?" He shook his head. "Shoot. It's no wonder he's online."

"Ain't seen you fishing much, Jennifer," Bo said, his eyes sparkling. "Truth be told, most days I've barely seen you walk outside."

"I do go outside. I mean, I do when it's not too cold. But you're right. I don't fish or hunt."

"What about George Strait? Do you fancy him?"

"Who's he?"

"My point exactly." Bo sighed. "Now that we've eaten your pie and dispensed our advice, I'll come by tomorrow with one of the new guys to work on your driveway."

"Someone new?"

Seth rolled his eyes. "We got three new men, arrived from Madisonville two days ago. They've got time on their hands."

"What about all that stuff you just said about Lincoln not trusting other men around me?"

"They won't be around you. You're going to stay inside and let these guys work." He leveled a look at her. "That means no walking outside with cookies, girly. Not yet."

She would've argued about that, except she was really grateful that she wasn't going to have to shovel her driveway anytime soon. "Thank you for taking care of the drive."

"It'll keep them occupied." He shoved away from the table and got to his feet. "You have a good afternoon. And honey, take my advice. Get off that app and don't give Phil here the time of day. He ain't worth it."

Seth shook a finger at her, just like he was an old-time schoolmarm. "Whatever you do, don't you go meet him. Trust me, that's a recipe for disaster. And let us know if he keeps calling you. If that happens, we're going to need to get your number changed."

She smiled at them but didn't promise a thing as she walked them to the door. If they noticed, neither man said a word. But she could still feel their warnings in the air after she closed the door.

Later, as she was sitting on the couch again, all by herself that night, Jennifer knew that she needed to be something more in the relationship department. She needed to be a lot more than just Lincoln's no-flirting neighbor.

CHAPTER 18

Nothing Bo was saying made Lincoln happy. "Tell me that again," he ordered when Bo paused to take a breath.

"Which part? The online dating, the pie, or that Ramon is going to be doing yard work over there tomorrow?"

He knew Bo was being half-serious and half-needling just to get a rise out of him, but that didn't make the conversation any easier to take. "You know what I'm talking about," he bit out. "I want to hear about Jennifer, dating, and this, this *Phil*."

"It's actually Phillip. It seems Jennifer wants a relationship, so she signed up. After messaging him for a spell, she liked him well enough to actually talk to him on the phone."

"What did they talk about?"

Bo gave him a sideways look. "Like I know the answer to that. For what it's worth, I did tell Jennifer that you weren't going to be happy about her connecting with strangers on the internet."

"But she didn't listen to you, did she?"

"Why should she? She's a grown woman. Plus, you ain't her father, and she ain't your responsibility."

He gritted his teeth to keep from spouting off everything he was thinking—which was that while he definitely was *not* her father, but he *wanted* Jennifer to be his responsibility. After rolling his neck to loosen some of the tension sinking in, he snapped, "Anything else I need to know?"

Bo's eyes glinted. "About Jennifer or everything else?"

After years of working together, Bo had picked today to become a jokester. "Everything else. What's going on with Mason?"

"He seems to have settled in. You know he worked hard on the repairs to that house. Plus, he says he's been staying away from his old buddies."

"Do you believe him?"

"I do." He shrugged again. "We'll see if he continues to walk the line."

Lincoln nodded. He'd learned that half the work of keeping someone on the outside was giving them opportunities to make the right choices. Trust was a factor too. If a person didn't want to change, he wouldn't. It was as simple as that.

"I need to head up to Madisonville and meet with a guy who's due to get paroled next week. You good on the construction sites?"

"Seth is heading over to the one in town tomorrow. Charlie and Emmitt are at another. They're supposed to reach out to me if they have trouble."

"Sounds good." He stood up. Though it was tempting to walk away, he knew Bo deserved more than that. "Hey. Thanks for checking up on Jennifer today and talking to her. Thanks for filling me in too."

"No prob. Do you want some advice?"

He raised one eyebrow. "That depends. Is it going to tick me off?"

Bo half-smiled. "Probably . . . or not."

"What is on your mind, then?"

"If you like this woman, you need to speak up and do something about it."

He did like Jennifer. He liked her a lot, but that didn't mean they had a future, did it? "Come on. We both know it's not that easy."

"You're acting like any relationship is easy. It's not. If you take a chance with Jennifer, there ain't going to be one person who ain't going to support the two of you. And I'm not talking about just a bunch of ex-cons either. There are a lot of people in the community who respect you, Lincoln. Nothing would make people happier than to see you with a sweet, kind woman like Jennifer."

As much as he might have secretly wished Bo's words were true, Lincoln knew better. After all, he had tried to have a relationship before. Rayla had been both jealous of all the time he had to spend away from her and uncaring about what he was trying to accomplish. It had ended after they'd both said a lot of things they regretted and could never be forgotten.

Furthermore, he didn't want Jennifer to get tainted by some of the stuff he had to deal with. He liked her how she was. He was glad she wasn't street smart. What would he do if she changed because of him? Or worse—what if she somehow got hurt because of him?

"Jennifer deserves someone better than me. We both know that."

"I don't necessarily agree—but if that's your decision, then I'll support you." He turned to leave, but then, with his hand already on the doorknob, he turned back, "But, Lincoln, if you're not going to tell her how you feel, you need to let her make her own way. Okay, I'm outta here."

• • •

The next day, Lincoln replayed Bo's words in his head the whole seventy-minute drive to Madisonville. At first, Lincoln had been so shocked when Bo had relayed the news, he'd hardly been able to do more than simply gape at the guy.

Now, he felt more confused than anything. Confused about Jennifer's thoughts regarding him. Had that kiss meant enough to her that he'd ruined things by keeping his distance? And, if it had meant something, did she really want a relationship with him, of all people?

Then there was his mess of emotions. On one hand, Jennifer was everything he'd ever wanted. Someone sweet, honest. Kind. But those traits were pretty much the exact opposite of the man he was. He'd heard of opposites attracting, but he and Jen were about as far apart as Ross County and Antarctica or something. How could the two of them hope to have a real relationship if they had nothing in common to keep them together?

As he gave his name to the security guard before pulling into the parking garage, Lincoln couldn't help but reflect that relationships had been easier when he was locked up. He hadn't any choices and hadn't bothered to spend his time wishing for things to be different. All he'd ever done was hope and pray that he'd make it out of there. And then he had.

After parking, he scanned the information about Adrian, his newest prospective tenant. In for a couple of drug and theft charges. Done two years, no problems, seemed to have kicked his habit and wanted to move on.

Lincoln hoped that was the case.

After going through the metal detector and another security check, Ernie walked him into a room where he and Adrian could speak privately. The room was small, only about six by seven feet. In the center was a table bolted to the floor and two plastic chairs. All of the walls were bare and painted stark white, with a single window, which was being monitored. As familiar as the room was, it was the smell that got to him like it always did. There was a combination of sweat, bleach, and old shoes that never seemed to change. It always made him want to take a step back and search for a window.

"Thanks, man," he said to Ernie.

Ernie clapped him on the shoulder. "It's good to see you. How you doing, Lincoln? Haven't seen you in a while."

Over the last eight years, Lincoln and the older security guard had developed a friendship of sorts. Ernie hadn't been assigned to Madisonville when Lincoln was incarcerated, so the guy didn't have memories of Lincoln wearing an orange suit. In addition, Lincoln's program for newly released inmates had been given quite a bit of recognition of late. He had a high success rate of keeping parolees out, helping them to get acclimated and to obtain work.

Lincoln's visits had gone from being barely tolerated, to grudgingly accepted, to what it was now. Almost as if he was a coworker—or at least someone who was on the same side.

"I've been good. Busy. You?"

"Same old, same old." Leaning against the open doorway, he smiled. "I have a grandson now."

Lincoln shook his hand. "Congratulations."

"I just got to make it two more years. Then I'll get my full pension, and I can spend my days fishing and chasing kids."

"I'm glad for you. If anyone deserves it, it's you."

"All right. You're here for Adrian, yeah?"

He noticed that Ernie didn't seem real thrilled about that. He scanned the paperwork and spouted off Adrian's number. "That's the right guy, yeah?"

"It is. I'll go get him."

Ernie's comments were pretty unusual. He'd escorted at least a dozen guys into this room over the last three years and had never sounded so aloof. Every once in a while, Ernie would even go so far as to mention how he was glad the guy was going to have Lincoln to look out for him. That had been the case with Mason.

So Ernie's response was sending out warning bells. "Hey, wait a sec. Is there something I need to know about this guy?"

Ernie shrugged. "Nah, he's just . . . well, he's got a mouth on him. Kind of full of himself, which is always pretty odd when a man's this close to getting out." He left before Lincoln could ask him any more questions, which was also unusual.

Reminding himself that every case was different and that even when he'd been on the verge of getting out, he hadn't been every guard's favorite person, Lincoln sat down to wait.

Ten minutes later, Ernie escorted Adrian into the room.

Adrian looked as young as he was—twenty-four—had a good amount of tats on his forearms, and he walked with a rolling gait. Everything about him projected a confidence that was incongruous with his handcuffs and orange jumpsuit. Adrian eyed Lincoln suspiciously until Ernie motioned for him to sit down.

"So you're Lincoln Bennett," he blurted.

"I am."

"I've heard a lot about you."

"Like what?"

"Like you found your faith in here."

"That's true." Lincoln raised an eyebrow. "Anything else?"

"That a lot of men who do work for you don't come back in here."

"I don't make miracles. I just give men opportunities—if they're willing to take them."

Adrian grunted. "Too bad you couldn't get me out of here today. I can't wait to leave."

Lincoln didn't fault Adrian for saying that, but something in the man's tone set him off. "I don't pull strings, just trying to help out guys who want a hand after they're released."

Adrian smirked. "I can't wait to get a hand."

Lincoln was getting a pretty good idea of why Ernie had negative feelings about the guy. He looked over at the guard, who was still lingering by the door with a look of distaste on his face. "I've got this, Ernie. Thanks."

"All right." Ernie walked out and shut the door behind him. Lincoln knew that a guard would be standing at the door in case Lincoln knocked to be let out and another guard would be watching and listening to the conversation in case there was a problem or Lincoln made a hand signal to show he needed assistance.

After a moment, Adrian rolled his eyes. "That guy. Wish he'd die already."

"The guard is a good man. Decent."

"Yeah, right." Adrian shifted impatiently, cursing under his breath about the handcuffs. "Any chance you can take these off while we talk?"

"No."

Adrian's frustration wasn't anything that he, or any other guy he knew in the prison, hadn't felt a time or two. It wasn't easy to try to have a conversation while handcuffed. It was like the brain was at war with itself. Lincoln remembered constantly feeling as if he was off-balance. But that said, Lincoln was starting to feel uneasy about this kid. He hadn't expected a choir boy, but this guy should've been showing him *some* respect.

Lincoln folded his arms over his chest. "You're due to be paroled in six days. What are you hoping to do when you get out?"

Adrian raised his eyebrows. "Do you really have to ask?"

"Whatever. Beyond the obvious. What about the rest of your life?"

The guy's face turned into a mask. "What's it to you?"

And . . . that was all he needed to know that the guy wasn't right for him. Irritated that he'd already put so much effort into the man and made the trip up to the prison for no reason, Lincoln allowed his expression to turn icy.

"Now, it doesn't mean much. I've decided you're not right for my program." He moved to stand up.

Adrian's expression turned slack. "What are you saying?"

"I'm saying I've been putting in a lot of time on you, making inquiries, checking you out. More than one person thought you'd do well with the program I run, but it's obvious you won't. So we're done."

"You can't do that."

"Yeah, I can." Still ticked off, Lincoln flattened one of his palms on the table. "What did you think was going to happen here? Did you think I was going to be okay with you not showing me respect?"

Adrian looked like he was about to swallow his tongue, but his pride was still too far in the way to allow him to do anything decent. "Hey, man . . . you need to calm down."

"I'm calm. Calm enough to encourage you to ask around to some of the guys who've been here a while. Ask them about me. Then, if that means anything at all, maybe you'll take what I'm about to say to heart."

A muscle in Adrian's cheek twitched but he remained silent.

"Here it is, kid. There's a verse from Galatians that I take with me and it's served me well. It's Galatians 3:23. Look it up if you're interested."

"And if I'm not?"

"Then remember this—the outside world ain't like it is in here. And I'm not talking about jumpsuits and handcuffs. I'm talking about freedom and boundaries and obligations. I don't care who you are, it's hard to make it on your own on the outside. Most men fail."

"I'm not gonna end up back in here."

"Good. But I'd bet a grand that with the chip you've got on your shoulder, you're going to be wearing that getup again within a couple of months. If you even last that long."

He knocked on the door. "I'm ready."

"Wait!"

Lincoln ignored him. Didn't turn around when Adrian started yelling and spouting off threats.

When the door opened, Ernie was accompanied by two more guards, both of whom looked a lot younger and stronger. Ernie gave Lincoln a half smile as they walked down the hall.

"I guess it didn't go real well."

"Nope. You called it. I should start asking you who I should take on."

"Nah. You do all right. I don't always see the potential. That guy though . . ." Ernie sighed as he led Lincoln down the hall. "He's not ready to change. Not yet."

"I'll officially tell the warden, but he won't be going into my house. I don't trust him."

"Too bad for him, but good for you." When they were almost to the exit, Ernie added, "There's another guy whose time here is just about up. Young guy but cut from a completely different cloth. He might work out for you."

"What's his name?"

"Jerome. Sorry, can't remember his last name."

"Shoot me an email if you can give me either his number or name, and I'll take it from there."

"I will." Ernie held out his hand. "You take care, Lincoln."

"You too. Go fishing soon, buddy."

As he walked out, he couldn't help but think that he had dodged a bullet. Just thinking about Adrian getting anywhere near Jennifer made him ill. There was just no way.

●●●

It was only later, when he was driving home, that he started wondering if Adrian had been really such a bad fit for the house or if he'd simply been thinking about the chance of him getting near his neighbor.

That was the crux of it. He was no longer thinking of Jennifer as part of his obligation to Ginny but as the woman he admired. No, it was more than just admiration—his feelings had gone from respect to admiration to liking to something a whole lot more. He cared about her. A lot. The fact was, she'd gotten under his skin and he'd found himself thinking about her at odd times during the day.

Okay, he'd begun thinking about her all the time. He felt protective of her, wanted to take care of her. He didn't want anything bad to touch her—especially a guy like Adrian, who was so wrapped around the axel of his life and his experiences in prison that he'd forgotten a lot of the basic tenets of how to treat people.

But, what did that actually mean? Was he really all that worried about Adrian and the rest of the guys targeting Jennifer . . . ? Or was he worried about the rest of the world?

The answer was plain to see, of course. Even if she didn't know it—and even if he wasn't fully ready to admit it—he yearned for Jennifer Smiley to be his. After a lifetime of making do and giving up and putting everyone else's needs first . . . Lincoln wanted her in his life.

CHAPTER 19

Something was going on with John Lincoln Bennett, and Jennifer wasn't sure what to do about it. He'd started showing up at her house at least once a day, and at odd times too. In the last three days, he'd shown up while she was still having coffee, in the evening when she knew there was a party going on at his place and, just yesterday, in the late afternoon to shovel her driveway.

Every time, after she got over her shock, she'd say hello and then offer him a cup of coffee or a beer or even a glass of iced tea. To her surprise, he'd accept. Yesterday, after he'd shoveled her driveway, he'd guzzled half a glass of tea and eaten four peanut butter cookies. Even more confounding was that Bo and Seth were nowhere to be found during these visits. She'd honestly begun to think that he didn't leave his compound without one of his right-hand men. Now she was wondering if he'd had an argument with them.

Because the alternative—the idea that he was coming over by himself because he wanted to spend time with just her—well, that was a little hard to believe. Not only had he made it clear that she was his obligation, but there was also her grandmother's past to contend with. Jennifer felt tainted by it, and unsure how she felt about Lincoln's part in MeMe's loan shark past.

So pretty much everything between them was different now. Especially since she was currently attempting to get up the nerve to go on a real date with one of the men she'd met on Match Link. After Lincoln had started coming by again, she'd been tempted to forget about the app, but some of the women she worked with had encouraged her to at least go on one date. A date is just a date, they'd pointed out. It didn't have to mean anything more than that.

She would have stewed on the pros and cons some more . . . if Lincoln hadn't been sitting just a couple of feet away. Clyde, who'd slowly begun to spend more time with Jennifer, was in the room too. She'd bought yet another cat condo, and it was right next to the kitchen table. Clyde was resting on the top floor and cleaning a paw.

But instead of talking about Clyde, Lincoln was watching her knead bread as if she were doing something unusual.

Tired of the way he was frowning at her, she said, "I promise, this is how you knead dough. I'm doing it right."

He stood up and leaned on the other side of the counter. "I wasn't doubting you, babe. I was just wondering why you're making it in the first place."

"Um, because fresh bread is really good?" Deciding to put him to work, she pointed to the metal loaf pan. "Oil that, would you?" When he looked at a loss again, she pointed to the paper towels and the industrial jug of canola oil. "Put some on the paper towel and then rub it around."

He did as she asked. "Any particular reason you've got so much oil?"

"Because I bake a lot, and I get tired of running to the store . . ." She divided the dough into thirds and started rolling it into balls, then putting each one in the pan. "Why?"

"No reason." He grinned. "Just asking. So, what happens next?"

"Since the dough's already risen once, I just have to let it rest and rise for about forty minutes then pop it in the oven. Forty minutes after that, the whole house will smell amazing and I'll have a loaf of hot, fresh bread."

"Shame I'll miss it."

"Are you sure you have to go?" The moment the words were out, Jennifer wished she could take them back. She'd sounded disappointed.

"Afraid so. Bo's picking up a new guy from a prison down south today. He's going to need me around for a spell."

"What you do is really nice, John." She draped a dishcloth on top of the bread then turned on a faucet.

His eyes widened in surprise before he clamped it down. "It's not nice."

She turned back to the sink. "Sure it is. You give a lot of people hope."

"Having this program helps a lot of people out. But it's not like I do it out of the goodness of my heart. I get paid for it."

She was pretty sure that whatever money he received for helping out ex-cons wasn't much. "Do you help out because you wished someone would have done that for you?" She hated to think of Lincoln getting out of prison and being all alone.

"Ginny did."

"Did she really?"

"What is that supposed to mean?"

She shrugged. "You know. It's basically because of her that you were in prison in the first place."

"I've never blamed anyone but myself, Jennifer. I knew what I was doing."

"Still, I don't think she did a whole lot out of the goodness of her heart."

He grunted. "Does anyone?"

"I don't know," she said slowly. "I mean, I suppose that there are some people who help others just to help. But maybe they have other reasons as well."

"Ginny wasn't a saint. That's a fact. But I never needed her to be."

"Even though it's been hard to comprehend everything I learned about her, I don't think I needed her to be perfect either."

When Lincoln frowned, Jennifer tried to think of another way to explain herself. But just as she was about to start talking, they heard a knock at her door.

Lincoln tensed. "You expecting anyone?"

"No, but that doesn't mean much." After all, when had he ever let her know he was coming over?

When they heard the knock again, this time with more force, Lincoln headed to the front door. "I'll get it, babe. It's probably Seth or one of the boys."

She followed, just to see who it was. But the older man at the door wasn't anyone she'd ever seen before. She would have remembered him too. His skin was slack, and his brown eyes looked vaguely yellow. He also had the look of someone who'd recently lost a bit of weight. His clothes kind of hung on him, though she figured any man would pale next to Lincoln.

As for Lincoln? He was glaring at the guy and had moved to stand directly in front of the opening. There was no way this guy was going to get inside without Lincoln moving.

"Lincoln?"

"I'll deal with this, Jennifer," he replied, still staring at the man with a look of distaste. "You go back into the kitchen, yeah?"

She didn't move and was just about to remind John that they were in her house when the older man spoke.

"Look at you, Lincoln Bennett. Playing house with my daughter."

The voice, the words . . . it all made Jennifer's blood run cold. Stepping closer so she could see around Lincoln, she met the gaze of the man on the other side.

"You're Jennifer." He smiled, revealing bad teeth. "I wouldn't have guessed it, but you turned out all right."

It took a minute, but she realized she was staring at Eric Smiley. A man she hadn't seen since she'd been barely old enough to talk.

Lincoln's expression was ice-cold as he continued to block Eric's way into the house. Jennifer wondered if Lincoln was preventing her father—if that was really who this man was—from getting in or if he was keeping her from getting any closer to the interloper.

Lincoln didn't need to worry about her, though. If Jennifer hadn't already had a creepy feeling about him from her mother's stories, the letter she'd read of his had told the rest of the story.

"Why are you here?" she asked.

"That's how you're going to greet your long-lost dad?"

His voice sounded slimy—or perhaps that was simply the way he made her feel. "Maybe you are my father, maybe you're not. All I know is that you are definitely not my dad." She closed her eyes in frustration. Her voice sounded thready and strained.

"Jennifer," Lincoln murmured, "you don't need to do this."

She knew Lincoln was trying to shield her, and she was grateful for that, but there was no way she wasn't going to get some answers. For too long, she'd held her anger and disappointment about his absence deep inside. "You didn't answer my question. Why are you here?"

"I heard you got the house. I wanted to see it."

Beside her, Lincoln's posture eased a bit. She saw why. Seth and two other men had just pulled up and were walking toward them.

Her father heard the footsteps and turned abruptly. "You boys didn't need to join us. I'm not here for trouble."

"You okay, Jennifer?" Seth called out. "Boss?"

"I'm fine." But even to her own ears, she could tell that her voice was shaking.

"Glad you're here," Lincoln said.

"Charlie here saw him pulling in the drive," Seth said.

"I wasn't sure what to do, so I called the house," Charlie said.

"You did good. I'm proud of you."

"Well, I sure as hell ain't good," Jennifer's father said loudly, interrupting. "Jennifer, tell these guards of yours to give you some space and let me in. I want to see this house."

Maybe she should feel bad for not demanding Lincoln go. After all, Lincoln had enough problems without adding hers to his plate.

But there was no way she wanted to be alone with her father. He was leering at her in a way that was about four steps beyond creepy. He also looked desperate, like there was just about nothing he wouldn't do to get what he wanted. Honestly, Jennifer was afraid of this guy. And that said a lot, considering the men she now trusted implicitly.

Clearing her throat, she said, "You need to go on your way. I'm not going to let you in." Not only did he creep her out, but she was also vividly aware that he didn't see her as anything other than a way to get the property. She didn't mean a thing to him.

But at least that wasn't a surprise.

Eric jerked his head to the side. "This is *my* house."

Fueled by Lincoln's reassuring presence and the knowledge that the other men were there too, she spoke her mind. "It's not your house. Ginny left the house to me."

"That's only because she didn't know where I was."

Jennifer glared at him. "That's on you. You left the area."

"That ain't exactly the truth. I've been around." Sounding almost amused, he added, "Sometimes, I've even gotten pretty close." Almost smiling, he added, "Jennifer, you might not have seen me, but I've seen you."

If they had been alone, Jennifer would have reached for Lincoln's hand. Instead, she made do with stepping a little closer to him. By her side, Lincoln seemed to become even more formidable.

Eric stuffed his hands in the front pockets of his jeans. "Don't you start thinking you can ignore me. I've got a lawyer. I have rights, you know."

Wanting to deny everything he was saying, Jennifer shook her head, but something in his eyes told her that he wasn't just messing with her. "I don't want to see you now. I can't."

"How come? You got something special planned with this guy?" He laughed. "Don't worry. I'll stay out of your way."

Obviously ready to toss Eric off the porch, Seth stepped forward. Lincoln stopped him with a hand. "You aren't making a lick of sense, Eric. Ginny's will was iron tight, and she cut you out of everything. I suggest you move on."

"Jennifer, are you sure this is what you want?" her father asked.

Seth spoke before either she or Lincoln had a chance to say another word. "It is exactly like that. She don't want you here, and that's enough for me. Turn around and head to your car."

Her father fisted his hands but then suddenly shrugged. "I'll be seeing you, Jen," he said before turning away and loping to his car, a white Chevy Cavalier that had seen better days. All of them stood motionless until he backed down the drive, turned, and then vanished from sight.

When he was finally gone, Jennifer couldn't have stopped the tears from escaping her eyes if she'd tried. Just as she hiccuped, Lincoln wrapped an arm around her and pulled her into his chest.

Not caring that Seth, Charlie, and the other guy were watching her fall apart, Jennifer wrapped her arms around Lincoln's waist and held on tight. Right now, it felt like Lincoln was the only person she could trust, especially since she wasn't even sure if she could trust herself.

Still holding her close, Lincoln exhaled, then ran a hand down her hair far more gently than she would've ever dreamed he was capable of. "I know," he murmured. "He's an . . . He's not worth your time, Jen."

"I can't believe he showed up." She trembled, thinking about the consequences on her life of having to see him often.

Lifting his head, Lincoln said, "I don't want her alone. When Bo gets in, Seth, you put Craig or someone in charge of the new guy and then fill Bo in on what's happened."

"Got it."

"Then you two come up with four or five guys to come over here. Keep 'em on rotation. Tell 'em not to worry about payment. I'll take care of them."

"No one's going to want money to look after Jennifer, boss," Charlie said.

"I appreciate that, but Seth, you offer it just the same."

"You going to stay here a while, boss?"

"Yeah."

Listening in, Jennifer pulled away. "You don't have to do that."

Meeting her gaze, his expression softened before he flicked his attention back to the men. "Give me two hours."

She knew he had obligations. People who were counting on him. Forcing herself to step away from Lincoln. "Guys, thank you, but I'll be okay. No one has to stand around here and babysit me."

"I know he's your dad and all Jen, but he's trouble," Seth said. "He's not going to make things easy for you."

"I know. But, um, I'll talk to a lawyer too. Or something."

"Accept the help from your friends," Lincoln murmured. "It's how it is right now."

Her friends. She realized then that Lincoln was exactly right. She wasn't alone, not any longer.

Pride might make her feel good for about two minutes after the men left, but then she would be scared out of her wits. She was on two acres and was at a complete disadvantage where her father was concerned. She didn't know why he was there, and she didn't know anything about his past.

Plus, when was she ever going to learn? Doing everything by herself hadn't ever done her any favors.

Looking at him, she nodded.

Ten minutes later, after the other men had left, she had the oven on and had started to focus back on her dough.

Lincoln had taken up residence back in his chair and was half texting on his phone and half grumbling about Clyde, who had just hopped on top of the table.

"I'm not loving this cat, Jen," he grumbled.

When she found herself stifling a giggle, Jennifer realized something pretty important. It didn't matter about their pasts or their differences. All she knew was that she didn't just need *someone* in the room with her. She needed Lincoln.

CHAPTER 20

After another thirty minutes had passed and her bread was in the oven, Jennifer looked up at Lincoln. He was still sitting in that chair like he didn't have a care in the world—except maybe an ornery cat. She knew that wasn't the case, though. When he wasn't complaining about Clyde, he'd been either frowning or texting on his phone.

"I really do appreciate you staying here for a while," she said for at least the third or fourth time. "I don't know what I would have done if you hadn't been here." If he wasn't still there.

"There's no need for you to keep thanking me. I'm glad I was here. I don't like thinking about you dealing with Eric by yourself. Especially since he shouldn't have shown up in the first place."

"It's going to be a bit until the bread is done. Would you like me to make you something to eat?"

Looking concerned, he stood up. "Do you really feel like cooking?"

She nodded. "I can't just stand here." Especially since when she wasn't worried about her creepy father, she remembered how good it had felt to be held in his arms.

He walked into her kitchen. "What strikes your fancy?"

It was three o'clock. If he stayed there a full two hours, he wouldn't be leaving until almost five. She knew he wouldn't go home and make himself something decent for dinner. He'd no doubt start barking orders and meeting with the dozen people or so who'd been waiting all day to get a few minutes of his time. "Chicken and dumplings?"

He smiled slowly. "You got time for that?"

"I do. Is that okay?"

"Yeah, babe. That . . . that sounds real good. Want some help?"

"Thanks but not today." The way his phone had been lighting up, he wasn't going to have time to chop up vegetables with the amount of texting that was going on. She went to the refrigerator and pulled out celery, carrots, and a package of chicken she'd just thawed out that morning.

"All right then." After glaring at Clyde, who was now sitting in the chair he'd just vacated, Lincoln sat down on one of her barstools next to the island. "So who taught you to cook? Was it your mom?"

She shook her head as she filled up a big pot with water. "My mom is a pretty good cook, but she wasn't around a lot when I was little." Thinking back on those years, she said, "She was always working, I'm afraid."

"Her parents didn't help her out?"

"I think they did a little bit." She thought about it as she chopped an onion into fourths and tossed it into the water. "I've never asked her how they felt, but I have a feeling that they probably weren't real pleased with her choice in men. They were never all that fond of Ginny either. She was . . . well, she was a little too rough around the edges for them."

She shrugged. "Anyway, to answer your question, we had a neighbor lady who watched me a couple of times a week. She's the one who encouraged me to learn to cook."

A line formed between his brows. "All this time, I never really thought about what your mom had to do to make ends meet. I only knew that Caroline was better off without Eric."

Jennifer smiled at him. "That was the general consensus." She threw in the carrots and celery and the chicken and set the pot to boil. "Of course, my mom never had anything to say about him, and MeMe never really did either. When I was twelve or thirteen, I used to think my grandma didn't want to talk about my dad because I was so sensitive about being one of the only kids I knew who never saw her father. But then later, she confided that my father didn't seem capable of ever making anyone else happy."

"Your grandmother used to say Eric was spoiled. Then, maybe lazy. Once she'd told me that he'd gotten too lucky, and he was too full of himself to ever hold down a real job." He rolled his eyes. "Eric was never too good at taking orders."

"And then?"

"And then? Well, then, she never saw him."

"He's always been gone and been such a disappointment to the two women in my life, and I've never sat around wishing that he was different. But now, after reading that letter? I'm worried, Lincoln. Ginny gave him a lot of money over the years."

"You have every right to be worried. Ginny made a lot of mistakes with him, starting and ending with giving him way too much money just to shut him up." A muscle worked in his jaw. "The truth is that Eric is nobody you want to know. I don't like you having to worry about him coming round when you're all alone."

"Maybe he won't come back."

He shook his head. "Sorry, but he will. He wants something."

"I know he doesn't want me. It must be the house."

Lincoln hesitated, then nodded. "I reckon so. The house is a hot mess, but the land is worth something. If he could manage to sell it, that is."

As lovely as the land was, it wasn't like she was sitting on prime real estate. Plus, after reading his letter and seeing her dad in person, Jennifer knew that even if her father got the land and sold it, the money wouldn't last long.

It didn't seem like her father was the type of man who believed in long term financial planning.

"MeMe left the house and land to me in her will. Even after my mom talked to the lawyer, she said that it was rock solid. Could my father even have a case?"

"Usually I'd say no, but with Eric, I'm not certain. He has a history of getting what he wants."

Satisfied that the broth in the pot was simmering, she walked to his side. "I'm afraid of that too. My mom said he was manipulative. He had to be really good at twisting things around since he'd gotten my grandmother to keep giving him so many chances."

"I figure everyone has an Achilles' heel. Eric was definitely your grandmother's worst one."

Lincoln sounded so certain about that. "Did you see him much when she was alive?"

"Sometimes. Most of the time, no."

That surprised her. She'd thought that her father left the area soon after she was born. "He was here that often?"

Taking her hand, he pulled her toward the couch. When they were sitting, he even went so far as to rest her legs over his own. She'd never been positioned like that before, but it didn't feel like being manhandled at all. Instead, with his heavy palm just resting on her calf, she felt connected to him. She also felt reassured—and that maybe Lincoln needed this closeness as much as she did.

"He was only ever around when he needed something. Ginny let him stay when she was in the mood to forget how much he'd hurt her in the past."

"She never told me any of this."

"She wouldn't have. She loved you, Jennifer." Concentrating on their topic, Lincoln sighed. "To be honest, especially now that you and me know each other, I think your sweet nature and innocence was something that she valued."

Jennifer rolled her eyes. "I'm not that sweet or innocent."

"Compared to her, you are." He raised one shoulder in a half shrug. "That's why she kept things from you. She didn't want you to know her bad side." His blue eyes were penetrating. She knew what he was saying.

What he was implying.

Lincoln was once again giving Jennifer a choice. She could continue cleaning out the house and barn. She could continue throwing out garbage and putting trinkets in donation boxes and keep on feeling good about her efforts.

But what she was also doing was getting rid of all the things that signified who her grandmother was. In its place would be a clean building, a clean slate, and a whole lot of unblemished memories that Ginny had carefully given her.

Or, Jennifer could force herself to actually look at some of the debris that littered the home of the real Ginny Smiley. Like what she'd found out with the loans and the blackmail, and how her grandmother had used Lincoln when she'd needed to use force to get her way. She'd also be forced to break down those walls around her heart, even if it hurt a little bit. But wasn't feeling something worth that hurt? Living a few feet apart from the rest of the world hadn't done her much good. It had kept her safe, but it had also prevented her from ever experiencing love, pain, or even joy.

Returning to the discussion, Jennifer said, "I already know about the loans and blackmail, Lincoln. Are you saying that my grandmother had a bunch more bad habits?"

"I'm saying that Ginny Smiley had a curious sense of right and wrong and was ruthless when it came to getting what she wanted." His voice gentled. "You saw her a couple of times a year. When she knew you were coming, she'd be thrilled. She cleaned things up. Baked you cookies. Kept people like me far away."

"But?"

"But that wasn't how Eric grew up. He grew up seeing Ginny in action. He learned a lot from her about getting what he wanted. I'm not saying his problems are completely her fault . . . but a lot of people might say that they're not surprised that Eric turned out to be so spoiled and mean."

His speech wasn't exactly shocking, but it did make her feel tainted. This was her grandmother and her father he was talking about. She already knew she wasn't a hundred percent her mother's daughter. But if that was true, did it also mean that she wasn't zero percent her father's?

She rose from the couch and paced across the room. "Lincoln, I don't know what I'm supposed to do now."

He walked to stand in front of her. "There isn't anything for you to do. It's history, Jen."

"But that history is sordid."

"So? A lot of history is sordid. But just because it makes a person uncomfortable, it doesn't mean it didn't happen."

She agreed with him . . . but she also now started to understand why people fought so hard to tear down some monuments. They were hard to face. And this house, in a way, was her family's monument. Why was she fighting so hard to keep it?

Why hadn't she listened to her mother's advice and simply sold the house off and moved on?

"I think I need some time to think about this."

He stared at her curiously. "To think about what?"

"About what I should do next."

"There isn't anything for you to do, babe. It's just like you said. Your grandmother loved you enough to leave you this house and the land it sits on. You've been happy here, right?

She nodded.

"Then I want to make sure you stay happy. Me and Seth and the rest of the guys are going to do our best to make sure that your worthless father doesn't try to steal it from you."

"And then?"

"And then you can spend your days working on your computer, taking care of that cat, and baking bread." He looked down at his feet. "Or whatever else you want to do. I'll make sure of that."

"I don't think it's that easy." Her throat worked as she weighed her options again. "Maybe . . . maybe I've been thinking about all of this all wrong. Maybe I should consider selling the house after all. Not to Eric or anything, but to someone, and then I should go back."

His expression shuttered, betraying his hurt. "Would you really do that? You could just up and leave?"

"I don't know. Maybe." The timer buzzed on the oven. Glad for the distraction, she hurried to the kitchen and pulled the pan out of the oven. The monkey bread was a perfect golden brown and smelled like heaven. "The bread's done," she said, stating the obvious. "Would you like some before you go?"

"No." Still standing in the living room, he looked at his phone's screen. "It's gotten late, and I've still got a ton to do. I better get on out of here."

Still pretending that she hadn't just hurt him, Jennifer pulled out a knife. "Would you like a piece for the road? It's no trouble."

"Thanks, but I'm good. I'll have someone come over and stay out on the front porch for a while. He'll knock on your door, so you won't be scared."

"That won't be necessary." But, of course, her voice sounded strained.

"It is. If Eric comes back, call me." He took a deep breath. "And, if you decide not to call, don't give him the time of day, okay?" After another pause, he added, "I'm not just saying all this to be a jerk, Jen. Listen to what I'm saying. Your grandmother's secrets might hurt, and I might be a disappointment, but your father is going to do whatever it takes. He'll *hurt* you." His blue eyes filled with pain. "Do you understand? He won't care if you end up bleeding and broken either. I promise you that." His words were so intense, she just stood there, trying to process it all. "Lock that door after me," he said as he walked out.

A cold burst of air filled the kitchen, startling her. Looking out the window at Lincoln's retreating back, she was stunned to see a sprinkling of snowflakes swirling around him.

It had started to snow yet again.

Huh. It looked like the world hadn't stopped turning after all. It only felt like it.

CHAPTER 21

Lincoln had messed up. He'd told her too much. She was innocent, at least to the ways of the world—*his* world. Well, she had been.

In Jennifer's world, people stopped at stop signs. Even in the middle of the night when there wasn't another soul around. She didn't take risks, and even when she did, the risks she was taking weren't very reckless at all.

And he?

Well, he had just about the worst timing known to man. Only he would decide to make sure Jennifer knew that her grandmother was even worse than she previously thought on the same day her long-lost father walked back into life.

Lincoln had always considered himself to be smarter than that. Now Jennifer was entertaining all kinds of crazy notions about selling that house and moving away. Leaving Ross County forever. Leaving him to figure out how to get her to stay without coming off like a controlling jerk. He had to come up with a plan too—because he was in love with her.

In. Love. With. Her.

In love with everything about Jennifer Smiley. He loved her looks, her demeanor, her naivete. He loved the way she cooked to make herself feel better, the way she cooked to make him feel better. He loved how she felt in his arms, how she kissed, and how she was slow to trust. He loved knowing that he'd been one of just a few lucky people to get close to her.

Selfishly, he even loved how she'd softened his edges and made him want to be gentle with her. He wanted to be better when he was around her, and even more patient with the men he'd sworn to be there for.

And now it all might be gone.

Approaching his house, Lincoln saw Mason had door duty. The guy had a pissed-off expression on his face, but it cleared as soon as he spied Lincoln.

"Hey, boss."

Knowing the guy was still doing his best to stay on the straight and narrow, he stopped. "Mason, how's everything going around here? Everything good?"

"Sure, boss."

Lincoln reckoned he should give the guy points for following Bo's directives, which was to handle problems without getting into a fight or handing them over to somebody else.

However, after Eric's appearance, he wasn't up for any more guessing games. "I appreciate you keeping things professional, but I'd appreciate knowing the truth about what's going on. I got a slew of texts, but nobody came right out and said what the problem was. What's wrong?"

Mason swallowed hard but answered. "It's the new guy. I didn't know Adrian was going to show up here. We didn't get along in Madisonville, but that ain't your problem. I'll handle it."

"Hold on, now. Bo picked up *Adrian?*" He could have sworn that Bo was going to chat with the other guy Ernie had in mind and then bring him back. "How did that happen?"

Whether it was Lincoln's glower or the new, harder tone to his voice, Mason looked even more uncomfortable. After visibly getting a handle on himself, the kid said, "I'm not sure, boss. I only know what did happen."

"Where is he now?"

"In his quarters, I guess."

Lincoln had a couple of rooms that the guys could use for a week or two when they first got released. Usually he didn't mind. Most of the men knew that living at Lincoln's wasn't a ticket to his good graces or to nonstop parties. It was actually the opposite.

He'd never intended to have any men live with him, but then he'd discovered it made a lot of sense. Some guys found the transition from being watched and monitored twenty-four seven to living fully on their own to be a difficult one. They did stupid stuff, which in turn put Lincoln's program in jeopardy.

Lately, though, Lincoln had started thinking that it was time to get everyone out of his house again. It had begun to feel like he could never get away from all the guys and their problems. Plus, he'd realized that he was a lot more patient and understanding with a man's transgressions when he had a break from time to time.

Unfortunately, he hadn't gotten rid of the rooms yet.

"Sounds like I need to go see what is going on." After taking two steps, he walked back to Mason. "Hey, this is important so listen up."

"Yeah?"

"There's a guy who's back in town. His name is Eric Smiley."

"Jennifer's dad?"

Lincoln nodded. "Under no circumstances is he supposed to be on the property. If you see him, send him on his way and text me or Seth right away. Understood?"

"Yeah." His eyebrows rose then a look of consternation filled his eyes. "Ah, boss . . . what if he's with Jennifer? Do you want me to send her away too?"

"He won't be. Jennifer only met him today. And, just for the record, don't you ever send Jennifer away. Ever. If she shows up here, it's because she needs something. You bring her straight to me. And by that, I mean you escort her."

"And if you aren't here?"

"Then you help her or ask Bo or Seth to." He paused. "Understand?"

"Yes, boss."

"Good."

Pleased that something was finally going right, Lincoln lifted his chin to Mason before heading down to the basement to look for Bo and Adrian.

The basement was right out of the mid-'80s, and he'd never felt all that compelled to modernize it. The eight-foot ceiling was made of tiles and there was industrial gray carpet on the floor. The main area looked like a teenage boy's wish list, or at least his back in the day. There was a beat-up pool table, a foosball table, two pinball machines, a Coke machine filled with sodas, and a seventy-two-inch flat screen on the wall, hooked up to a game console.

It was a favorite hangout for the guys—some of them were barely more than teenagers themselves.

Walking through the space, he was struck by the quiet. Though he'd just been thinking that he needed *more* quiet in his life, silence wasn't what he'd been expecting down here.

Then he heard Bo down the hall. He didn't sound pleased.

Walking into the second room, Lincoln knew why. Adrian sat on a cot with his shoes off and had a plate from his kitchen on the bed.

Both men looked up at him when he entered.

Lincoln was in no mood to be played for a fool. "What's going on here, Bo?"

Bo twisted his neck a bit until it popped. "When I went to pick up the other guy, Adrian here was waiting for me. Turns out he talked his way into this house with the warden."

The warden wasn't exactly Lincoln's favorite person, but he'd been more than fair with Lincoln and his program.

But that said, he had enough problems on his plate without dealing with Adrian's attitude. "Pack up your belongings. You're out of here."

For the first time, Adrian looked scared. "Look, I'm sorry for going over your head, but I was desperate. I didn't have anywhere else to go."

Bo rolled his eyes. "I saw your paperwork. You have a cousin in town."

"I do, but he's knee-deep into his motorcycle club, his MC. My parents are dead and so are my two brothers. I'm telling you, I had nowhere else to go."

Lincoln didn't like feeling wrong, and he wasn't sure if he had been wrong about Adrian. But there was something about the expression on his face that told him there was more to his story than he'd let on. He sighed. "I'm not good with surprises, and I've already had my fill of them about three hours ago. So if you want someplace to sleep tonight, you'd best be upfront and tell me the truth."

"I can do that."

Lincoln waited, but Adrian said nothing more. Leaning against the door, he spoke again, deliberately allowing his tone to be harsh. "What are your plans? And not just for tonight."

Adrian gazed at him. Looked at them both, then seemed to come to a decision. He picked up his backpack and pulled out a piece of paper. "I want to finish this," he muttered, handing the slip of paper to Bo.

Looking like he was about two seconds from tearing it up, Bo unfolded the sheet and quickly scanned it. Then blinked and studied it more closely. "This is a college transcript."

If Bo had said it was a list for Santa Claus, he wouldn't have been more surprised. "Say again?"

"I took classes in prison."

"Okay . . ." A lot of guys took a course here and there. Most were to get a GED. A good amount of them never finished the first class. He'd only met one or two guys who'd taken college courses.

"Boss, he has twenty-one credits total." He shook the paper. "And get this, they're all As."

"What are they in?"

"Math and applied chemistry."

"Wait a minute. Are you saying you're smart, Adrian?"

He looked down at his feet, like he was embarrassed. "Yeah."

"What do you want to do, you know, after you finish college?"

"I want to get into nursing school."

Bo's eyebrows rose practically to his hairline. "You want to be a nurse?"

"There's nothing wrong with that," Adrian said. "A lot of guys are nurses now. It's a good job. It's good money too."

Lincoln was impressed despite himself. "You're serious, aren't you?"

Adrian shrugged. "I just need some time."

"Why didn't you say any of this when we met last week?"

"I was afraid."

"Of what? Me?"

"No. Of what would happen if word got around at the prison. You know how nobody wants you to have dreams. Not even the guards. Not really."

Lincoln actually did know what Adrian meant. Half of surviving prison life was forgetting about everything else. Once a guy started thinking about what he could be doing, or wished he was still doing? Well, that was a dangerous thing. Everyone saw that as a weakness, and it was the downfall of more than one man.

He glanced at Bo. Bo stared right back at him, which was enough of a signal that he was in favor of Adrian staying for a spell.

Well, so be it. Hadn't he learned a thing or two about forgiveness back in prison? Didn't his favorite verse in Galatians say that a man was held in custody until faith set him free? Maybe it was time to put some of those teachings into practice.

"We'll give it two weeks."

"Thanks, man."

"Don't you be thanking me. This isn't a charity ward. You've got to pull your weight. Bo or Seth will tell you what to do. And you've got to be able to prove to me that you're in communication with that college of yours. If you intend to go to school, then I want to see that you're working toward that. Got it?"

Adrian nodded.

"We mean it," Bo added. "There's no reason to do anything special for you. A lot of guys don't end up staying out. They're back in the pen in less than a year. Nobody's going to be your babysitter."

"I got it."

"Then you'd best get up, take that plate back to the kitchen, and get on work detail," Lincoln said. When he noticed Adrian appeared a whole lot more humbled, he turned and walked out . . . wondering all the while if he was making the right decision.

Like everything else, he figured time would take care of the future.

Feeling more exhausted than ever, he walked back upstairs, nodded to a couple of men playing cards, grabbed a beer out of the fridge, and headed to his room. Then, when he was finally alone, he sat down on the easy chair and allowed himself to go over his conversation with Jennifer.

Telling the truth about her grandmother—and his role in her practices—had been one of the hardest things he'd ever done. Telling her about her father and Ginny's role in his upbringing had been almost as bad.

He'd hated watching the hope in her expression fade to doubt and eventually morph into pure disappointment. It didn't matter if it was better for her to know the truth either. Sometimes even good medicine was hard to swallow.

That said, he allowed himself to mourn everything that could have been with her. He'd fallen in love with her and he'd had vague hopes of some kind of future with her. Maybe they never would have married, but he had hoped to be close to her. For her to lean on him.

He'd loved holding her in his arms. He'd liked everyone knowing that she was off-limits. That she was his. He wanted to be hers too. Who was he kidding? She already owned his heart. She didn't even have to ask, and he'd handed it over. Now he didn't know how he'd ever get her back. It wasn't like she was going to forget the things he'd done, just like he couldn't go back in time and not do them.

Taking another long pull from his beer, he set it on the side table and stared at the black screen of his TV. At a loss. Through the crack under the door, he heard the faint rumble of the other men's voices. The house was good. Good enough.

Against his will he kept straining to hear another voice, something softer, sweeter, higher pitched.

But, of course, there was nothing there.

CHAPTER 22

"You need anything ma'am?" Charlie asked after a brief tap on the front door. "Sam is on his way over. He'll stay until around one, then be relieved."

Jennifer was torn between breathing a sigh of relief and feeling guilty for making the guys do so much extra work. "Do you know Sam?" When Charlie raised his eyebrows, she shook her head. "Sorry. Of course you do. What I meant was, do you think he's trustworthy?"

"He is."

"Oh! Well, then, maybe he should come in and sit on the couch tonight."

"That's not possible."

"Because . . ." she prodded.

"Sam can't very well keep watch if he's hanging out inside the house, ma'am."

"I get that, but it's really cold out. There's snow."

Charlie looked amused. "He'll be all right. He'll only be here a couple of hours."

"All right." She didn't want to argue about how the guys were watching her place. But boy, was she going to feel guilty about Sam being outside in the cold while she was snug in bed.

"Don't worry so much. We're all used to standing watch outside. Someone's always outside Lincoln's place too."

"Really? I didn't know that."

"We're all on rotation and have been for years. So this ain't nothing new for us."

It was nine o'clock. Time to let him go and get herself in order too. "Well, um, please thank Sam for standing out in the cold to keep me safe."

"Will do. Lock up now."

"I will. Good night, Charlie."

"Night, ma'am."

She closed the door, flipped the deadbolt like she should, and then walked back to the small sitting room off the kitchen. She'd been watching some reality show on her laptop and sipping peppermint tea. Neither had appealed to her. The tea was lukewarm, and she couldn't care less about which celebrity was marrying whatever other star.

All she could think about was the news she heard from Lincoln.

For the last five hours—from the moment Lincoln had left her house, Jennifer had been trying to unravel her mind. She wasn't having much luck. She supposed it was no surprise, though. In the span of two hours, she'd been delivered the perfect storm. Her father's appearance, which had been shocking. Then, on the heels of that was the news about her grandmother enabling his behavior.

The sad part about Lincoln's news was that it hadn't been shocking, not really. There had been a part of her that had known something was wrong with the journal and letters she'd found. She'd known that they didn't make sense. Didn't mesh with the picture she had of her grandmother.

So the fault had been her own. She hadn't wanted to believe that the woman she'd idolized for so long had been so ruthless when it came to things she wanted done.

But instead of coming to terms with that, she'd blamed Lincoln, who had not only been the first person to tell her the truth, but he had also been completely honest about his role in MeMe's life. When he'd left, she'd felt terrible. She'd been angry at her worthless, conniving father, at herself for being so vulnerable, at her grandmother for living so many lies, and at him. For no real reason except that he was Lincoln—exactly the man he claimed to be.

He'd known that too. But instead of getting mad at her, he'd made sure she was being protected.

Which meant, of course, that she had a lot to learn about being loyal and accepting other people.

Ding.

She picked up her phone and glanced at the screen. Maybe Lincoln had decided to text her?

He had not. It was another text from Austin, a guy she'd only recently met on her dating app.

Yesterday, Jennifer probably would've ignored it. Contrary to what she'd said to Bo and Mason, she wasn't sure if online dating was for her. But in that moment, since she was feeling so blue, she opened the app and read the message.

Then read it again.

It was only four lines, but it was so nice. It wasn't full of flowery compliments that she knew didn't mean anything. Instead, he talked about his dog, how he worked from home too, and he wondered if she was the type to love all the snow or hate it.

It felt so sincere, she responded before doing what she usually did—which was to analyze every single word and debate exactly what it meant to her.

> First off, I don't feel all that strongly about the snow. I live in Ohio, which means it snows from time to time in the winter. I don't know if my blasé attitude about frozen rain is a deal-breaker for you or not.

> To answer your questions, I kind of have a pet. It's a cat that I inherited. I'm pretty sure he's only staying until he finds someplace better. What is your dog like? And, yes, it is good to meet someone who knows what it's like to work from home. It's not for everyone, but I've always enjoyed the quiet.

She read off her reply, her finger hesitating over the last part about how she admitted to liking the quiet. She feared it made her sound a little too introverted. But then she reminded herself that she didn't really care whether Austin wanted to go out with her or not. It was just nice to communicate with someone who had no idea about her grandmother or father.

After she pressed send, she picked up a book, intending to

at least try to read for a while until she fell asleep. But to her surprise, Austin replied again, and his message made her smile.

Huh. Maybe Match Link wasn't such a bad idea after all.

• • •

After almost another week passed, Jennifer said yes to dinner with Austin. She was still fairly wary about meeting someone in person, but she knew she had to get over that hang up. Plenty of women had begun good, solid relationships with men through Match Link. Besides, he seemed a whole lot better than Phillip. Feeling lonely even though guys were constantly around and watching over her, Jennifer knew she had to do something proactive.

She was still confused about the house and her original goal of cleaning it out. So much so, she'd even asked Wayne not to come over for two weeks.

Now that she had a date on the horizon Jennifer was regretting the decision to say yes. Regretting it a lot. She didn't want to meet Austin for dinner. She didn't want to get to know him better either.

But, unfortunately, she couldn't think of a reason to say no either.

And that, in a nutshell, was how her life was—in a constant state of doubt and confusion. She found herself dreading the moment she saw Lincoln again. But then, just as often, she would feel depressed because he hadn't come around.

When she'd discovered five or six of her grandmother's journals, her first instinct had been to take them to a shredding service. But then, just as she was getting ready to carry them out to her car, she'd opened one of the books to a random page and started reading. And then continued to read for the next two hours.

Yes, wishy-washiness had become her constant companion, and she hated every minute of it. She'd do one thing, then toss and turn all night and regret it the next. She was exhausted, cranky, and completely confused about every decision she'd ever made. Even decisions about her job and schooling.

Honestly, the only thing she didn't regret was her father's absence.

Bo had told her that Eric had been seen around town quite a bit. The man had been sitting in bars, talking to old friends of his, drinking cheap vodka. In other words, not doing much of anything at all. Bo had warned Jennifer that the very fact that Eric hadn't heeded their warnings and stayed away had been a bad sign.

Jennifer hadn't disagreed.

Her father was undoubtedly biding his time, but for what, she didn't know. Jennifer had no idea if he would show up at her doorstep with a lawyer or pop up in the middle of the grocery store and cause a scene. All she did know was that sooner or later he was going to get tired of waiting. She just hoped he'd do something before she reached her breaking point.

When her phone rang and she saw it was her mother, she answered reluctantly. "Hey, Mom."

"Has he come back yet?"

This was how her mother now started every conversation, thanks to Jennifer giving in to a moment of weakness and relaying all that had recently happened. But of course—just like everything else—Jennifer was regretting that decision.

"I told you that I'd let you know if he did, Mom."

"Jen, you didn't tell me about Eric showing up on your doorstep until three days after the fact."

"I know, but—"

"Have you heard anything about him at all?"

"Only that he's still hanging around town, drinking bad

vodka, and waiting," she joked. It was a pretty lousy joke, but Jennifer hoped it would lighten her mother's tone.

It didn't. "You need to contact a lawyer."

"I already spoke to MeMe's lawyer, remember?" She'd called him two days ago. "He said the will was ironclad and that there was nothing Eric's lawyer could do about it."

"I don't know if that makes things better or worse."

Her mother's comment sent chills up her spine. She was a lot of things, but she wasn't the type of person to start spouting off comments foreshadowing doom and gloom.

If Mom had been trying to get her attention, though, she'd certainly done that. "Why would you say that?" she asked quietly.

"Because Eric is lazy, Jennifer. He doesn't do much without a reason—and that includes waiting for you to give him the time of day." She sighed. "As much as I hate to say this, you also know that he's probably not waiting around to start a relationship with his long-lost daughter."

That hurt. She hadn't expected her father to suddenly start feeling paternal, but hearing her mother say the words pinched her heart.

She swallowed hard, hoping to control her voice enough so that she would sound calm. Thoughtful. "I realize Eric doesn't want to know me, Mom."

"I've made you upset. I'm sorry." After a pause, she said, "I'm just so irritated that this man is once again making me be the bad parent."

"I'm twenty-eight years old, Mom. I'm not going to get upset because my mom isn't doing what I want. Believe it or not, I'm pretty strong."

"I know you are. However, you also have the sweetest heart. It's there, under all those layers of defenses you've slipped on in order to hide it."

"Mom—"

"There's nothing wrong with your soft heart either. It's been such a blessing and I've always admired it—and have wished on more than one occasion that I was more like you." Her voice softened. "One day, you're going to meet a man who will find it to be everything he's ever wanted or needed. I just pray that he'll value it enough to help you protect it too."

Where was this coming from? "I didn't know you thought of me like that." She hadn't even realized her mother thought things like that at all.

"Well, I always have. Ginny did too. Maybe that's why she gave you that house, because she wanted to help you take care of yourself." She grunted. "And now that loser ex-husband of mine has ruined your peace."

"I'm okay. The guys next door are watching over me."

"The prisoners?" Her mother's voice dripped with derision.

"They're ex-cons, Mom. They're also good men."

"They can't be that good if they went to prison, can they?"

Jennifer was way, *way,* too tired to go down that path. "How about this? I trust them to come running if I need help. That counts for a lot. Besides, I've met plenty of men and women who never spent time behind bars who are complete snakes. Such as Eric Smiley."

"You have a point there." Her mother's voice turned soft. "You know, it still isn't too late. You could put the property up for sale and come home to Cincinnati. Then you wouldn't have to deal with Eric or worry anymore."

"I'm not going to let him win and scare me off." Feeling her spirits lift, Jennifer realized even saying the words out loud had been good for her. Maybe she'd finally made a decision about the house after all.

"It's not letting Eric win to protect yourself, Jen."

But it would, she realized in a startling sense of clarity. If she ran away, she'd be running away from everything she'd recently gained. Her independence, her newly discovered backbone . . . and even her grandmother's memories. She'd also be running from her new circle of friends, who she really valued. She'd be running away from Lincoln too, and she couldn't do that either.

Jennifer was sure that if she did run, she wouldn't feel any better. Going back home would be retreating into her solitary life, and somehow, she just didn't think it would suit her anymore.

"I know you love me, Mom. I love you too."

"I might not have said it enough, but you're a wonderful woman, Jen. I'm proud of you and . . . well, I would be ruined if you got hurt."

Her mom's words meant a lot. A lump formed in her throat as she realized that she'd needed to hear those words for some time now. "I'll do my best to stay unharmed, then," she said lightly.

"If you don't call or at least text me every couple of days to tell me that you're all right, I'm going to call you. Don't make me worry, Jen."

She closed her eyes, feeling guilty. Yet again, she'd been living in her vacuum, acting as if no one was affected by her decisions other than herself. "I'll do better about keeping in touch. I promise."

"I hope so."

Practically the minute they hung up, Jennifer received another text from Austin.

> Looking forward to our date.

Feeling disgusted with herself, she tossed her phone down. Well, at least one of them was.

CHAPTER 23

Kevin Heilman was a sergeant in the county sheriff's department and had worked with Lincoln off and on over the last eight years. Lincoln had learned the hard way what a mistake it was not to work with the local sheriff's office. Back when he'd first gotten out, his tendency to avoid law enforcement officers at all costs had created a lot of unnecessary problems that could have been deterred if he'd simply been open and direct with the local law.

Of course, he hadn't been the only one to have to overcome previously held prejudices. Not too many people had been excited about having a bunch of ex-cons hanging out and even sometimes all living on one property.

Now, while things weren't exactly smooth sailing between him and the sheriff's office, Lincoln and Kevin had a fairly good working relationship.

Which was why Lincoln had asked him to meet at the

Palace, a local diner that served exceptional food, even though it looked like a fixed-up shack.

Kevin stood up when Lincoln got in. "I'm glad you called," he said as he reached out to shake Lincoln's hand. "I love this place and I can never get anyone else to come here with me."

Lincoln grinned. "As long as everyone else stays away, we can always get a table."

"Courtney would probably rather have the business."

"Maybe, maybe not." He happened to know that Courtney had a lot of love for fishing, snowmobiles, and her grandchildren. She might not want to be busier than she already was.

Taking a seat, he glanced over at the chalkboard menu. "What's on the menu today?"

"We're serving all-day breakfast. Ricotta pancakes, eggs benedict, some kind of omelet, French toast with bananas, and the usual Palace breakfast."

"Ah, man." The usual included biscuits, sausage, gravy, and three eggs.

Kevin grinned. "I know. I came here hoping for eggs and bacon, and now I can't decide whether to go for French toast or the usual."

"Best make up your mind, Officer," Tamara, Courtney's daughter, said as she approached. "It may be breakfast, but I ain't got all day, you know."

"Fine. I'll have the usual."

"Eggs?"

"Yes. Over easy."

"Coffee? Juice?"

"Both."

She smiled his way. "And you, Lincoln?"

"Same, except scramble my eggs."

"You got it," she said before sauntering off.

Kevin flipped over his coffee mug as he leaned back in his chair. "She likes you a lot more than me."

"What can I say? I'm a nice guy."

He rolled his eyes but didn't say anything as Tamara returned to fill their coffee cups and drop off tall, thin glasses of fresh-squeezed orange juice.

After Lincoln took a fortifying sip of the juice, he got down to business. "I think I'm going to need your help, Kevin."

He sat up, his expression all-business. "What's going on?"

"It has to do with my neighbor, Jennifer Smiley."

"I haven't been down that way in ages. She bought Ginny's old place?"

"She's Ginny's granddaughter. Sweet woman too."

"What's going on?"

"Ginny's son, Eric, has popped up out of nowhere. He's Jennifer's dad but they've never had contact."

"Can't exactly say that's a bad thing."

"I agree. Heck, I'm pretty sure Jennifer feels that way too. I'm afraid he's going to make trouble for her."

Kevin had pulled out his phone and was typing in notes. "Why do you say that? Has he threatened her?"

Thinking of how slimy the guy had been, Lincoln sighed. "No . . . not in so many words. But he wants the house. Or, rather, he wants the money from the sale of the house. He feels it's his right, even though Ginny's will was ironclad. She made sure of that."

"What's been going on?"

"Bo's seen him hanging around town. A couple of the guys think they've seen him driving by her property."

Kevin paused and glanced at Lincoln again. "You're keeping that close of an eye on her?"

"Yeah. She needs someone looking out. And yeah, I want that someone to be me," he finished. He might not be ready to declare his love for her to the general population, but he was no longer afraid to put it out there.

"I see." Kevin smiled, just as Tamara returned with two plates heaped high with biscuits and eggs. "Thanks, Tammy."

"You know I don't answer to that, Sergeant. But you're welcome. Enjoy."

When she sauntered off again, Lincoln grinned. "She's never going to go out with you that way."

"She might, especially if you're off the market."

"I didn't say that."

"You didn't need to, Lincoln. This meeting said it all."

"I guess it does," he said sheepishly. Even though things between him and Jennifer weren't at their best at the moment, he couldn't deny that she was special to him. "Kevin, look. I know you can't do anything about Eric right now. But I'm asking you, as a friend, that if I call you about needing help, will you not wait to respond?"

"I wouldn't have waited even if you hadn't asked."

"Yeah, I know, Kevin. I know responding to calls is your job. But what—"

Kevin cut him off. "Lincoln, it absolutely *is* my job. But what I'm also saying is that we're friends too. Plus, it's not like you ever call about stupid stuff. If you ask for help, I'll know without a doubt that you need it." He leaned forward slightly. "I won't wait, Lincoln."

"Thanks."

Kevin shrugged it off, just like Lincoln knew he would if their situations were reversed. "Tell me what else is going on. Got anybody new in your crew?" he asked as he speared a bite of eggs.

"As a matter of fact, I do. Guy's name is Adrian, and he's a piece of work."

"Uh-oh."

"Yeah, I wasn't too impressed with him when I met him at the prison. I told him not to reach out to me. But then he did. He showed up at my place and wheedled his way into one of the rooms."

Kevin's eyebrows rose. "What did you do?"

"While I was chewing on him, he pulls out his freaking college transcript. It was filled with credits that he'd earned while incarcerated."

"Impressive."

Lincoln nodded. "Turns out he's smart and wants to finish college and be a nurse."

A fresh smile played on the sergeant's face. "So . . . let me guess . . . you gave him another chance?"

Lincoln wasn't one to blush, but he could have sworn that his cheeks were heating up. "I might have done that."

Kevin started laughing. "I might have to stop by your place just to meet this guy."

"Come on over if you want. Though he'll probably ignore you the whole time. Like I said, he's got an attitude."

He chuckled again just as Tamara came back with a filled coffee pot.

"You men want a refill?"

"None for me," Lincoln said.

"I'll take some," Kevin said. When she finished pouring, he smiled at her. "Thanks, Tamara."

For a split second, the waitress looked like she was about to smile back. Then, the door chimed as a couple wandered in. After practically tossing their checks on the table, she walked over to greet the newcomers.

Kevin sighed. "She's never going to give me the time of day, is she?"

Not wanting to come right out and hurt the guy's feelings, Lincoln shrugged. "Never's a real long time, buddy."

"Thanks for letting me know."

Fifteen minutes later Kevin was long gone, and Lincoln was sitting in his truck and glaring at a text he'd received from Bo while he'd been watching Kevin attempt to flirt with Tamara.

> Just stopped by to check on Jennifer. She's got a date tonight with some guy she met online. What do you want to happen? Do you want me to tail her or no?

The string of profanities Lincoln let fly made him glad he was alone. Unfortunately, letting loose hadn't helped a thing though. All he was doing was thinking about some clown escorting her into some restaurant, as if he had any right to be by her side.

Even the idea of such a thing had every part of him screaming in protest. But what could he do? She was a grown woman and was obviously not pining for him.

Because that sucked for him, and he felt even more ticked off, he texted Bo back.

> No. We ought to have a party tonight, anyway. It's been too long since everyone let loose.

> Sure about that, boss?

He stared at the four words for a long moment. He could almost feel Bo's disappointment seeping through. He didn't blame the guy either. He was disappointed in himself too.

But there were some things he couldn't control and some people he couldn't order around. Jennifer and her needing to date losers from Match Link was one of them. Gritting his teeth, he replied to Bo once again. It was painful, but the right thing to do.

Positive

Lincoln was almost disappointed when Bo didn't question him again.

CHAPTER 24

The Lakeside Inn had a fancy name, considering it wasn't near a lake and was located in the middle of a shopping center. Plus, it was a little run-down on the outside, despite its attempt at being "upscale."

Jennifer had been taken aback when Austin had suggested it as their first date. It was a little off the beaten path, a little too dark and fancy, and the owners had the reputation of being rather inattentive.

At least, that had been her impression when MeMe had taken her there four years ago when Jennifer had come for a long weekend.

MeMe had been friends with the owners for decades and seemed to think the steaks and fish were terrific. But Jennifer's steak had been too rare, the vegetables overdone, and the server had gotten mad at her when she'd asked if they could cook her meat some more. She'd spent the majority of the evening attempting to get someone to refill her water glass while MeMe had eaten every bite of her catfish like they'd been dining at Emeril's in New Orleans.

So she wasn't really looking forward to her date, the restaurant, or the meal. She hoped that she was wrong on all counts.

Standing in the kitchen, she looked down at her outfit and wondered again if she'd made a wrong choice. Her sweater dress was a little more snug than anything she usually wore, and the smooth brown leather boots with the two-inch heel were a whole lot fancier.

The boots were also going to be a challenge if the parking lot was icy—but the alternative was for her to wear something with some tread on them, which meant she'd have to change her outfit yet again.

After shaking her head at her doubts, she threw on her coat, grabbed her purse, and got out of there. Three hours. She just had to make it through the next three hours, and then she could come home, put on old sweats, and veg out in front of the TV for a couple of hours.

"Wow, Miss Jennifer. Look at you all dolled up," Seth said from his spot on her front porch. When the wind picked up earlier, Jennifer had tried to convince him to come inside, but he'd refused, saying he liked having a good view of the street.

Since they were both standing under the front porch's light, she struck a pose. "I know, right? I even have lipstick on."

"I heard that you got yourself a hot date." He didn't look too happy about it.

Over the last two weeks, she'd given up having any thoughts about retaining her privacy while having a bunch of men actively trying to keep her safe.

"It's just a first date, Seth. Nothing special." Since he still didn't look happy, she tried to joke. "Hey, at least you'll get the night off, right? No babysitting duties for you."

But instead of looking pleased, he looked worried. "Want some company?"

"Like, would I like you to come along?"

He nodded, looking completely serious.

"Thank you, but I don't think that's going to help my first impression much, do you?"

"He'll get over it. Or, hey, how about I just stay in my car in the parking lot? That way I'll be nearby if you need something."

Seth was the nicest guy in the world. "Thanks, but no thanks."

"Sure? I don't mind. Lincoln's got a party going on tonight anyway."

She hated that she hadn't known about the party and that she cared about what Lincoln was doing. "I'll be fine. Have a good time tonight. And don't worry. I'll get Austin to walk me to my car when it's over."

He curled a lip. "His name is Austin?"

"Come on, Seth. There's not a thing wrong with that name."

"Where are you going again?"

"The Lakeside Inn."

His eyebrows pulled together. "That place is kind of a dump. The steaks are overpriced, and the parking lot is dark."

"It wasn't my choice, Seth. Hey, maybe it's gotten better anyway. Everything deserves a second chance, right?"

He rolled his eyes. "Whatever. Just be careful."

"I will. Don't worry."

• • •

But two hours later, as she was sipping lukewarm decaf and listening to Austin talk about his exercise routine, Jennifer figured that she'd been wrong after all.

Some things absolutely did not warrant a second chance. Both the restaurant and her date were proof of that.

"That's why I'd be happy to come over," he said.

Come over? "I'm sorry, I guess all that good food has made me a little sluggish. What did you just say?"

"I just offered to come to your place. You know, to show you some of my moves that the trainer taught me," he said, his tone a little harder. "What do you say?"

"I say no." When his expression turned cold, she felt even more uncomfortable. "I'm sorry. I guess that came out wrong." Boy, her dating skills were rusty. She didn't have to be that blunt.

Austin rested his elbows on the table. "Really? What did you mean then?"

This was so horrible. "I meant, thank you, but I don't want to see your moves." And she couldn't even believe she was saying those words! Deciding just to get the whole experience over with, Jennifer added, "Austin, you're a nice man, but I don't think we're going to work out."

"You're dumping me?"

"I don't think you can dump someone after only one date."

"You're not even giving us a try, Jennifer. I've put in a lot of time with you. We've been texting and talking for days now."

She'd now bypassed uncomfortable and was moving into *ick* territory. "Well, I'm sorry, but you know how online dating goes." When he was staring at her silently, she started to get a little worried. Austin was acting really mad. Almost furious.

She'd had enough. Mentally calculating the cost of her meal plus her portion of a tip, she threw three twenties on the table. "You're making me uncomfortable," she said in a low voice. "I'm going to go."

When he didn't say a word—didn't even move, Jennifer

grabbed her purse and strode out of the restaurant, anxious to put as much space as possible between her and him.

Only when the door closed behind her did she realize that she'd left her coat inside. The hostess had taken it when they'd arrived. Though everything was telling her to go back inside and wait for it, she simply didn't have the nerve. She didn't want to see the hostess, who would know that their date was a disaster. Really didn't want to see Austin who looked seconds from making a scene.

And, since it was pitch dark and she had to go to the parking lot by herself—the dark parking lot, thanks to the lone light post sporting a dead bulb, she started walking faster.

She had her keys in her hand and the little flashlight on the end of her keyring on. The tiny beam helped her negotiate slick spots, but she was definitely lacking in the safety department. As her foot slipped, she frowned. She'd been a fool to wear these boots. If she wasn't careful, she was going to break her neck.

Just as she pressed the unlock button on her key fob, she was jerked to the side. Her feet slipped out from under her and she stumbled, then fell to her knees.

"You don't leave. You don't leave me until I say you can."

She couldn't see his features, but Jennifer knew she didn't need to see much to know that Austin was determined to hurt her.

She jerked from his grip.

"Listen." Uttering a stream of profanities, he hit her cheek hard enough that she felt like he'd broken bone. Her nose started bleeding.

She screamed. Screamed as loud as she could, even as he jerked her to her knees and tried to drag her deeper into the parking lot.

He was threatening her, giving her all kinds of directives

in between promises of retribution for ignoring him, and she screamed again.

When he hit her mouth, her lips were cut, either from his fist or from her teeth. By this time she figured it out, it didn't really matter. All that did was that something far worse was in store for her if she didn't fight. She struggled again, but he was holding one of her wrists and jerking.

Then she felt her dress's neckline tear.

Knowing what was next, she whimpered. Everything inside of her wanted to close her eyes and pretend it wasn't happening. Pretend it was just a bad dream.

But when she felt his mouth on the nape of her neck, felt his teeth when they scraped her skin, Jennifer returned to reality.

"No," she said.

"That ain't going to stop me." Laughing, he grabbed at the hem of her dress.

Which made her realize that she now had nothing to lose. "Help!" she called out. "Help!" she yelled again as she kicked him as hard as she could with her boot.

He grunted. Released her.

When he reached for her again, she rolled away and screamed with all her might.

"Ma'am?" a voice called out from the distance.

"Help!" she cried again as Austin reached for her hair.

"Here!"

"We're on with the police," a big, burly pair of guys yelled as they came barreling toward her. And then, just as Austin slapped her hard, they tackled him.

Austin thudded to the ground with a cry of pain. One of the burly guys hit him again.

"Ma'am, Miss?" the other man said as he gingerly reached for her. He flicked on his phone's flashlight and shined it on her.

The glare was blinding. Even though her brain knew the man was only trying to help, she pulled back and cried out in fear.

Right away, he lifted his hands. "Easy now. Okay," he said in a gentle voice. "I won't touch you." Pulling out his phone, he said, "Look, I'm going to call 911 again and tell them that we need an ambulance. Okay?"

The glow from his phone's screen illuminated his face enough for her to see that he was almost as freaked out as she was. Though it hurt to speak, she whispered. "Okay."

"Good." He smiled softly at her before he started talking on his phone. "Hey, my buddy Brandon just called and said that we needed some cops at the Lakeside Inn? Yeah, well, we just found the gal this uh, guy was attacking. She's gonna need an ambulance. Hmm? What? Oh, yeah, she's conscious, but she's bad-off. Okay. Yeah. I'll hold." Looking her way, he said, "Cops are almost here, and the ambulance is right behind them. Five minutes at the most. You're gonna be okay, right? Anyone can hold on for five minutes, right?"

His words were barely registering. "Austin? Where's he?" she whispered.

"That guy? Oh, he's under Jackson's knee. Don't worry, honey. Jackson wrestled in high school and college. He can pin anyone without hardly a second's thought."

"Thank you," she whispered.

"No prob, ma'am. We're just glad we were here. I have to tell you, we almost didn't come. This place has the worst steaks." As she heard the sirens blare, the man stood up. "Hey, I'm gonna wave him over here. Hang tight. I promise Jackson ain't gonna let him get near you again. And I've got two girls. I'd never hurt a woman. It's gonna be okay."

She didn't know the man. Heck, she probably wouldn't even

be able to point him out if she saw him in a lineup. But that didn't matter. She'd recognize his voice anywhere.

And more importantly, she trusted him. She closed her eyes.

"Miss? Miss, it's Officer Drury," she heard a woman's voice say through a cloud. "The ambulance is three minutes out. Hang in there."

She started crying.

"Is this your purse, ma'am? Is your phone inside? Is there anyone you'd like to call?"

"Lincoln," she murmured. When the officer held it up, Jennifer called out her security code, then nodded when she asked for permission to scroll through her contacts for Lincoln.

When she saw the officer click a button then hold the phone to her mouth, Jennifer finally relaxed. Lincoln was going to be with her soon. And when he came, everything would be better.

CHAPTER 25

Lincoln wasn't sure what had compelled him to tell Bo to answer his phone. Usually, when he was dealing with a problem in the house, he let it ring or go to his voice mail. And he really did have a problem. About an hour after they'd tapped a keg for the impromptu party, Adrian had gotten into a fight with Emmitt, one of the guys who was two weeks from transitioning out of Lincoln's program.

From what he and Seth had been able to discern, Adrian had essentially jumped Emmitt and caused enough damage to warrant an x-ray and twelve stitches on his face. Seth was dealing with him.

Adrian's actions had been bad enough that Lincoln knew he would have to contact his parole officer in the morning. In the meantime, it was up to him to get to the root of the problem and decide if the transgression was severe enough to step away and let the authorities take over . . . or intervene on the guy's behalf.

These meetings weren't all that rare, but Lincoln hated them.

He liked to be the guys' advocate, not play God with their future. Unfortunately, at least once a month, he had to intervene.

All that was why he'd shelved his cell in the basket near the door to his office, like he'd requested Adrian and Seth to do.

But when his phone started ringing again after stopping for the briefest minute, Lincoln knew something was going on. "Bo, grab it, will you?"

"Yeah, sure boss." After giving Adrian a death glare, Bo walked to the basket and fished out the phone. Immediately, his whole posture shifted. "It's Jennifer, boss."

He'd thought she was out on that Match Link date. "Really? Well, answer it, will you?" It was after nine. Late for her to be calling, especially since he couldn't ever recall her ever calling just to say hello.

Adrian shifted on his feet. "Lincoln, what—"

Still watching Bo, Lincoln raised a hand. "Hold on, Adrian."

For once Adrian did as he was asked.

"Hey, Jennifer, what—" Bo's body tensed. "I'm sorry, who is this?" His voice turned quiet and serious. "What? Ah, no, ma'am. Yeah, he's right here. Hold on." Putting his hand over the mouthpiece, he called out, "Lincoln. You need to get this now."

Already reaching for the phone, Lincoln glanced at Bo. "She okay?"

"No, sir." Looking even more worried, he added. "Cop's on her phone."

He took the phone, his heart now beating faster. "This is John Bennett."

"Do you go by Lincoln?" a brusque, female voice asked.

"Yes. My legal name is John Lincoln Bennett." Vaguely aware of Bo opening his office door and signaling for a couple of other guys to join them, he barked into the phone. "Who is this? What's going on with Jennifer?"

"This is Officer Drury. Jennifer asked me to call you."

"What happened? Is she okay?"

"Sir, she's getting loaded up into an ambulance now. Heading to County hospital."

Already imagining her little sedan crunched in some collision, Lincoln felt his mouth go dry as he wrapped his hand around the edge of a table. "Officer Drury, is she okay?"

Lincoln could hear sirens and some more conversation in the background. "Sorry, Lincoln. Hmm? Oh, hold on." After another pause, she said, "Sir, I'm sorry to let you know that she's been attacked."

"Attacked?" He took a deep breath of oxygen. "I'm sorry, ma'am. Did you say Jennifer's been attacked?" He felt like the whole room went silent.

Or, maybe he was just running out of oxygen. "What happened? Where is she? Officer, is she okay?"

"I need to pass back her phone. She's conscious and asking for it."

She was conscious. He felt like he'd just been hit across his midsection with a crowbar.

"Sir, are you still there?" The cop's voice was filled with compassion.

"Is she dying? I need something."

"She's sustained multiple injuries, but none are life-threatening. She'll be at County. Should I tell her you'll meet her there?"

"Yeah." He shook his head. "I mean, yes, ma'am. I'll be there shortly. Thank you for calling. I'm on my way."

"Very good." She clicked off before Lincoln could respond.

When the line went dead, Lincoln figured it was just as well. He didn't know if he was capable of saying another word.

"Boss?" Bo called out.

Feeling like he was in a tunnel, Lincoln turned to him. To his surprise, in addition to Bo and Adrian, three other men were standing in the room as well. All were staring at him intently. "Jennifer was attacked," he said slowly. "She's . . . she's alive, though."

"And?" Bo asked.

"And, uh, she's getting loaded up into an ambulance and is on the way to County hospital." Finally, his brain kicked in. He felt his jeans' pockets to make sure he had his wallet and keys. "I gotta go."

Bo shook his head. "I'll take you."

They had a good twenty guys there drinking beer, Emmitt at urgent care with Seth, and the fool Adrian was standing in his office like he didn't have anything better to do. "No need. I've got this."

"Lincoln, sorry, but I'm not gonna let you drive right now. Let's go."

"What do you want to do about this guy, boss?" Mason called out.

His body relaxed slightly. It looked like Mason had finally decided to step up. "Fix it," he said simply.

Reaching for his coat, he strode out of his office. He was vaguely aware of Bo pulling on his coat and grabbing his cell, and he was now murmuring something into it.

All the men in the living room were silent and staring at him. It seemed the news had already spread like wildfire.

When Dillon, a fairly new recruit, joined them, Lincoln gave Bo a look.

"We're going to need him to stay with your truck, boss. I'm going into the hospital with you."

"I'm perfectly capable of checking on Jennifer on my own."

"I'm not worried about that. I'm worried about what's going to happen when you find out the whole story."

Right now he couldn't care less about that. "I won't be leaving her side."

"I understand, boss. But you pay me to weigh every possibility and this is one of them. Trust me."

Dillon kept his expression blank, and so far, he hadn't met Lincoln's eyes.

As Lincoln got in the passenger seat and Dillon pulled out in an old Ford sedan right behind them, Lincoln stopped caring. "We're a good thirty minutes away."

"Less than that now. Don't worry. We'll get there."

Lincoln nodded. But it didn't escape his notice that not once had Bo said that Jennifer was going to be all right.

He racked his mind, trying to remember the last time he'd exchanged more than a few words with Jennifer. It had been days.

"When did you last talk to Jennifer?" he asked Bo.

"Two days ago, maybe," he replied as he sped down the highway. "She talked to Seth about this date. Not me."

"Did she tell him about what she was doing tonight?"

"I think so, but I'm not really sure. Seth didn't say much." He passed a truck going under the speed limit. "But it ain't like we've had much time to talk. It's been a busy night."

"Yeah, I guess so."

"Seth can tell you about it later. He's meeting us there."

"I thought he was with Emmitt?"

"Seth left him after I called." His fingers drummed on the steering wheel as he slowed for a red light. "And before you start asking why he's heading there too—it's because he wanted to."

A surge of jealousy flared before he tamped it down. "They've gotten close."

Bo shrugged. "You know we all like Jennifer. She's like a sister, you know? A nicer, sweeter one," he said as the light turned green. "Seth says he's gotten to know her because of Wayne, but honestly, I think he just likes to stop by just to see if she's been baking. He brings her things, too."

This was news to him. "What kind of things?"

"Oh, you know. He brought her a chicken the other day."

"A what?"

"He was at the meat market, and some dude was selling high-priced organic dead birds. You know how Jennifer loves that stuff."

He did not, but he was starting to realize that he'd put up so many barriers between them that he didn't know her all that well. Pulling out his phone, he called Seth.

He answered on the first ring. "Boss, I'm standing outside the emergency room doors. Where you at?"

"We're maybe five out. Listen, Bo said you saw her this evening. Did she tell you much about what she was doing?"

Seth waited a couple of seconds then spoke. "Yes."

"And?"

"She had a date at that Lakeside Inn."

He frowned. There weren't a lot of choices for dining, but that place was known for being a dive. "And you didn't think to tell me that?"

"I . . . No, boss."

Seeing the sign for the hospital lit up in the distance, Lincoln forced himself to calm down. Whatever happened wasn't Seth's fault. "We're almost there."

Bo didn't offer to drop him off. Just parked in the back of the lot and directed Dillon to keep an eye on the truck—and to keep his phone handy in case Bo called him.

Lincoln barely waited for Bo to finish speaking to the guy before striding forward and nodding to Seth.

When they entered the emergency room entrance, Lincoln

strode directly to the attendant on duty. It was an older man who looked bored and like he'd rather be sleeping.

"May I help you?" he asked in a monotone voice, barely making eye contact.

"I'm here for Jennifer Smiley. She was just brought in by ambulance. Where's she at?"

The attendant sat up straighter and straightened his glasses. "Hold on, now. We can't let just anyone wander in." He started shuffling through a number of assorted forms in front of him. "Are you family?"

"I'm close enough. I'm her fiancé," he said before Bo or Seth could say a word.

"May I see your ID, please?"

Pulling it out of his back pocket, Lincoln handed his driver's license to the man, who wrote down his name and then asked him some questions about his vehicle and phone number. He was antsy about the wait, but Bo gave the guy most of the information.

Five minutes later, he gave Lincoln a visitor's badge and a slip of paper to show the attending nurse.

"Thanks," Lincoln said.

"No problem." Looking hard at Bo and Seth, the man added, "You can go on back, but they can't. We only allow one visitor at a time."

"All right. Thanks." Clipping the badge on the collar of his gray Henley, he breathed a sigh of relief. Though it wasn't anything out of the ordinary, Lincoln could tell that Bo was irritated about having to sit in the waiting area.

The guys' concern for both him and Jennifer made his heart clench. He didn't often think that he was blessed, but these guys were everything a man would want by his side. "I'll be in touch," he said before walking through the doors.

CHAPTER 26

It was the smell that got to him. Cold, sterile, canned air and pungent medicine.

When Lincoln walked through the double metallic doors, he saw a woman in uniform standing nearby. She looked to be in her late twenties. When the nurse whispered something to her, she approached Lincoln.

"Hi there. Are you John Lincoln Bennett?"

"Yeah. That's me."

She held out her hand. "Maeve Drury."

"Thank you for calling me," he said as they shook hands.

Officer Drury was a little thing, shorter than even Jennifer, but she looked tough. "So I hear you're now Miss Smiley's fiancé?"

"Yep." He didn't blame the woman's incredulous look. He knew how he looked—and that she probably didn't believe a woman like Jennifer would ever wear his ring. But, whatever. All that mattered was that he'd almost gotten to her side. "Where is she? And what happened?"

The cop pointed to a drawn curtain. "The doctor's in there. It's going to be a moment."

As much as he wanted to barge in, he didn't want to be in the way. Besides, now that his brain was clearer, he needed some answers. "You said she's been attacked. What happened, exactly?" he asked again.

"As far as I can tell, she was out with a man, and when she was walking back to her car, he came up behind her. A couple of men heard her scream for help, and they ran over."

She'd been screaming for help. Hating the images filling his brain, Lincoln leaned his head against the wall. "Where's the guy who grabbed her? Any idea?"

Amusement lit her eyes. "We've got him down at the station. One of the men who came over to help used to wrestle. He pinned the assailant down on the pavement."

"Sounds like I owe that guy a thank you."

When he looked her way again, Officer Drury was frowning up at him. "Sorry to ask, but are you sure you two are engaged?"

"Jennifer asked for me, yeah?"

"She did."

"Then that's all that matters, right? She trusts me."

Compassion filled her eyes. "She was anxious to talk to you."

"I'd really like to see her now." The last thing he wanted was for Jennifer to think she was alone in this place.

"I understand. But, all the same, I'm going to stay a moment. We got the guy, but I want to make sure he stays locked up for a spell. I'd like to ask her some more questions." She looked about to add something more when they both heard a cry come from Jennifer.

"I'm sorry. I can't stand here any longer." He reached for the cubicle's curtain.

Officer Drury reached for his arm. "Lincoln."

Keeping his voice low, he looked her way. "You can come with me, but I am not standing out here while she's crying."

And with that—not caring a lick about what anyone else thought—he parted the curtain and entered. To his relief, Officer Drury stayed behind.

There was a doctor in scrubs, a nurse, two machines, one of which held a bag of IV fluid. And, looking so small and frail lying there, Jennifer.

Taking it all in, he realized that his heart literally hurt. She'd been badly beaten and was lying on the examination table on her back. Someone had removed her shirt but hadn't put a gown on her. A thin blanket was covering her body and chest but not her feet and calves. Her legs were bare. Two pink bra straps were curved around her shoulders.

She was also shaking like a leaf and crying.

Seeing the tears and her obvious pain finally shook him out of his reverie. He strode forward, barely aware of anyone else in the room. Crouching down, he carefully used the side of his thumb to erase the tear tracks that ran down her face. "Jen? Jennifer, baby. I'm here."

"Lincoln, oh, thank God." Her free hand reached toward him as the rest of her started shaking.

The doctor cleared his throat. "Sir? Sir, she's sustained two fractured ribs. Please take care."

"Of course." With more care, he ran a hand down her arm. Jennifer leaned closer to him. "You're not alone, babe," he whispered.

"John," she whispered as her body started to shake with fresh tears.

Never had his given name sounded so good. "Hush, now."

"You need to move to the side, sir," a nurse said.

Lincoln did as she asked. "I'll move wherever you want me, but I'm not leaving her." He could no more ignore the look of pain and fear in Jennifer's eyes than he would be able to stand still in front of a moving train.

And that wasn't even taking into account everything he was feeling as he started cataloging her appearance.

Jennifer's face was swollen, there were traces of blood on her nose, lips, and cheeks, and what wasn't smeared with blood was black and blue. She had scrapes on her arms and a quickly applied bandage on her hand. Her pretty blond hair was in disarray, and if he wasn't mistaken, he was sure there was another patch of blood streaked on the blond strands.

But what he couldn't seem to look away from—or come to terms with—was the mark just above her collar bone. Blood was there too; it was bruised and slightly swollen. But he recognized it for what it was all the same. Someone had bitten her.

He'd been involved in numerous fights in prison. A couple before that. He'd even broken up several at his house. All of them had raised his adrenaline and created a flash of anger that he always tried so hard to control.

But nothing—*nothing*—he'd ever experienced had prepared Lincoln for the flare of fierce anger that rushed through him now. If the animal who'd attacked Jennifer was in the room at that moment, he would have killed him. Absolutely, without any regrets. He'd gladly go back to prison if it meant that he avenged her. Almost glad that the nurse had moved him farther to the side, he tried to get his temper in check.

"Sir, are you family?"

"I'm her friend and neighbor. I told the officer out there I was her fiancé. My name is Lincoln Bennett."

"Well, Lincoln, do I need to get the police officer back in?" The doctor, who looked barely out of medical school, was staring at Lincoln like he was part of the problem. "You aren't responsible for this, are you?"

Lincoln's body went cold. Of course the guy didn't know him from Adam, but every fiber of his being rebelled against even being thought of as a person who could do this. "I am not."

The nurse inhaled sharply. "Dr. Evans, the officer said the man who did this is in custody."

"Oh, sorry."

In another lifetime, Lincoln might have taken offense. Now he couldn't care less what the doctor thought. All that mattered was that he helped Jennifer.

"Lincoln? John?" Jennifer whispered. "John, are you still here?"

Ignoring the doctor and the nurse, he leaned down. "Yeah, baby. I'm here. The doc is gonna fix you up." When he felt her tremble again, he brushed a lock of hair from her face. "What will help you, babe? Do you want me to step outside?"

"No!" Tears slid down her cheeks. "Please, don't leave."

Well, there was his answer. They'd have to forcibly remove him from her side. Looking directly at the doctor, who looked both touched and embarrassed, Lincoln pressed a kiss on a patch of skin near her temple. It looked to be one of the only spots on her face that was unscathed. "I'll stay here then, Jen."

"Her pulse rate has gone down, doctor," the nurse said.

"All right, fine . . . but Lincoln, is it?"

"Yeah?"

"I need you to help keep her calm, not make things worse." The doctor's brown eyes looked at him for a long moment. Which made Lincoln realize that the bite mark wasn't the worst thing he was going to have to deal with.

His respect for the man rose a notch. As long as this Dr. Evans was also all about Jennifer, Lincoln would be on his side. "I understand," he said. "I'll be fine."

Whatever the doc heard in Lincoln's voice must have reassured him, because he returned all his attention to Jen. "Jennifer, do you remember if you received any other bite marks?" he asked quietly. No, calmly, just like the doc was asking her if she'd like ice in her glass of water or something.

To his amazement, the emotionless approach seemed to help her. "I don't think so. But I . . . I think I have some scratches on my back. And my knee is real sore."

After quietly giving some directives to the nurse, the doctor spoke to Jennifer. "Do you remember when you were in the ambulance? The EMTs cut off your boots."

"I remember."

When they started peeling back the blanket, Lincoln took care to avert his eyes. He might have imagined what she looked like without her clothes on, but he'd never wanted to see her like this. He kept them firmly on her face, especially when she sought him out.

He ran his thumb over her knuckles. "I'm still here. Not going anywhere."

"Your knee is banged up and bruised, but I don't think there's any internal damage," the doctor said after he spent a few moments moving the joint and speaking to the nurse. "Could you roll on your side toward Lincoln so we can see your back?"

Once again, the calm, detached manner seemed to help. Without a word, Jennifer rolled toward him.

"If you could maybe put a hand on her shoulder, sir?" the nurse asked. "I think that will help keep her steady."

As he leaned closer, half tucking her face into his chest, he caught sight of the scratches on her back.

He inhaled sharply. He'd assumed the scratches had been from the pavement. But there were four deep gouges, made with a man's nails. He'd made those marks intentionally.

Doing his best to pull himself together, Lincoln glanced at the doctor and nurse.

They seemed just as surprised by the sight.

"Okay, Jennifer," the doctor said as he helped her lay back down on her back. "We're going to clean these up for you. Is there anything else? Did he scratch you anywhere else?"

"Scratch? Um, I don't think so."

"All right." After giving Lincoln a warning look, the doctor quietly added, "Now, did he touch you any place else?"

"Else?"

"Yes."

Lincoln noticed that the nurse was pointing to a rip on the side of Jennifer's panties.

"Dear, do you remember if you were violated?" the nurse asked in a soothing tone.

Jennifer's eyes widened. "I'm sorry?" She looked at Lincoln in alarm.

Lincoln knew she was in shock and confused. And, as much as he hated to add to her pain, there were some moments when only plain speaking did the trick. "Honey, were you raped?" he asked.

"No. No!"

She was trembling so badly, Lincoln was torn between attempting to soothe her and helping the nurse and doctor see to her needs. "Babe, did he try? Maybe he touched you—"

She shook her head. "No. Just this."

She looked so uncomfortable, he was worried she was embarrassed. "Jennifer, are you sure? Because if something—"

"I'm sure. John, I was screaming and those guys came." She started shaking. "I promise."

Exchanging a look with Lincoln, the doctor nodded. "All right then." He pulled off his gloves. "Cassie here is going to clean you up. We're also going to give you some antibiotics intravenously. That drip is going to take a couple of hours."

"Do I have to stay here much longer?"

Dr. Evans looked at Lincoln again before speaking to Jennifer again. "It's up to you whether you'd like to spend the night here. I can admit you, which will let you get some sleep, or we can put you in a private room for a couple of hours."

"I want to go home."

"Do you have someone to help you when you get there?" the nurse asked. "You're going to be sore."

"I'll be there," Lincoln said. "I'm not going to leave her side."

"All right then." Raising her voice, the nurse said, "Jennifer, since you have Lincoln here, I'm going to put a small sedative in your IV. It won't put you to sleep, but it might make cleaning these wounds easier to handle."

"Okay."

Lincoln thought Jennifer's voice was already slightly groggy sounding. If the medicine was already working, he was grateful for that.

"Lincoln, if you could sit in the chair by her IV, that would be helpful."

"All right. Of course." He moved to the chair, carefully pressed her other hand in his, and then watched the nurse wash Jennifer's face, then neck, then the assorted scrapes on her legs and arms. Finally, he helped the nurse turn Jennifer again so that the scratches on her other side could be thoroughly cleaned, covered in an ointment, and bandaged.

By that point Jennifer had her eyes closed most of the time.

When she was all done, the nurse glanced at both the bag of fluid and the time. "She'll need to be here at least another two hours, sir. Do you want to get a cup of coffee or something? I'll stay with her."

Remembering Bo and Seth, he stood up. "Thanks. I'll be back within ten minutes."

"You can even take fifteen." Cassie smiled. "I won't mind sitting down for a few minutes."

"Thanks."

After walking out of the room, he stopped and pressed the back of his head against the hallway wall. Every muscle in his body felt like it was bunched up, and his head was so full of warring emotions, he didn't know whether to hit something or cry.

He took a couple of seconds to pull himself together then headed out to the waiting room.

To his surprise, Bo and Seth had joined him, as well as Charlie. They all stood up when he approached. "Seth, I didn't expect you and Charlie to still be here."

Seth shrugged. "We all care about that girl. There's no way I wasn't going to be here."

"How is she?" Bo asked.

"She's got some fractured ribs and a lot of cuts and bruises. Some worse than others." There was no way he was going to mention that bite mark in the waiting room. "It took a bit for the nurse to clean her up."

"But that's all?" Bo asked.

On another day, Lincoln might have snapped at his second in command for crossing the line. But he knew that they'd all been fearing the same thing. "I think so. She said she hadn't been raped." His voice was ragged.

There were a thousand questions in their eyes, but each of the men was used to biding his time. "Is she staying here over-night?" Seth asked.

"No. The doctor suggested it, but she didn't want to. They've got her on an IV and are transferring her to a room for a spell.

It's got a light sedative in it, so she's resting. When that's finished, I can take her home."

Looking at the three other men, it hit him that he'd used to only regard Seth and Charlie as a responsibility, but they'd become some of his closest friends. Not only were they there for him, but for Jennifer as well. He'd always be grateful for that.

"Is Dillon still out with my truck?"

Bo grinned. "Yep. He's doing a good job too."

"He's probably also freezing."

Seth shrugged. "He'll be all right."

"Listen, the kid should get on back. I'm going to be here at least another two hours, likely three. I'll call you when we get back to her house."

Before he could say another word, Bo turned to Seth and Charlie. "Seth, you stay here with Lincoln and help him get Jennifer home. Charlie, you come with me. We'll send Dillon home and then I'll send you over to Jennifer's house."

"And?"

"You'll make sure everything's okay and that there are some lights burning for her."

"Got it."

"Don't forget Adrian," Lincoln said.

"I haven't. Mason is sitting in your kitchen with him. Last I heard they were eating grilled cheese sandwiches."

"What about the party?"

"That closed down when y'all left," Charlie said. "Most of the guys either went home or are playing cards. Everyone's been waiting to hear about Miss Jennifer."

Satisfied that everything was under control, Lincoln was anxious to get back to Jennifer's side. "Seth, would you find me a cup of coffee in this place and bring it to the room? They'll let you drop it off, I reckon."

"You got it, boss."

Feeling better now that he was reminded he wasn't alone in this, he turned to face all three of them. "Thanks," he said.

To his surprise, it was Charlie who spoke up. "Don't thank us for this, boss. We wouldn't want to be anywhere else." He looked down at his boots. "At least twenty other men wanted to be here too, but Bo put a stop to that."

"It's true," Bo said. "But I figured Jennifer had enough to deal with without knowing all our ugly faces were hanging out in the lobby."

"I'll let her know that everyone wanted to be here. She'll appreciate that." Just as he turned around, he muttered, "Get me that coffee, Seth."

As he walked down the hall, he heard a couple of chuckles, which made him glad. At times like this, he realized that they had all come a really long way.

Further than he would've ever imagined. Right before he entered Jennifer's room, he paused and said a brief prayer of thanks.

CHAPTER 27

The first thing Jennifer was aware of when she came to was that she hurt all over. The second thing was that she was in her own bed and not in a hospital room.

The third was that she was about to throw up.

Sitting up with a jerk, she tore off the covers and lowered one foot to the floor. She was prevented from moving that second foot by the arm that suddenly clamped around her waist.

Stunned and scared, she cried out and tried to twist free.

"Jennifer, what the heck?"

She blinked. Lincoln was sitting in the most uncomfortable chair in her house next to her bed. His eyes were bloodshot, and he looked pissed off. "I'm gonna be sick," she said around a gag.

Just as she tried to lurch to her feet again, Lincoln used his other arm to bring over a trash can and held it under her mouth.

Just in time.

Sitting on the edge of her bed, all she was aware of was how awful she felt, that she was ruining her grandmother's kitschy pale-yellow wicker trash can, and that Lincoln was for some reason witnessing every minute of it.

And, it seemed, he was holding her hair away from her face.

When at last it felt like there was nothing left in her stomach, Jennifer collapsed against her mattress again. "I'm sorry," she said, though she was pretty sure the word came out as a slurred "soy."

"Emmitt, get in here!" Lincoln called out.

"Yeah, boss?"

To her shame, Lincoln handed the trash can to the guy. "Get rid of this for me."

"Can too?"

"You want to keep the trash can, babe?" Lincoln asked, as if she wasn't slowly dying of embarrassment.

Keeping the wicker would mean Emmitt was cleaning out her vomit. That was about two steps more than she'd ever want another person to do. "No."

"Throw the whole thing out, Emmitt," Lincoln said, just as if he was asking the guy to grab him a soda or something.

Without a word—or really even a look in her direction—Emmitt walked out of the room and closed the door behind him.

She pulled the covers up and moaned in embarrassment.

Pure compassion filled Lincoln's cobalt-blue eyes. "How are you feeling, really? Are you going to get sick again? If so, I can ask Emmitt to hunt down another one of Ginny's ugly-as-sin trash cans. There's a slew of them around here."

It was time she came to terms with the fact that there wasn't a thing she could do at the moment about the state she was in. After checking in with her stomach, Jennifer shook her head. "I think I'm good."

Looking pleased, Lincoln got to his feet. "Stay there. I'm

gonna get you a washcloth and something to rinse out your mouth." He paused. "Or, do you have to go to the bathroom?"

Suddenly she realized that she really did. "I do."

"Okay, then."

Next thing Jennifer knew, John was carrying her. Luckily there was a small bathroom connected to the bedroom. Otherwise poor Emmitt would've gotten even more of an eyeful.

"I can walk, John."

"Humor me." He kept going until he was helping her stand up next to the toilet.

To her surprise, he looked like he was ready to help her get on the toilet too. "I've got this. Go on out."

"Babe, stop being so shy."

There was being shy and there was retaining at least a portion of her self-respect. "Leave."

Muttering under his breath, he turned on his heel. As soon as he closed the door behind him, she relaxed enough to grip the countertop nearby to combat the wave of dizziness that took over her. Then, finally, she was able to do her business. Taking care not to look at her reflection, she turned on the sink to wash her hands.

The second the water started running, the door opened again. "You decent?"

She didn't know what she was. She supposed decent was a good enough description. "Yes. I mean, I'm okay."

"No. You're not," he said quietly as he moved closer.

There was so much force in his words, she glanced his way and was confronted with pure pain in his eyes. It was enough to make her quit arguing and concentrate on putting toothpaste on her toothbrush. She'd half expected Lincoln to take over that task too, but he just stood there and watched her scrub her teeth and spit.

When she inadvertently spied her reflection, complete with

swollen eyes, nose, cheeks, and more than one scab forming on her lips, she closed her eyes in horror.

Austin had hurt her so badly.

Without a word, John bent down, turned the tap to warm, and located an unused hand towel. As soon as the water warmed, he helped her wash her hands, then quietly placed the lid on the toilet. Finally, he helped her sit down before gently wiping her face with the warm towel.

It felt so good—and it had been so long since anyone had cared for her like this, she kept her eyes closed and simply appreciated his attention.

When he was done, he tossed the used cloth on the floor and picked her up again. She leaned against him until he deposited her back in bed. Clyde, who'd jumped into the center of the bed when she'd been in the bathroom, meowed his displeasure.

"Move, cat."

Clyde gave him an evil eye before jumping off the bed and trotting out of the room.

Only then did she decide it was time to figure out what was going on. "John, how long have you been here?"

"Since we brought you home around three this morning." He looked at her intently. "Do you remember last night?"

Stark flashes of pain, followed by images of Austin ripping her dress, then the white room at the hospital, and finally Lincoln's hand in hers floated to the surface. "Yes," she said. "I mean, I remember parts of it." When he just looked at her and waited, she said, "I remember what happened, and the police officer calling you. I remember the hospital and you holding my hand."

His expression flickered before he swallowed hard. "Do you remember us taking you home?"

"No. Who is us?"

"Seth and me."

"Seth saw me like this too?" Though she was talking about her face, Jennifer looked down at herself and saw she had on her baggy baby-blue knit nightgown. It was soft and worn and probably the least attractive night garment she owned.

"Babe, the nurse put you in an old hospital gown. I wrapped my coat around you. Seth saw you in that."

It was a testament to how bad she looked that Lincoln wasn't making fun of her for being shy again. "I see." Still putting the pieces together, she touched the hem of her nightgown, which came up to about mid-thigh. "And this?"

"After I got you home, I helped you get it on." Lincoln's face was a hard mask, almost like he was just waiting for her to act offended that her privacy had been violated.

She wasn't going to say a word about that. "Thank you."

One eyebrow rose. "That's all you've got to say?"

"Thank you very much?" Even though it hurt, she smiled slightly.

"You're welcome." He fussed with her covers for a minute, smoothing the sheet, then rearranging the blanket and down comforter over that.

When he looked satisfied with his efforts, he sat on the edge of the bed. "It's time for some pain pills, but you need to eat something with them. What do you want?"

"If I mention something, does that mean poor Emmitt's going to have to cook it?"

His lips twitched. "Probably. Or I will."

Jennifer wasn't really hungry, especially since she'd just disposed of her stomach's contents. But her back was hurting her and so were all the other marks and scrapes. "Maybe a can of soup and some crackers?"

"Emmitt can probably handle that. I'll be right back."

When she was finally alone, she looked around the room

and saw a half dozen signs of his night. There in the corner was the hospital gown he'd mentioned. On the side table was a mug of half-drunk coffee. A glass of water with a straw in it. Two prescriptions. His cell phone. It was clear that Lincoln had stayed by her side all night. He'd tended to her, helped her in probably a dozen different ways that she'd never realize.

What would she have done if he hadn't been there? She probably would've been lost without him.

No, she'd be more than that. Jennifer blinked, realizing she wasn't just referring to the last twenty-four hours. Somehow, this intimidating man had become the person she trusted the most in the whole world.

When Lincoln returned, he was holding a bowl of soup in one hand and a bag of crackers in the other. "We hunted around and found a can of chicken and stars. That will have to do."

"It'll be fine."

He pulled over his chair and leaned closer to her. "I'm not in a hurry to burn your mouth, so let's take this real slow."

His statement struck her as funny. She smiled at him before opening her mouth like a baby bird.

It did take a while to get down about half the soup and a couple of crackers. But Lincoln must have deemed it enough because he opened up one of the prescriptions and handed her a pill. "This is for pain. The next one is an antibiotic."

She frowned, until she remembered her shoulder where Austin had bit her. Reaching up to touch it, she felt just the hint of a bandage before Lincoln pulled her hand away. "No, baby. Leave it alone."

Feeling her cheeks heat, she murmured, "I guess you saw what he did."

"I did." His expression darkened. He handed her the pills and the glass of water. "Take this."

She swallowed and handed him back the glass. "I hope I don't have a scar." What would she do if she had to stare at the marks from Austin's mouth every day for the rest of her life?

"The doctor told me he didn't think you would scar too much from that. But if you did, the nurse told me you can get plastic surgery."

It would be expensive, but worth it. "I guess I'll see what it looks like." Noticing that he was glowering, she raised an eyebrow. "What?"

He shifted uncomfortably. "Jennifer, I'm trying my best to give you time, but it's killing me not to ask what happened."

Her former self would have kept everything bottled up inside. But this new version of her? Well, she realized that keeping the details of Austin's assault a secret wouldn't help her at all. It was going to hurt, but remembering it only in her dreams wouldn't help her much either.

"I can talk about what happened. I mean, some of it."

"The cop who I talked to, her name was Officer Drury, I think, told me that she's going to stop by later to speak to you again." A muscle in his cheek jumped, but his voice was calm when he spoke. "Do you want to wait to talk to her? Or, I can try to put her off a while."

"I'll talk to her when she comes. I'm pretty sure I remember talking to her, but I can't remember what I said." She frowned. "Everything is pretty fuzzy."

"I bet."

Seeing how tense he was, she said, "We can talk now, if you want. It might help me get my head together before the police come."

"All right. So, this guy you were with—"

"His name was Austin."

"He's in police custody. You don't have to worry about where he is or if he's going to hurt you again."

That was a relief, but not just for her. "To be honest, I would worry more about you."

His eyes narrowed. "What do you mean by that?"

"I'm afraid if he wasn't in jail or wherever they have him—that you would go after him yourself." Realizing that she was making him sound like her own avenging angel, she quickly added, "I mean, you might if you had felt strongly." She hoped he understood that she was trying to keep him from a second stint in prison.

"I would have thought about it." He ran his fingers through his hair. "So yeah, I'm glad he's locked up too." Lincoln shifted in his chair. It was obvious that he was waiting for her to talk some more.

But no matter how she tried, it was becoming pretty obvious that finding the right words was nearly impossible.

"This is hard, but you have the right to know. I mean, if it was reversed, and someone had beaten you up, I'd want to know the whole story. But, it's all kind of a blur."

"Tell me what you can, then."

She liked the sound of that. It sounded doable. She didn't have to recall every detail. Taking a deep breath, she said, "I hurt and I feel gross. Violated. I'm mad that this happened to me. But mostly I just feel embarrassed."

"There's no reason for you to be embarrassed."

"I think there is. I knew better than to meet Austin for dinner. Everything I've read about online dating said to keep it during the day and short for the first two or three dates. Plus, I regretted saying yes almost immediately. I should have listened to my instincts and canceled." She glanced at him then looked away. "But I was afraid I was being silly. And, well, I guess my feelings were hurt too."

"Because I was staying away from you again."

"Yes, but I'm not blaming you, John. What happened to me was my fault."

He shook his head. "Honey, not a bit of what happened was your fault. Half the people I know—both men and women—are on dating apps and never have a problem. You should be able to expect to go out with a jerk, have a bad time, and then go home."

The way he described it made her chuckle. She had experienced dates like that. "I guess you have a point."

"What happened at the restaurant?"

"It was the longest dinner of my life. Austin was full of himself and even made a couple of suggestions about how I should wear more makeup. You know, maybe try to lose weight."

"Which we both know you don't need to do."

That was definitely a conversation for another day. "Anyway, it was pretty obvious that I wasn't having a good time. He said he wanted to come to my house. I said no, and he was rude about it, so I got up to leave. I even left money. He was mad at me, like I owed him something, you know, for the meal, but I ignored him and got out of there.

"But when I stopped at my car—and yes, I already had out my keys, John, he . . . well, I guess he grabbed me."

"He jumped you." Those two words sounded as if they'd been pulled from his throat and he was choking on them.

"I guess he did. One minute I was standing there, the next minute he was pulling me toward the back of the parking lot, near some bushes and trees and covering my mouth with his hand." Remembering the feeling of hopelessness, she shuddered. "I couldn't breathe."

At last, she dared to look at Lincoln.

The expression on his face was so dark, she feared it had been a mistake to tell him anything at all.

CHAPTER 28

Officer Drury showed up in the midafternoon. Lincoln was relieved that Sergeant Heilman was by her side. It wasn't that Lincoln didn't trust Officer Drury; it was more like he trusted Kevin completely. Watching them confer just outside of Jennifer's front door, Lincoln forced himself to exhale.

He was so keyed up after hearing Jennifer's story, he'd been seriously doubting that he was going to be able to hold it together for much longer. At least with Kevin being here, he had a half-decent chance of not going completely ballistic.

But Lord Almighty, who could blame him?

Jennifer's recounting had been painful and made bile churn in his insides—and it wasn't only because of what had happened to her. Lincoln knew she was strong and would get through Austin's attack even stronger.

No, what had been hardest for him to bear was that he couldn't do a thing about it. He couldn't fix her, and he couldn't bear her pain. Then there was his need to "fix" the whole situation. There was believing in right and wrong, and then there was needing to go after the guy who hurt the woman he loved.

And yeah, there was that. It had taken some of the worst moments in Jennifer's life to make him realize that he needed to tell her how he felt. Even if nothing ever happened between them, he wanted her to know what she meant to him.

Two raps at the door brought him out of his stupor. He strode to the door just as Bo did. "Boss, you want me to stick around or go?"

"Stick around, if you can, 'kay?" He didn't want to finish the thought, but he reckoned it was pretty obvious, at least to Bo. He was going to need the man's help to get his act together if he started to go off the rails.

Opening the door, Lincoln shook both of the officers' hands. "Kevin. Officer Drury."

"Didn't expect to see you here, Lincoln," Kevin said.

"Jennifer needs me."

"How is she doing?" Officer Drury asked.

Lincoln shrugged. "Well enough, I guess." Glancing at Bo, he said, "Ma'am, you might have met him last night, but this is Bo."

"My real name is Sam Beauman," Bo said.

"Mr. Beauman," Officer Drury murmured.

"Call me Bo, if you please," he said as he shook hands with the officer and Kevin. "Nobody's called me by either Sam or Beauman in years."

"I can do that. Now, who are you, exactly?"

"Most days I work for the organization and supervise newly released ex-cons. Other days, I guess I'm Lincoln's right-hand man."

"I see."

But it was real obvious that Officer Drury was still a little confused by him being at Jennifer's house. "Why are you here now?"

Lincoln opened his mouth to state that he couldn't see the hell why it mattered, but Bo answered. "Because it's the right thing to do."

Drury looked like the answer was as clear as mud, but she merely nodded as they walked into Jennifer's living room.

"Where is Miss Smiley?" Kevin asked.

Lincoln gestured to the stairs. "She's in her bedroom. Have a seat and I'll go fetch her."

The officer looked at the stairs with a frown. "If she's in too much pain to get out of bed, we can go to her."

He didn't think there was any way in the world that Jennifer would want to talk to two strangers in her bedroom, but Officer Drury might have had a point about the stairs. "I'll go see what she wants to do."

Walking up the stairs, he tried to guess how Jennifer was going to want to handle things. She might only want one officer to speak with her privately, or maybe only him and Officer Drury but not Sergeant Heilman.

After a brief knock, he cracked open the door. Her bed was empty. "Jennifer?"

"Hmm? Oh, I'm here. I was just putting on a robe. What do you think? Am I covered up enough?"

She was in a voluminous, thick, white terry cloth robe that skimmed her ankles. It was cinched tight around her waist and wrapped snuggly so there was only the smallest portion of her throat showing at the top.

"I reckon you are, but you've got nothing on your feet. Want some socks or something?"

She wiggled her toes. "No. I'm not a real fan of socks." She took a deep breath. "So the police officer is here?"

"There are two of them. One is Officer Drury. She was at the hospital with you last night. The other officer is Sergeant

235

Kevin Heilman. I know him; he's a good man." Noticing that she hadn't moved, he added, "Jennifer, they wanted to know if you were okay with coming downstairs or if you wanted them to come to you. It's up to you."

"I don't want them in my bedroom, John." Looking perturbed, she added, "That's okay, right?"

Lincoln figured that right now she was feeling like the only safe place in her world was this bedroom. He rushed to reassure her.

"Babe, you don't have to have anyone in here that you don't want." He held out a hand for her to take, because that was where his mind was now. He didn't want her to feel like she was alone in this even for a moment.

She walked to his side and slipped her palm against his. He was pleased to notice it felt calm and dry. "Will you stay with me?" she asked.

Jennifer would never know how relieved that made him. "Of course I will, if that's what you want." Wrapping an arm around her waist, he smiled. "I think Bo is hoping you'll let him be nearby too."

"For you or me?"

He couldn't believe it, but she'd made him chuckle. "For both of us, I reckon. He's still worried about me going off the rails."

She nodded, not really giving him an answer, but Lincoln figured it didn't matter. He'd discover what she wanted soon enough.

"Let's go get this over with, Jen," he said as he slowly guided her down the steps. After about five, Lincoln reckoned he should've just carried her in his arms, but he knew she needed at least this small amount of independence.

When they walked into the living room at last, Lincoln felt

three pairs of eyes studying the way he had one arm around Jennifer's waist and the other hand holding her elbow. He reckoned his feelings for her were evident for everyone to see. Weeks ago, Lincoln knew he would've tried to appear more circumspect. As far as he was concerned, his private life was nobody's business but his own.

Now, however, he wanted everyone—most especially Jennifer—to know how important she was to him.

Even if she never loved him back, Lincoln figured that her leaning on him was something to be proud of. It even might be enough.

CHAPTER 29

Both officers and Bo stood up when she and Lincoln entered the living room. Feeling those three sets of eyes actively studying her, Jennifer was vividly aware that she was in bare feet, an old nightgown, and a massive robe. She was clean—thanks to the careful bath she'd taken after Lincoln's soup—but she still felt dirty and ugly thanks to Austin's attack.

Lincoln had shifted slightly and was now only holding her hand. However, he didn't seem to notice or care that she was squeezing his palm so tight that it was likely cutting off his circulation.

"Jennifer, like I told you, this here is Kevin Heilman, he's a detective with the sheriff's department. Next to him is Officer Drury. She spoke with you last night, both at the scene and at the hospital."

"Hello, Jennifer," Officer Drury said kindly. "It's good to see you on your feet."

"Thank you." She tried her hardest to remember conversing with Officer Drury, but she couldn't recall much beyond the woman calling Lincoln. How could that be? "I'm sorry. I . . . I don't remember much beyond you helping me with my phone."

"No worries," she said easily. "That's why I came over here today."

Jennifer nodded. When she caught the sergeant's eye, she looked back down at her feet.

"Come on. Let's sit down," Lincoln said. He directed her to her grandmother's loveseat. The same one that Lincoln had once said was the most worthless piece of furniture in the house. She'd privately agreed with his assessment but was now glad that she hadn't asked any of the guys to take it to the thrift store. She and Lincoln were a snug fit. But instead of feeling cramped, she liked the feeling of his body next to hers. He made her feel protected and not so alone.

The two officers sat down as well, just as Clyde sauntered in and rubbed against Officer Drury's leg. She bent down to pet the cat. Clyde miraculously allowed the caress before going back into hiding.

Looking amused by the cat's antics, Bo stepped toward the back of the room. He stood against the wall, watching carefully as always.

After exchanging a look with the officer, Sergeant Heilman pulled out a notebook and an electronic tablet. After something buzzed, he turned to face her, his expression impassive yet concerned.

When he spoke, she decided his tone matched his demeanor. "Jennifer, I'm very sorry about what happened to you. As you know, Mr. Austin Carson is in custody. We've been speaking to him and digging into his past. He's been arrested before. I'm sorry to say that it doesn't look like you are the first woman he's reached out to on social media and later assaulted."

"I see." She didn't know if that made her feel better or worse. Was she in good company . . . or should she have known better?

Officer Drury spoke then. "I know it doesn't seem right, but his prior record is a good thing for you. Because of that, we can keep him detained for a while, at least until we press formal charges and then maybe even longer."

"She's right, Jen," Lincoln murmured. "Every reason they have to keep him locked up is a good thing."

"Okay," she said.

The sergeant spoke again. "Jennifer, as difficult as this is going to be, I need you to tell us everything you know about Austin, starting from when you first made contact. No detail is too small."

"We'd also like to log into your social media accounts and phone records, Miss Smiley," Officer Drury said.

"Of course, but there isn't that much to say."

"That's fine," the sergeant said. "Now, if you could tell us when you first met him online, we could get started."

Suddenly Lincoln's presence next to her felt wrong. Just imagining his reaction to her words made her feel sick. Plus, did she really want him to hear all about how stupid she'd been for the last week?

No. No, she did not.

"John, I think it would be better if you left."

"Better for who?"

"Both of us."

After staring at her for a few more seconds, Lincoln got to his feet. "Jen, I think we should talk about something first."

She didn't move. "I don't believe that's necessary."

"I promise it is. Please, babe?"

Jennifer could count the times on one hand that John had spoken to her in that soft, pleading tone. Couldn't remember too many other times that he'd whispered please to her.

It wasn't like him to let down his guard, to be vulnerable. "All right, then." Getting to her feet, she glanced at Officer Drury. "I'm sorry. I'll be right back."

To her surprise, Officer Drury didn't look irritated at all. Instead, she simply nodded. "Take your time."

When they were alone, she said, "Lincoln, this is going to be hard enough without you hearing everything."

"Why? You know I'm on your side, right? I care about you, Jennifer."

"I know that. Of course, I know that. It's just . . . I don't want you to hear what an idiot I was. If you hear about all the things I did, all the things I wrote, you're going to never be able to unhear those words. And I don't think I'm going to be able to take that."

The line had returned in between his brows. "What do you think I'm going to do? Or say?"

"I don't know." Maybe he wouldn't say anything. But surely, he would think she'd made a lot of mistakes and could've acted smarter. He wouldn't be wrong, either.

"None of what happened was your fault. I'm not gonna think that for a minute." He took a deep breath. "Jennifer, don't you get it? I love you."

He loved her. Her bottom lip was trembling, and she bit down hard on it to stop.

He ran his thumb over her bottom lip, freeing the bruised tissue. "Don't hurt your lips, babe. You're hurt enough, yeah?"

Still overcome, she nodded.

"Now, let me stay by your side, okay? I don't want to interfere. I want to be there for you. I don't want you to have to do this all alone."

"All right." She released a shaky sigh.

"Good. Now let's go get this over with."

"I'm sorry," she apologized when they joined the others. "I guess I'm still shaken up."

"You take your time, Jennifer," the sergeant said. "This isn't easy."

She realized that no one was now looking at Lincoln like he was a threat anymore. With some surprise, she realized that they'd been able to watch her and Lincoln talking in the kitchen.

When she felt Lincoln's arm rest just on the top of the loveseat behind her back, she started speaking. "I guess I should start off by saying that I haven't had a lot of luck in the dating department. So, um, after I felt that I wasn't having very much luck with the men I was meeting in person, I decided to try online dating."

"What she's trying to say was that Lincoln was sure he wasn't good enough for her and made the rest of us promise that we wouldn't ever flirt or even think about dating her," Bo supplied.

Not wanting to go down that road, she said, "Anyway, I had heard that Match Link was a pretty good site, so I grabbed an old picture of me, wrote a profile, and decided to see what would happen."

"And Austin reached out to you right away?"

"No. I heard from several other men first. Austin reached out after I'd been online for about a month."

Both police officers leaned forward. "And then what happened?" Officer Drury asked.

Jennifer took a deep breath and relayed everything. Told them about the emails and the texts they exchanged. The phone call and her decision to meet Austin at the restaurant.

Sitting beside her, Lincoln sat motionless and silent. She had no idea if he was holding every thought in tightly or if nothing she was saying was a surprise. Jennifer knew that she didn't really care what or how he was feeling or inwardly reacting. At least not at the moment.

All she allowed herself to concentrate on was the fact that he was there and that he believed in her.

That knowledge enabled her to speak more easily about everything. She sloughed off her guilt and embarrassment and shared the dinner conversation, her disappointment, and then, at last, his attack.

And when Officer Drury shared that the more details she could supply would help put Austin away for good, she made herself return to that moment and shared everything she could.

Lincoln remained motionless the entire time, though there must have been something in his expression because she noticed Bo staring at him intently the whole time.

An hour later, the interview was over. Lincoln helped her get to her feet, and she shook the officers' hands. Then she collapsed back on the couch while Lincoln walked the officers to the door.

"You did good, girly," Bo said. "You should feel real proud of yourself."

She shrugged, not willing to take a compliment for sharing her story. "I just hope it helps put him away."

"I saw how the cops were reacting. What you were saying made a difference. I'm sure of it."

She smiled at him. "You might have heard the cops' words, but I only noticed you watching John. Did he do okay?"

"You were the one sitting next to him, girly. You tell me."

Jennifer couldn't believe it, but she giggled. "Bo, we need to put you on a game show or something."

"And why is that?"

"Because you are the best liar I've ever met."

He pressed a hand flat on his chest. "Now you're just breaking my heart."

"Are you giving Bo grief again, babe?" Lincoln said as he returned.

"Maybe a little bit."

He smiled at her. "Jen, you want water or hot tea?"

She never would have guessed it, but Lincoln was a whiz at making hot tea with milk and honey. "Hot tea? Do you mind?"

"Wouldn't have asked if I minded. Now, how about I help you get upstairs so you can lay down?"

"I can handle the stairs on my own."

"Jennifer—"

"John, I need to climb those stairs for myself."

"Fine. I've got to talk to Bo for a sec, but I'll be in with your tea after that."

"Take your time." When she was about halfway up the stairs, she realized both men were still standing there. "Hey, Bo?"

"Yeah?"

"Thanks for being here."

"No place else I'd rather be."

Two minutes later, when she walked into her bedroom and laid down on the bed, her robe still securely fastened around her, she heaved a sigh of relief.

Clyde meowed his hello, then carefully maneuvered next to her back and curled in a ball. The cantankerous cat's display of affection lifted her spirits slightly and made her feel a small bit of hope.

The last twenty-four hours had been hideous. Some of the worst moments of her life. But she was surviving, just like that crazy cat.

And, she was learning, survival was all that really mattered. Survival . . . and knowing that Lincoln Bennett loved her.

CHAPTER 30

Once Lincoln heard Jennifer close her bedroom door, Lincoln felt his hands clench. If he'd been in his own house, he knew his fist would have already gone through a wall. Instead, he rested his head against the paneling and breathed deep.

"You've got to calm down, boss," Bo said.

"I'm working on it."

"She's hurt, and she's hurting, but she's going to be okay."

"I know. I just . . . " His jaw clenched. "I'm just trying to come to terms with the fact that the only reason Jennifer wasn't raped was because two fifty-year-old guys happened to be in the vicinity."

"But they were."

"Yeah, they were. Thank the Lord."

He walked into the kitchen, filled Jennifer's stainless steel kettle with fresh water, and placed it on the burner.

As much as he wanted to be there for Jennifer, he realized that his emotions were still in turmoil.

Losing control wouldn't help the woman upstairs.

He sighed. "I hear you." After getting out a mug, squirting some honey and milk inside the way Jennifer liked it, he said, "I think I need to get out of here for a few hours."

Bo nodded. "Seth and Mason are on their way over. After I brief them and make sure Jennifer's good, I'll leave with you." He paused. "Will that work for you?"

Lincoln knew he was being managed, just as he knew Bo's question wasn't exactly an inquiry. Bo was just going through the motions.

"You sure about Mason?"

Bo nodded again. "I'm sure. Jennifer knows Mason and trusts him. The guy's got some growing up to do, but he's always treated her kindly. We know that he thinks the world of her. She'll be at ease with him—and Seth will be here to keep him in line."

Seth would. He was usually quiet and reserved around Jennifer, which seemed to put her at ease. Mason, in contrast, was like a puppy around the girl, always so eager to please. He'd heard Mason make Jennifer laugh more than once. If he and Bo couldn't be around to look out for Jenifer, those two were the next best thing.

"Yeah." He stopped, realizing that he wasn't making a lick of sense. His mind was turning to mush. He needed some sleep or he was going to regret it. "Sorry. I mean, you're right. Right about everything. Thanks."

Bo shrugged off the praise. When the kettle started whistling, he said, "Go take her some tea and tell her what's going on. Hopefully, all she'll do is sleep."

"Yeah, I'll do that." He knew he was always going to remember just how much Bo had had his back these last couple of weeks. He hoped one day he'd be able to return the favor.

Picking up the mug, Lincoln climbed the stairs. After knocking softly and hearing her faint answer, he entered her room.

Jennifer was back in bed, but she wasn't under the covers. Instead, she was lying on her side, the white terry cloth robe still wrapped tightly around her. Clyde was curled up next to her, looking almost nice.

When Jennifer saw Lincoln had her tea, she moved to sit up. The cat stretched out his legs but otherwise stayed put.

"Thanks, John," she said after taking a sip.

"Anytime." He set the mug on her side table, then perched on the edge of the mattress. "Why are you still wrapped up like that?" It was warm in the room.

"I don't know. I guess I needed to still feel secure."

"Want me to help you get settled?" He pulled on the corner of her sheet. "It's all pretty tangled up, you know."

"It's all right. I'm not too tired to straighten sheets." She smiled weakly. "Not as tired as you look."

"About that . . . I wanted to tell you that I'm going to take off for a bit. Bo's still here but he's going to leave after Seth and Mason arrive. They should be over shortly."

"That's not necessary. I'll be fine."

"I don't want you to be alone."

"Lincoln, Austin is in custody."

He hoped so, though he'd known of men who had done far worse get out on bond within hours against everyone's better judgment. Stuff happened. But more than that, he couldn't bear the thought of her needing something and not having anyone around to help her. Not today, anyway.

Not knowing how to put all of that in words, he shrugged. "I know you'll be fine, but they want to be here for you too. Might as well let them, yeah?"

She smiled. "All right."

"All right, then." He stood up. "I'll be back in a couple of hours."

"Take your time."

He felt her gaze rest on his lips. Maybe she was thinking about those kisses they'd shared? Maybe she was worried he was going to try something again.

Afraid he might, he got up and strode to the door. "Later," he said before walking back out. After making sure he had his cell in his pocket, he strode right by Bo, who was on his cell talking to somebody.

When Lincoln got back outside, the blast of winter hit his face, cooling him off. He stood still for a long moment, allowing the minute particles of ice to brush his face. He welcomed the slight sting. It served to wake him up and also to remind him that he wasn't God. He might always try to control his world and the people he cared about, but he still failed sometimes. No matter how much he might wish otherwise, in some ways he was just as vulnerable as Jennifer.

Especially where his heart was concerned.

When he got back to his place, he noticed a good number of cars were in the drive. He stepped out of his truck with a sigh. Though he was tempted to tell everyone to head out and give him some space, he knew that wasn't possible. Life moved on, and he wasn't the only person who mattered.

Determined to simply walk through the living room and head up to bed, he was shocked to see about a dozen guys standing in the space and facing him when he opened the door. No one was talking. Instead, each man was looking at him expectantly.

"What's going on?" he asked.

Dillon cleared his throat. "Everyone knows about Jennifer." He flushed. "I mean, Miss Smiley. Is she okay?"

Lincoln scanned the room. Every single one of these guys

had been out of prison for a while. Most had helped over at Jennifer's in one way or another. A couple had even shoveled her drive or helped Bo or Seth take stuff out to the thrift store or the dump. Just as importantly, everyone knew how much she meant to him. They deserved an answer.

"I think so," he said, weighing his words. "She, ah, met with the cops today and told them what happened. She's resting now."

"Do you need anyone over there?" another man asked. "You know, just to make sure she's all right?"

It was more than obvious that every one of them would have gone over if Lincoln would've let them. "Thanks, but Seth and Mason have got it covered." He nodded, which usually let them know they were dismissed.

But none of them moved.

He was so tired. Realizing how accustomed he'd gotten to letting Bo or Seth run interference, he scanned the lot of them. "Anything else I can help you all with?"

"What happened to the guy who did this?"

"He's locked up for now. The police have it handled."

When he saw their looks of doubt, Lincoln lifted his chin. "The guy had some priors, so that'll help him stay put. We need to let the cops handle it. Things aren't going to get better for Jennifer if one of you decides to interfere." He stuffed his hands in his pockets. "Trust me on this. Now, I've got a phone call to make, and then I've got to get some sleep. You all need to stand down and let cops do their jobs. I'm gonna be ticked if I have to spend a minute of my time on one of you when I've got Jennifer to take care of."

As soon as he walked to his suite of rooms upstairs, he pulled out his phone, made a couple of inquiries, and finally reached Caroline, Jennifer's mother. He'd realized in the middle of the night that she needed to hear what happened.

She answered on the first ring.

"Hello?"

"Caroline Smiley?"

"Yes?"

"This is John Bennett."

"Who?"

"Lincoln. Your daughter's neighbor."

"Oh. Yes, of course." There was a definite edge of suspicion to her voice now, right before worry took over. "Is everything all right?"

Reminding himself to play nice, he said, "I'm calling about Jennifer."

"What is this about? Oh, no. Has Eric shown up again?"

And . . . that was giving him a pretty good idea about why Jennifer hadn't asked him to call her earlier. Not knowing how to ease into the truth, he settled for blunt honesty. "Caroline, there's no easy way to tell you this. Jennifer was attacked last night."

"By one of the men living at your house?"

He gritted his teeth. "No. By a man she was on a date with."

"What do you mean by attacked?"

That was what she wanted to know? Not how Jennifer was or what she had been doing? "I'll let her tell you that. I just wanted you to know that she was taken to the hospital last night and then released, the perpetrator is in custody, and when I left Jennifer a few minutes ago, she was sipping hot tea and about to take a nap."

"I . . . I see." Her voice cracked. "Do you think I need to come up there?"

Caroline was her mother. Had he expected her to want to move heaven and earth to be by her daughter's side? Yes. Yes, he had. Then again, life wasn't full of people wanting to step up all the time.

"I can't answer that, ma'am," he replied at last. "I just thought you should know what happened."

"Thank you for calling. It was considerate of you."

"It wasn't a problem."

He loved her daughter. He was going to do whatever it took to be the man Jennifer needed—even if it meant dealing with her pain-in-the-rear mother. "I'll be in touch," he murmured before clicking off.

He pulled off his shoes and winced. He needed a shower. After that, bed. He knew he was about to collapse and needed to sleep before he did something foolish like go back over to Jennifer's and stay the rest of the day by her side. But first, he reckoned he had one more call to make.

"Yeah, boss?" Seth said when he picked up.

"Everything good there?"

"Yep. Bo left about five minutes ago. He stayed long enough to let Jennifer know we'd arrived."

Seth's voice sounded a little off. That was unusual, but he forced himself not to jump to any conclusions. "How's she doing?"

"I think she's asleep, boss. Ah, you want me to go upstairs and check?"

"Nah. But if she wakes up, let her know that I called her mother and told her what happened."

"Okay . . . anything else?"

"No."

"All right, boss. See you later."

"Later."

Lincoln ran the shower as hot as he could take it, cleaned off all the sweat and fear that he'd been wearing on his skin, then collapsed on his bed at last.

The last thing on his mind was that he was going to have to take that girl on a proper date. As soon as he figured out how to ask her . . . and what a proper date entailed.

CHAPTER 31

Jennifer had never imagined that a bunch of ex-cons could be her lifesavers, but that's what they had been. In the five days since Austin's attack, at least one of Lincoln's men had been nearby at all times.

Six months ago, if anyone had told her that she'd feel comfortable napping while two former convicts were lounging in her living room, she'd have thought they were crazy. But it seemed she would've been the crazy one, because she had never felt more secure or looked after.

Now she was sitting with Bo watching some British murder mystery series they'd both grudgingly become addicted to. She usually watched it with half her attention on the gorgeous gardens and houses.

Bo, on the other hand, enjoyed figuring out who the killer was—usually while also making fun of the detectives. Jennifer didn't blame him. She figured he had as much experience dealing with cops as anyone.

Today, however, he kept looking out the window and at his phone.

She decided to give him a little nudge out the door. "Bo, as much as I enjoy your company, there's no reason for you to be here, you know. I'm fine."

"You are healed up some, but I wouldn't call you fine, girly."

"Okay, how about this? I know I'm going to be fine."

"Yeah, well, I'm still going to stick around a little while longer, if that's okay with you?"

She almost smiled at his sarcastic tone. "Is there any particular reason? And don't tell me that you want to figure out who the bad guy is on the show."

"You know it's the gardener, girly. He's the only one who had the means and the motive."

She'd thought differently but kept that to herself. So far, they'd watched four episodes, and Bo's predictions had been right on the money every time.

Just as she picked up the remote to press play again, he blurted, "I heard your mother was coming up."

She thought he was joking. "Yeah, right."

"I'm serious. She's been talking to Lincoln."

"Bo, are you messing with me?"

"You know I don't talk smack about mothers."

His intent stare combined with the weird sixth sense that seemed to appear anytime her mother was near—and suddenly all she felt was inadequacy. Sighing to herself, she looked down at her outfit of old baggy gray sweatpants, V-neck white T-shirt, and one of Lincoln's flannel shirts that he'd left at her house a few days ago. "I wonder if I have time to fix myself up."

"Do you think she's really going to care what you're wearing?"

"I do. She's going to care, and I'm going to feel embarrassed."

"No offense, Jen, but the rest of you looks so bad, I don't think she's going to notice you're wearing Lincoln's old shirt."

She closed her eyes as she leaned her head against the back of the sofa. "Have you met my mother, Bo?"

"No."

That response probably said it all. Bo was the type of man who watched his words around her. No, he watched them around practically everyone. Whereas Mason practically vomited words, Seth was relatively quiet, and Lincoln was, well, Lincoln . . . Bo spoke quietly and softly all the time. She sighed. "By 'no,' I kind of feel like you're saying you're glad you haven't met her?"

"You know I don't know how to answer that."

"I guess you're right. Sorry." Just as she was about to suggest they go back to watching the show, her mother's white, shiny Escalade pulled into the drive.

Bo raised his eyebrows. "Is that her?"

"Yep. She's a fan of big, expensive SUVs."

His eyes warmed. "If Lincoln wouldn't hit me for doing it, I'd give you a hug and a kiss right now."

"Because?"

"Because you're a sweet thing, and it's going to be all right."

"How can you be so sure?"

He got to his feet and then held out a hand to help her up. "Because you're tougher than you look. That's why. Now, come on. Let's go greet your mother." Looking down at her bare feet, he groaned. "You should have had on shoes. It's twenty-five degrees outside."

"Not in here."

"One day you've gotta stop running around like a vagrant."

"Well, maybe one day you'll stop ordering me around."

"Doubt it." Still holding her hand, he gave her a little pull toward the door. "Come on now. You can at least stand here and look pretty while I go meet your mother."

Her mother had been about to ring the doorbell when Bo opened the front door. Maybe each of their appearances took the other off guard because they spent a good couple of seconds staring at each other.

Jennifer supposed it couldn't be helped. Her mother—like always—was dressed to the nines. Her blond hair, just a shade lighter than Jennifer's, was expertly cut and floated around her face and neck in gentle waves. She was wearing a soft red-cashmere sweater, gray wool slacks, and black boots. She was as slim as ever and her makeup was expertly applied.

Bo was dressed in his usual fashion too, in his faded jeans, a white T-shirt, and a black hoodie. His dark blond hair had recently been cut and he had scruff on his cheeks. As always, he looked way too handsome.

And of course, her mother noticed.

"Hi," she said after she seemed to get over the shock of standing so close to him. "I'm looking for my daughter Jennifer."

"I'm right here, Mom," she said.

"Oh, sorry, honey. I didn't see—" Her voice faded. "Oh, Jennifer." She pressed a hand to her face. "Lincoln told me, but I didn't realize . . ."

"I'm okay," she said quickly.

When her mother still stood motionless, just staring, Bo turned and grabbed hold of Jennifer's elbow. "Jennifer, go sit down, yeah? You're gonna catch your death in those bare feet, and then Lincoln's gonna have my hide."

Jennifer knew Bo was putting on his good ol' boy act, but still, she allowed herself to be led. She did it mainly because she felt foolish just standing in the doorway but also because her feet were cold.

And because it was a little hard to realize that the only thing her mother commented on was how bad she looked.

Bo's expression was like granite as he escorted her back to the couch and handed her a blanket. Then, to her surprise, he pressed his lips to her brow. "It's okay," he whispered before facing her mother and turning on the charm again.

"Mrs. Smiley, what can I get you?"

She darted a look from him to Jennifer. "My last name is Tate. I remarried years ago. Now, who are you?"

"I'm Bo."

"Bo . . . ?"

"My real name is Sam Beauman, but I don't answer to either of those."

"I see. And you're Jennifer's boyfriend?"

"I'm Jennifer's friend," he said quickly before Jennifer could explain their relationship. "I work for Lincoln. I'm staying with Jennifer today."

"Ah."

Jennifer felt her face flush, both from the way her mother was acting like Bo wouldn't be hanging out with her if it wasn't a job and by the way Bo was witnessing her mother's complete avoidance of her. "Do you want to have a seat, Mom? Or go to the bathroom or something? It's a long drive from Cincinnati."

"Yes, um, that would be great." She took off the camel hair coat she was wearing and tossed it and her purse on the chair closest to the hallway.

"How about coffee, Caroline?" Bo asked, just like he'd attended charm school.

"Coffee would be terrific. Thank you." She smiled. "Now, if you could show me where the bathroom is, Bo?"

"I'll be happy to." Looking at Jennifer, he said, "Coffee for you too, girl?"

"Thanks, but I'll get it."

"Sit," he mouthed over her mother's head as he led her down the hall.

When she was alone, Jennifer exhaled and tried to look at the bright side. Well, at least her mother wasn't treating her all that differently than she usually did.

And at least she had come, which was more than Jennifer would have guessed she would do. Pulling out her phone, she texted Lincoln.

> My mom is here. Thank you for reaching out to her.

A few seconds later, he replied.

> She's there already? I'll be there soon. Don't let Bo leave.

Jennifer smiled to herself as she put the phone down. She'd have to tell Lincoln later that Bo had already decided he was going to be her protector.

"I'm sorry about the way I acted when I arrived," her mom said as she walked across the room. "I was so shocked by the way you look, I didn't even give you a hug." She frowned. "Can you be hugged? Lincoln said you have some fractured ribs."

"I'd love a hug, Mom," she said as she leaned up to her mother's gentle embrace. When her mother ran a hand down her spine, Jennifer closed her eyes as the familiar scent of White Shoulders enveloped her. Her mother had started wearing that perfume years ago, and now whenever Jennifer caught a whiff, it always brought back memories of her pretty mother working so hard and trying to achieve perfection.

After they parted, Mom sat down on MeMe's favorite rocking chair. "Boy, I used to love sitting here when I was pregnant with you. I'm glad Ginny never got rid of it."

"I don't think she ever got rid of much. She was kind of a packrat."

"Really? I didn't remember that. I'll have to look around later and see what you've done to the house so far." She looked meaningfully at Jennifer's desk and computer in the room. "Besides converting this room into your office."

"It's a good place to work. The light is good." She also faced the driveway, which meant she could see everyone coming and going.

"I imagine it is." Her mother's smile faltered. "Are you okay, dear? I mean, really?"

"Yes. I was beaten up, but it could have been worse." She was tempted to tell her mother more, but she had no desire to describe her injuries again.

"So, he didn't rape you?" she asked just as Bo came in the room with a cup of coffee in each hand.

He stopped, obviously taken aback by the blunt question. Just as she was.

"No, Mom," Jennifer said.

"Okay then." Her mother brightened. "Oh, look. Coffee!"

"Here you are, ma'am," he said in a much cooler tone. He said nothing when he handed Jennifer hers, though his blue eyes were filled with irritation.

Jennifer didn't blame him. Her mom had a way of irritating her even in the best of times.

When he disappeared back down the hall, her mother smiled. "Well, no wonder you haven't wanted to come home.

I wouldn't either if I had men like him waiting on me hand and foot."

There were so many things wrong with that comment, beginning and ending with the fact that Bo was at her house and bringing her coffee *because she'd been so badly hurt.*

"Bo is a nice guy."

"He seems like it. Polite too. And he said that he worked for Lincoln?" At her nod, she said, "Doing what?"

"I don't know. Managing all the guys, I guess."

"Managing what guys?"

There was no way she was going to go down that path. "Mom, does it really matter?"

"No. I mean I guess it doesn't. Not really." She took a sip of coffee. "All I'm trying to do is find out how you're really doing, Jennifer. So far all I know is that you were attacked but not raped, some man is taking care of you, and you're in bad enough shape that Lincoln called to say I should drive up to see you in person."

"Is that not enough?" Lincoln said as he entered the room. Bo was right behind him and didn't look happy at all.

"Lincoln," her mom said as she gracefully rose to her feet. "I wasn't sure if I was going to get the chance to see you."

Lincoln shot her mother a long look before sitting down next to her. "Hey, babe," he murmured. "You doing okay?"

"I'm fine."

One of his eyebrows rose, but all he did was lean toward her and kiss her lips. "Sorry I couldn't get here earlier."

When he pulled back, her mother was frowning. "What's going on with you two?"

"Lincoln and I have become close," Jennifer said. That was an understatement, but it was as much information as she was ready to share. "Mom, are you spending the night?"

"I had planned on it, if that's okay?"

"Of course." Thinking quickly, Jennifer said, "I think the guest bedroom down the hall is clean and has fresh sheets."

"Don't worry about that," her mom said. "I'll fix it up if it needs fixing." Looking at Lincoln closely, she said, "Will you be spending the night too?"

While Jennifer wanted to sink into the floor from embarrassment, Lincoln stiffened, and Bo coughed into his hand, obviously to hide a chuckle.

"I've only spent the night one time, and that was the night I brought Jennifer home from the hospital," Lincoln replied in an icy tone.

"I see."

"The other guys and me have been taking turns staying here, but we've been sleeping on the couch, ma'am," Bo supplied. "So, there might be a pretty good chance that those sheets will still be in good shape for you."

"Why have all of you been here so much? I thought that man was arrested, Jennifer."

"He was," she agreed.

"He was, but he could get out on bail," Lincoln added. "Besides, no one wanted her to stay by herself at night."

Jennifer knew that Lincoln was still worried about her father showing up, but she wasn't in any hurry to bring that out into the open.

"I don't understand." Studying Jennifer more closely, she asked, "Just how hurt are you?"

Jennifer knew her mother wasn't meaning to be unfeeling, but there was no denying that she sounded that way. Bo was sending meaningful looks Lincoln's way, like he was just waiting for permission to toss her mother out the door.

Sitting beside her, Lincoln appeared so wound up, she

was sure he was going to get another migraine if he wasn't careful. It was time to defuse the situation, even if it meant she had to describe those injuries after all. "I have a sprained wrist, two fractured ribs, quite a few cuts and bruises, some of which needed stitches, and a creepy bite mark near my neck that I'm hoping and praying won't need plastic surgery to remove."

"He *bit* you? Are you serious?"

"I'm afraid so."

Lincoln got to his feet. "Did you bring a bag?"

"Hmm? Well, yes. It's in my vehicle though."

"Bo, go help Ms. Tate, would you?" When Clyde suddenly appeared, glaring at her mother, Lincoln added, "You might as well fill her in about the cat too."

"Sure thing, boss." He turned to her mother, his expression carefully blank. "After you, ma'am."

"Hold on. Did you say cat?"

"Don't worry about Clyde none. He's not too mean," he continued as he motioned for her to follow him out the door.

Jennifer hid a smile. It was more than a little obvious that her mother had been hoping Bo would simply take her keys and take care of everything, just like she was staying at a fancy hotel. She was glad Bo was making sure she knew she was staying someplace far different.

When they were alone, Lincoln said, "I'm not going to lie, babe. I'm about ready to put your mother in a motel."

"You know that there's only one motel around here and it's kind of sketchy."

"If that bothers her, she can go to the next town over."

"It's just one night, Lincoln. It will be all right."

"I might stay here on the couch tonight."

"Whatever you want."

He looked at her curiously. "Since when did you get so agreeable?"

"Probably about the time I realized how much I needed you," she replied. There was a time to play coy and there was another when only genuine words would suffice.

Maybe Lincoln felt the same, because his expression softened. "I need you too. Never doubt that."

The door opened again, bringing back in a burst of cold wind, Bo, her mother, a small suitcase . . . and Wayne.

The three people were a study in contrasts. Bo still looked mildly irritated, her mother seemed confused, and Wayne? Well, he was holding a cardboard box and looked scared to death.

Jennifer got to her feet. "Wayne, now this is a wonderful surprise. What brings you here?"

After kicking off his boots while still holding the box, Wayne walked to her side. "We have a present for you."

"Really? That's so sweet of you! Would you like a cup of coffee? It's fresh."

His lips turned up in a half smile. "*Danki. Kaffi* sounds *gut.*"

"Mom, would you mind going into the kitchen and getting Wayne a cup? He takes it black."

"Oh. Sure. I'll be right back."

Lincoln took the box from Wayne, looked at the contents, and grinned. "You did real good, boy. Now, take off your coat and get warm, yeah?"

As always, the boy did as he was told, though he kept sneaking glances at Jennifer. "You don't look so good."

"I know." She sat back down on the couch and motioned for him to sit too. "But I'm doing better. I promise."

"I'm real sorry that happened to ya," he said as her mother brought him the cup of coffee.

"Thank you, Wayne."

While he took his first tentative sip, Jennifer gestured for the box. "So when are you going to give me my gift? I'm dying to know what's in the box."

Wayne's whole expression lit up. "You can open it now if you want. Be careful though."

Just as she was about to reach for it, Lincoln picked it up and set it on the space next to her. She looked up at him and smiled. "Thanks." Then she heard a rustle. Confused, she looked down and felt her heart melt.

There was a little white-and-tan kitten, smaller than Lincoln's hand. It had longish fur and dark eyes and was staring back at Jennifer solemnly. "Wayne, you brought me a kitten?"

"I did." She heard him snicker the way he always did when she asked him obvious questions.

Ignoring him, she reached in and gingerly picked up the little furball and cuddled it close. The tiny cat had to only weigh three or four pounds. "Is it a boy or a girl? Do you know?"

"It's a calico, so it's a girl cat." When she mewed, looking directly at Jennifer, Wayne smiled broadly. "I think she already likes ya a whole lot more than Clyde does, Miss Jennifer."

"I hope so because I already love her." Unable to keep herself from looking anywhere but at the kitten's little scrunched up face, she said, "This is the best present. What made you think of getting me a kitten?"

"Well, *mei daedd* and I started thinking you might need a mouser to live in the barn. She'll be a good 'un."

"I can't let her live there!"

Looking amused, he nodded. "*Mei mamm* said you'd say that."

When the kitten started to squirm, Jennifer placed it on the ground. She scampered right over to Bo, then her mom, who knelt on the floor to pet her.

"*Danki,* Wayne," Jennifer said. "Thank you for bringing me such a special gift."

Blushing, he stood up and took a couple of steps backward, as if he wanted to be sure that Jennifer didn't try to hug him. "I should probably get on my way. I'll be back on Tuesday though to work. If that's okay?"

"Tuesday will be good."

"I'll walk you out," Lincoln said.

Worried about food, Jennifer called out, "What should I feed her?"

"There's cat food in the box, Miss," he said as he put back on his boots and walked outside.

"I'm going to head out," Bo said. "See you, girly."

When it was just the two of them, and one tiny kitten, her mother said, "You've surrounded yourself with a lot of interesting people."

"They're some of the best I've ever met," Jennifer said, just as they heard someone at the door again.

"I'll get it," her mom said. "Maybe Bo forgot his phone or something."

Thinking she was right, Jennifer leaned back on the couch to rest for a second . . . until her mother's gasp pulled her upright again.

"What are you doing here?"

"I have every right to be here, Caroline," her father said as he walked in. "More than you, I expect."

As she watched her parents face off, she shook her head in wonder. Seeing them together, she couldn't help but reflect that right then, at that moment, they didn't seem all that different. Both seemed intent on getting what they wanted . . . and both were completely ignoring her.

"Get out of the doorway," Lincoln called as he stepped

inside. After looking her way, he closed the door behind him and then leaned against it.

Her parents were still bickering. Lincoln looked like he was ready to toss both of them out on the snow.

Jennifer realized that if he did that, she probably wouldn't put up a fight. There was only so much family time a girl could take.

CHAPTER 32

Back when he'd been in prison, back when every moment had been monitored by cameras, guards, and the wary eyes of other inmates, Lincoln had often imagined his future. He rarely dwelled on what he wanted to eat or do the first couple of weeks and months after he got released. Much of that was a given.

Instead, he'd spend hours thinking about what he would do for the rest of his life. He'd wonder about what kind of job he'd get and if he would ever earn enough to have a house of his own. He tried to imagine having friends to hang out with because he liked them, not because there was nowhere else to go.

In true moments of weakness, he'd even imagine having a wife, maybe kids one day. A dog, for sure.

Some of his dreams had felt too big, almost embarrassing, given his past. Others, like earning a decent paycheck, had felt within his reach. But never had Lincoln ever imagined the situation he found himself currently in.

Most likely because it wasn't anything good.

Once again, he was in Jennifer's house. But instead of being alone with her, he was running interference between her parents. They currently seemed intent on ignoring him, their daughter, and it seemed, both a cat named Clyde and a tiny kitten.

For once, none of the other guys were around, and Lincoln was glad about that. The past week had been stressful, and all the men had stepped up, both helping stand guard outside of Jennifer's house, and picking up the slack in Lincoln's business so he could spend every spare moment with her. The last thing he wanted to subject them to was a pair of self-absorbed fifty-year-olds.

After glancing yet again at Jennifer to make sure she wasn't upset, he decided to put a stop to the bickering and get Eric out of Jennifer's life once and for all.

"Hey," he said. When neither parent gave him a passing glance, he tried calling out again, but this time with a bit more force. "Hey!"

Caroline, who'd been in the middle of some speech about junior high school fees, stopped midrant.

Eric turned to face him. "What?"

Lincoln peeked at Jennifer again. She was holding the kitten and seemed more amused than anything. Pleased he wasn't upsetting her, he strode toward the couple.

"Caroline, your speech about how expensive Jennifer was fifteen years ago isn't helping anything. Go sit down." As she complied, he turned to Jennifer's father. "Word on the street was that you'd left after finding out that this house was a no-go."

"I took off, but then came back a couple of days ago." Eric glanced at Jennifer before turning back to Caroline. "Seeing you is a real surprise."

"I don't see why," Caroline said. "I've always been the parent in Jennifer's life. The only parent. Instead, the real question is why you're here in the first place. I know it's not because you suddenly care about our daughter."

Eric stuffed his hands in his pockets but said nothing.

When he spied the hurt in Jennifer's eyes, Lincoln knew he would happily boot kick the pair of them out the door if he thought he could get away with it. Instead, he motioned for her to come to his side. She didn't hesitate. Still holding the kitten, she moved to stand in front of him. "You good?" he whispered.

"Good enough," she said in a low tone before answering her mother's question. "Basically, Eric here wants Ginny's house, but the will is ironclad, so he's out of luck."

"I have had a lawyer looking into this," Eric retorted.

"I have too," Jennifer said. "He said you have no case."

Eric shrugged. "There are ways around that."

Caroline tapped her toe. "Such as?"

When Jennifer leaned back against his chest, Lincoln knew it was time to shut the reunion down. Pulling out his phone, he said, "I ran out of patience with most people about two weeks ago. That means I'm not going to listen to the two of you bicker for another second. Eric, you need to reconsider your words. I've got the local sergeant on speed dial if you plan on making trouble."

Just as Eric smirked, looking like he was about to say something stupid, Caroline stepped forward and jabbed Eric in the center of his chest with one finely manicured white-tipped nail.

"You listen to me, Eric Smiley. You might be standing in your mother's house, and Lincoln Bennett might be as scary as anyone I've ever met, but the only person you should really be worried about is me."

Lincoln was so shocked, he simply waited for Eric to speak. But whether Eric was too surprised to speak or was attempting to come up with something constructive to say instead, he remained silent.

Caroline raised her voice. "I've got a lot of friends in a lot of high places and if you stay here another moment, I'm going to start calling in favors."

"What do you think they're going to do?" Eric asked.

"I know they'll do anything I ask."

Jennifer cleared her throat. "Mom, uh, maybe you should let Lincoln call Sergeant Heilman? He's really tough."

Her mother pivoted on her heel to face Jennifer and Lincoln. "No. Lincoln, I'm grateful that you're here for my daughter, and I'm happy that you two have found each other. But I do not need you to solve this problem."

Lincoln had to smile at that. "Yes, ma'am."

She turned back to Jennifer's father. "Eric, I might not have gotten along with Ginny all that well, but I sure learned a thing or two from her. Don't even think I don't know how to make your life miserable. We haven't been together for years, but I haven't forgotten a thing about the stuff you pulled when I was your wife."

"Oh, boy," Lincoln murmured.

For the first time since his arrival, Eric looked shaken.

Just as Lincoln wrapped his hands around Jennifer's waist, Eric walked right back out the door.

"He just left?" Jennifer asked. "Just like that?"

"It seems so," her mother murmured as she walked back to the couch. "Come sit down, Jen. You need to rest."

When Jennifer looked up at him, Lincoln nodded. "That's a good idea, babe. You go sit down with that kitten. I've got a phone call to make anyway."

He stayed in the room only long enough to make sure Jennifer sat. Then he strode outside.

Charlie was standing on the porch smoking a cigarette. "Hey, Lincoln."

"Charlie, I thought you were gonna keep an eye on Eric Smiley. Where did he run off to?"

"He's on the ground over by the barn."

"Say again?"

Charlie blew out a ring of smoke. "It was the craziest thing, boss. As soon as he walked out Miss Jennifer's door, he headed toward the barn. Bo tackled him and about two minutes later figured out why he was headed over there."

"Let me guess. The ammo in the barn."

Charlie grinned. "That old guy has guts, I'll give him that."

Walking over to where Bo was practically kneeling on the middle of Eric Smiley's back, he punched in Sergeant Heilman's phone number. Looked like he was going to need him to come out right away.

And, with any luck, the sergeant would find enough evidence to charge him with something good.

Lincoln would give just about anything for that guy to be out of his hair for a while.

CHAPTER 33

TWO WEEKS LATER

At last the cold weather had eased and the sun had come out. To celebrate the first warm day in months, Seth had helped Wayne coordinate a treat for Jennifer—her first buggy ride. He and his new horse, Ginger, had picked her up almost an hour earlier and taken her down the back roads near her house. Jennifer had been pretty sure that she hadn't smiled so much in ages.

Wayne had seemed to enjoy the outing as much as she had. He'd been almost chipper, chatting all about Ginger, the state of her hooves, and her fondness for apples.

Returning to her house, he'd just set the brake on his parents' courting buggy at the top of her driveway when Wayne whistled low.

"What do ya think is going on now, Miss Jennifer?"

"Hmm?" She'd been so delighted to have a ride in an authentic Amish buggy, it took her a minute to catch what Wayne was looking at.

But then she caught sight of Lincoln pulling something from the back of his truck. Something that looked like . . . a bench? "I guess I'd better go see, Wayne." When the buggy wiggled slightly—it seemed that a buggy brake didn't stop a horse's movements completely—she said, "Should I just hop down?"

"I'll help ya," he said as he gracefully leaped down then walked to speak to his horse.

"I've got her, Wayne," Lincoln said. "You hold on to Gingerbread there."

Gingerbread? Lincoln knew Wayne's family's horse? Still clutching the quilt that Wayne's mother had thoughtfully left in the buggy for her, she smiled at Lincoln. "Hi."

He grinned. "Hi yourself. You look pretty cute in the buggy, Jen."

"Wayne gave me the ride as a treat. And his mother made me this quilt." She held it up. "Isn't it gorgeous?"

"Absolutely. It must be your lucky day, babe," he murmured as he placed his hands on her waist. "Hop down now. I've got you."

And sure enough, he did. She was standing on the ground seconds later, holding the quilt with one hand and gripping his shoulder with the other.

"Got everything?" he murmured, sending chills down her spine.

"Yes. Oh, no, wait. I need my purse."

He reached in and handed it to her.

Walking to Wayne's side, she petted Ginger's forehead. "Thank you for the ride, Wayne. I loved meeting your new horse too."

He smirked. "I know." Turning to Lincoln, Wayne said, "Miss Jennifer was smiling like it was Christmas Day."

Lincoln chuckled. "That sounds like her. You heading home now?"

"*Jah.* Then I'm going to work at my new job at the hardware store."

"I'll be seeing you around, then. Thanks for your help today."

The boy shrugged it off. "It weren't nothing."

Jennifer smiled at Wayne. "Bye, Wayne. See you soon!"

Wayne chuckled as he guided the buggy back down her drive. Wrapping an arm around her shoulders, Lincoln guided her to the stone walkway that led to the porch.

As they watched Wayne drive off, Lincoln looked almost wistful. "I'm going to miss that kid."

"Me too." When the boy and the horse were out of sight, Jennifer pointed to the bench. "Want to tell me what this is about?"

"Not yet." Looking a little irritated, he added, "You weren't supposed to be home for another hour."

He'd been planning a surprise? "Lincoln, what's going on?"

"I'll tell you in a minute. Go on inside and put up your quilt or something."

There was no way she was just going to sit on the sofa and wait for him to come get her. "Want some lunch? I could make you a sandwich."

"Yeah, Jen," he said quickly. "A sandwich sounds real good. Thanks."

Since he had already turned away, she left him in peace and went inside. After placing the quilt on the arm of the couch, she peeked out the window at Lincoln. He was still standing next to the bench and looking irritated.

It was probably good that she was giving him some space. Something was clearly on his mind.

Walking into the kitchen, she washed her hands, opened the fridge, and started pulling out all the makings for a roast beef sandwich. After she sliced tomatoes and onions just like he liked them, she assembled everything and put it on the plate.

Then, deciding that Lincoln still needed a few more minutes of privacy, she turned on the kettle, and took a seat. It was amazing how accustomed she'd become to her new reality. She was very used to any of the guys from next door showing up at her house. They came over to do projects, visit, eat cookies, or just to check on her.

After everything that had happened with her father and Austin, Jennifer knew that they needed to be sure she was all right. Maybe she needed that reassurance too? She wasn't sure.

Of course, Lincoln's visits never affected her the same way. With him, her insides turned into a puddle. Sometimes she thought she even turned into a giggly woman she hardly recognized. But that was love for you. She wasn't sure what would happen between them—if anything ever would. But she knew deep inside that she'd never take her feelings for him for granted. Love and trust had never come easy for her.

"Jennifer, where you at?"

She got to her feet. "I'm in the kitchen." Looking at the empty counters she added, "Here's your sandwich. Do you want chips too?"

"Not yet. Come on out here."

Walking down the short, narrow hallway, she noticed that he had the front door wide open. "Lincoln, flies are going to get in."

"Close the door behind you then."

She did, then gasped.

Because there on her porch stood the white bench . . . and it was surrounded by about six rose bushes, each in a white ceramic container. "What's going on?"

"The guys told me rose petals would be good, but it seemed kind of a shame to pluck off a bunch of petals from perfectly good flowers." He paused and lifted an eyebrow. "Right?"

"Hmm? Oh, yes. Right." She knew her answer was useless,

but how else could she have responded? Who would have ever guessed that Lincoln Bennett discussed rose petals with anyone?

"Plus, this way, you'll always have flowers. You told me once that you liked roses, remember?"

She was still standing next to the door, staring at the bench and the pots. Her hands were clasped to her chest and she felt as if there was a rubber band on her tongue.

But since he was still staring at her, and now looking somewhat concerned, she nodded again. "Yes, I remember. Roses are my favorite."

A line eased in between his brows. She realized then that he was relieved. "Lincoln," she asked softly, "Why have you brought me a bench and six flowerpots?"

"Come sit down, Jen."

It only took five steps to get to the bench, but it felt almost like entering a new world. Especially when he looked at her sitting in the middle and smiled.

She scooted to the side. "Aren't you going to join me?"

"No. I've ah, got someplace else in mind."

Even more confused, she glanced at his truck. "Did you bring another bench?"

"As a matter of fact, I did not."

And then, like it was in slow motion, Jennifer watched him kneel on one knee in front of her. "John, what in the world?"

"Hush, now." After clearing his throat, he reached for her hand. "Jennifer, when I first saw you at your grandmother's funeral, standing so still and solemn, I knew you were something special. Later, when you walked into my house, passed a dozen ex-cons while carrying a cake, I pretty much lost my heart right then and there. You were everything I ever imagined a woman could be and everything I never dreamed I would ever find."

He took a breath. "Then, when you accepted me as I was,

even though I was nothing you ever hoped for, I knew it would break my heart to let you go."

Jennifer was so overcome, she knew she couldn't say a word if she tried. She settled for squeezing his hand.

"I almost lost you a few weeks ago. For a moment there, my world went dark. I was afraid I might have lost you for good." He took a breath, and when he started speaking again, his voice was all gravelly. "I realized that it was time to stop living in regrets and start planning a future. I realized that I no longer had any regrets about what had happened to me in the past. Not my childhood, not what I did for Ginny, not even my stint in Madisonville. Because all of that brought me to you." He sighed. "And that's when I knew."

She had tears in her eyes. Blinking them back, she murmured, "You knew?"

"I knew that it didn't really matter anymore what our pasts were like, or even what the future had in store for us. I knew I needed to stop being afraid."

She had to remind herself to breathe.

"You already know that I love you, Jennifer. I can't promise that I'll ever be worthy of you, but I'm sure going to try. I'll do everything in my power to make you happy. To keep you safe."

While she tried to catch her breath, Lincoln shifted, and pulled a platinum ring from his pocket. "Jennifer Smiley, will you marry me?"

John Lincoln Bennett was kneeling before her. She was sitting on a bench he'd built and was surrounded by six pots of red roses because he couldn't bear to tear the petals off of flowers. If such things could happen, then all miracles were possible.

Jennifer had known she'd loved him for weeks now—but never more than at that very moment. She held out her hand. "Of course," she said with a smile.

He grinned as he got to his feet and slid the ring on her finger.

Her engagement ring had a thick band and an enormous emerald-cut diamond in the center of it. She stared at it in awe. "John, this is beautiful," she whispered.

"I was hoping you would like it."

"I more than like it. I love it." She giggled at his pleased expression. "It sure is big, though."

If anything, Lincoln looked even more pleased. "It's three carats."

"Three?" She had a rock on her hand. She tilted her hand this way and that. Each time, the diamond caught the light and practically stole her breath away. Reaching for him, she leaned close. "John, this ring is amazing. It's absolutely gorgeous too . . . but you didn't have to do this. I love you. You know that, right? I would've said yes to any ring."

"I didn't want anyone who looked at you to ever doubt for a moment that you're taken. I figured three carats would do the trick."

Getting to her feet, she hugged him. And then she started crying.

And then time stopped because he was kissing her and holding her like she was going to disappear if he didn't.

When he pulled away at last, she started tearing up again and sat down on the bench and gazed at her finger. Her life was different now. She was no longer by herself. She was Lincoln's fiancée.

Looking pleased, he sat down next to her and held her left hand between the both of his. "Your hand looks real fine. Perfect. Can we get this wedding done soon?"

What could she say?

"Of course, John. But, maybe you could give me at least a couple of days to get used to being engaged?"

Without cracking a smile, he nodded. "Yeah. Sure, babe. I think I can do that."

CHAPTER 34

FOURTEEN MONTHS LATER

"Jennifer, it's the middle of the night. What are you doing up?" Lincoln frowned. "And, why the heck are you standing out here without a coat on?" he asked as he turned around and strode into the living room. "It's freezing."

Bemused, Jennifer watched her husband stride through the house, grumbling to himself as he grabbed the quilt Wayne's mother had made for her off the couch. She knew by now that there was no reason to say much, Lincoln might be married and *almost* domesticated, but he was still the man she'd first met nearly two years ago. He could be gruff and bossy. He also tended to bark and grumble from time to time about all sorts of things—most especially about the two cats who sometimes seemed to rule the house.

However, Jennifer also knew that Lincoln loved her so much that he never bossed her around without her welfare in mind— and that his bark was about ten times worse than his bite.

Striding back outside, now armed with her favorite quilt and a pair of socks, he glared at her. "Are you smiling at me?"

"Never." It was really hard not to smile. But of course, she wasn't trying all that hard either. "Did I wake you up?" she asked.

He pulled her to the white bench he'd built for one of the best days of her life and placed her on his lap. Seconds later, socks covered her feet and the quilt was wrapped around the both of them.

"I woke up when I realized your side of the bed was cold. It's four in the morning, babe. How come you're up?"

"Snow glow." The moon was out, and its glow reflected on the freshly fallen snow. She loved sleeping with the curtains open but the snow glow—as she liked to call it—always woke her up.

"Tomorrow night, we're sleeping with the curtains shut."

"Okay."

Patting her tummy gently, he nuzzled her neck. "Now, how's our baby?"

"Good." She was now fifteen weeks along and was slowly getting used to the idea that they would have a son or a daughter in just a few months. She was also learning something new about her husband. He was sure that their marriage and her pregnancy were miracles. More than once he'd shared that he'd never expected to be so blessed.

He sighed. "Okay, then."

Sitting on the porch, warm against him, and enjoying the feel of the cold, brisk air against her cheeks while the rest of her was protectively wrapped up in her husband's arms, Jennifer sighed happily. Realizing that he was relaxed as well, she looked out at their front yard. She loved how sometimes it felt as if they were the only two people in Ross County.

She knew Lincoln appreciated the peace and quiet even

more than she did. At first, she'd worried that Lincoln moving in with her would feel stifling to him after a while. After all, he'd been used to living with a whole lot of men. They weren't quiet men either. His home had been filled with lots of people, noise, music, and responsibilities. He'd also been surrounded by some men who were closer to him than brothers. Men who had risked a lot for him . . . and for her. She'd been so concerned that he'd hate not being in the thick of things.

But she'd soon discovered that Lincoln didn't regret the change at all. In fact, sometimes it seemed like he'd settled into wedded bliss easier than she had. He seemed to enjoy everything about living with a woman—from her makeup on the bathroom vanity, to the candles she burned in the evening, to all her "girly" quilts and pillows and picture frames that were scattered all over the house. He'd even argued when she'd told him that she was going to switch out her shabby-chic pink floral comforter with something a little more manly.

And now, here they were, expecting a baby.

"What are your plans for today?" she murmured.

"First, I plan to get some more sleep. Then . . . I'm meeting with Vanessa and Simon Brown."

The names sounded familiar but she couldn't place them. "Who are they?"

"They opened up the Back Porch," he said, naming the new restaurant in town. "They said they'd be amiable to have a couple of the guys work there."

"Really? That's great."

"Yeah."

She knew this was Lincoln-speak for being really happy. For the last six months, he'd been working hard to convince various businesses in the area to take a chance on "his" men from Madisonville so the guys wouldn't always have to work construction. "You're on your way, then."

"Hope so." He shifted so he could see her face in the snow's light. "There's a long way to go, but it's a good first step. But if I can end up here with you, then I guess anything can happen."

Jennifer felt the same way about her life with Lincoln. When she'd first met him—and was introduced to all the men he supported in so many ways—she'd been scared to death. She'd taken every television movie and sensational headline about ex-cons and rolled it into her psyche and had been afraid to trust.

But soon she'd learned that it wasn't the men in the house she hadn't trusted—it had been herself. She'd been so hurt—by her father's abandonment, her mother's silence, and even her grandmother's secrets—that she had retreated into a life so tightly controlled that she'd hardly even knew who she was.

Then, little by little, she'd taken small steps to see the world around her. And Lincoln had helped her see the many possibilities that were in it.

Life on Edgewater Road hadn't been easy. She'd struggled, but she'd also found more happiness than she'd dreamed possible.

"I think I'm ready to go back to bed," she announced.

"Me too." He stood up, grabbed that quilt, and took hold of her hand. Led her inside and closed the door behind them. After flicking the deadbolt with a click, he flung the quilt on the edge of the couch.

And then, he stood to the side and motioned for her to precede him up the stairs. Just as he always did. Because he had her back.

Once Jennifer was lying back in bed, she watched as Lincoln pulled the curtains shut, encasing the room in darkness.

She felt him climb into bed, the side nearest the door, of course. "Sleep, baby," he whispered.

For a second, she wondered if he was speaking to her or their unborn child. But it didn't really matter. All that did matter was that she was lying in the dark, relaxed and content with her husband beside her.

Her heart had never been so full of bright hope.

ACKNOWLEDGMENTS

Some books seem to write themselves, but this wasn't one of them. For *Edgewater Road,* I needed as much help and support as I could get!

I'm so thankful for my longtime critique partners Heather Webber, Cathy Liggett, Hilda Knepp, and Julie Stone for helping me fine-tune the beginning of this book multiple times. I also owe a great deal to my agent Nicole Resciniti for her encouragement and support during this novel's publication journey.

I'm so thrilled that this novel found a home at Blackstone Publishing, and particularly grateful to editor Vikki Warner for chatting with me on the phone about both this book and the potential to create a series in the middle of central Ohio. I'm also indebted to editor Ember Hood for her careful eye and honest remarks. I know this book is a whole lot better because of her input! Thanks also go out to the grand marketing and publicity team for championing this novel and to the amazing Alenka Linaschke for her perfect cover!

Finally, this book wouldn't have been written without my husband Tom's support, as well as the support of our many Ohio friends who reached out during the middle of the pandemic just to make sure I was still writing.